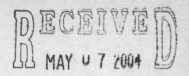
Cynthia Rogerson is Californian and has lived in the Highlands since 1982. Her short fiction has been published in numerous anthologies and journals, and has been shortlisted for the Macallan/*Scotland on Sunday* Short Story Prize and the Neil Gunn Prize. *Upstairs in the Tent* is her first novel.

Praise for *Upstairs in the Tent*:

'The ... narrative creates an intrigue and suspense that will keep the reader turning pages ... Interlaced with gentle humour, Rogerson's style [gives] her novel the urgency and directness of the spoken word ... A compelling and affecting story written with accomplishment and flair and radiating a humanity and sense of place that's worthy of Neil Gunn'
Inverness Courier

'a delicious little series of baby's-eye view snapshots of the world ... both in the womb and out of it, drawn with a warmth and confidence which avoids sentimentality'
Glasgow Herald

'The structure of *Upstairs in the Tent* is mosaic-like, layered, and its wide-ranging point of view suits Rogerson's ability to inhabit all of her main characters convincingly. She sketches them with just the right amount of detail, chooses just the right aspects to emphasise'
Scotland on Sunday

'Sharpened with a quicksilver humour ... light and at the same time profound, *Upstairs in the Tent* is [a] quirky and impressive début'
Highland News Group

Upstairs
in the Tent

Cynthia Rogerson

review

First published in 2001
by REVIEW

An imprint of Headline Book Publishing

First published in paperback in 2002

10 9 8 7 6 5 4 3 2 1

ISBN 0 7472 6734 0

Typeset by
Letterpart Limited, Reigate, Surrey

Printed and bound in Great Britain by
Clays Ltd, St Ives plc

HEADLINE BOOK PUBLISHING
A division of Hodder Headline
338 Euston Road
LONDON NW1 3BH

www.reviewbooks.co.uk
www.hodderheadline.com

(For the man in the train)

Acknowledgements

The writer would like to thank her large and lovely family, whose complete indifference to her literary endeavours gave her the stubbornness to finish this book. But she expects them to change now.

She is indebted for research and editorial advice to Janet McInnes, Michel Faber, Andrew Greig, Angus Dunn, Merideth Sigrist, Geraldine Cooke, Fee Murray, Doris McCann, Violet Bent, Caroline Bowes, George Pirie, Pat Gulliver and Moira Forsyth. Financially indebted to the Scottish Arts Council. And generally in debt to everyone else.

Continuous technical support provided by Alan.

PART ONE

My house breathes, like. I've haird it
In and oot, hello and goodbye
Coom back, stay awa
Ken fit I mean? It's dead creepy, but I like it.

                                   Overheard on a bus

I'm naked to the bone,
With nakedness my shield.
Myself is what I wear:
I keep my spirit spare.

                                   Theodore Roethke

Once there was a little boy
He lived in his skin
When he pops out
You may pop in.

     Anon, from The Mother's Gift, *1812*

How it Begins

Of course, nothing really has a beginning, any more than it has an ending. No beginning, no end, only change. Back and back it goes, till you could end up blaming Aristotle for your repossessed car. But for simplification, and the satisfaction of blaming Roddy, Mhairi considered *that* afternoon the beginning. She'd been having one of those loud pretend orgasms she used to think were orgasms.

Whoaa, whoaa, said Roddy, as if she were a runaway mare and he the strong gentle cowboy, talking her, rocking her back to docility.

She slowed, took deep long breaths, made mewing noises, rubbed her head against his chest. (They'd both seen the movies, knew their roles. He played the man, and she the girl/woman.)

Roddy extracted himself. Rolled and lit a cigarette. She watched him. His gaze was towards the window, but it was inwards he focused. Working out the logistics. He stole a glance at his watch. Two shreds of tobacco stuck to his lip, and while he picked them off, and while Mhairi shifted slightly to minimise the leaking out, while the sun shone through the never-washed windows, and outside a red bus stopped to let people off and on, while all this and countless other things were happening, certain cells deep inside Mhairi began a minute vibration. The greatest act in the circus, the multiplying act of the ages; also an echo of recent events, only much tinier.

Whoaa, whoaa!

Roddy farted and coughed, stubbed out his cigarette. Mhairi got up to use the toilet, wrapping a sheet around her. If she noticed the tingling, the quivering fairy dust inside her, she didn't say. She looked quickly in the mirror, thought she looked different, but attributed that to the dope. She moved slowly, clumsily, back to bed. Roddy was up and dressed.

Do you have to go now?

Aye. I'm late as it is.

Workaholic. But you'll be back tomorrow, will you?

He shrugged nervously.

What's that suppose to mean?

It means I'll try. Right?

Well, try hard.

Don't I always? Aren't I your best man?

She threw a pillow at him. Idiot! You're my only man.

Too bad you're only number three on my list, then.

In your dreams, poser.

Believe what you want, Mhairi, I'm offsky.

Suit yourself.

Aye, I do that, alright.

And Roddy was out of the door and down the stairs. Mhairi got up quickly and ran to the window. The bastard was whistling. Whistling! And swinging his arms to beat the band.

(And within her, the miracle; from something to somebody.)

4

Four Months Later, Somewhere Else

Was Kate. Someone's mother, someone's daughter, formerly someone's wife.

Kate in her house. A whitewashed stone building with a view of the sea, on the west coast of the Highlands. Kate was usually either inside her house looking out of a window, or outside her house, looking at her house. It was a pleasing house from every aspect. Solid, symmetrical, humble, secretive; like hundreds of other stone houses. If she was away shopping or working at the pub, she always greeted the house when she returned. Hello, house, she would say, opening the door. It's just me. I'm back.

There was a rusty caravan out the back, a muddy strip of veg plot, a rowan tree and plum tree, both wind-warped, and a winding weedy path that led to the porch door. A pair of downstairs windows, topped by two narrow dormers poking out of the slate roof. Two chimneys, one that rarely smoked and one that frequently did. The walls were white from a distance, but the harling had shades of yellow, green and grey, with crack lines wrinkling around the windows. The house was old but worked. It was Kate's skin.

Hogmanay just gone, Kate took no heed of it. Why toast a shortened lifespan? And as for being happy about a thousand years passing, well. The millennium, when it came, would have to manage without her.

So there she was, a woman of forty-one dirty winters and teasing springs, not caring that she straddled the turn of the century, standing in her kitchen and looking out of the sink window. Lyle Lovett in the background. It was a fine morning, but she hardly noticed. She looked, but only because it was the obvious place to rest her eyes while washing dishes.

Perhaps the window looked for her, noticed that the hard coldness had gone. A clear and warm suffusing of soil and stone was taking place. Spring? Maybe for an hour or two.

She finished washing up and opened the window a crack. Noticed, at last. The air swirled over her face, entered her lungs and blood. She tilted her head back, let her eyelids flutter down. Took a deep breath. Her concerns fell away and she opened the window wider to watch them glint into nothing, reabsorbed into the world, which knew their true unimportance. Felt light.

And then, the old two-second spiralling torrent of clarity. This spring, this year, would be different. She would:

> Try to like Mhairi.
> Swim in the sea.
> Dig the whole garden.
> Enrol in a course.
> Quit the pub job.
> Get central heating.
> Get Mhairi to like her.

Do sit-ups, push-ups.
Stop listening to gossip.
At least stop passing it on.
Stop reading Trollope.
Stop reading Binchy.
Buy iron tonic.
Dye her hair.
Shave her legs.
(Well, maybe not.)
Be friends with Mhairi.
Buy expensive lipstick.
Scavenge the winter sales.
Buy a gaudy brooch.
Drink lots of water.
Sell Jack's sheep.
Read literature.
Be nice to her mother.
Be nice to her daughter.
Be nice.

All this, despite her resolution to make no resolutions. It was always like that. Ambushed by renewal urges, just as she was reconciled to stagnation. Giving entropy a run for its money again.

Looking out of the window, a light breeze lifting her frizzy, greying (but not grey yet!) hair, she spotted big Murdo and wee Murdo walking up the track to her house. Irritation instantly flooded back. Her lips pressed and all her concerns gathered together and flew in a dark flock back through the window to lodge securely in her gut. Caw, caw.

Fuck it, she said. Nothing for it but to fill the kettle. They would come regardless, and might have good news this time.

It was and it wasn't.

Jamie

There's this man, or boy, and he's invisible. It's a strange life. Of course, belonging exclusively to himself, he clings to it anyway; not even sure it's stranger than every life, and perhaps he's right.

This person, currently called Jamie, cannot imagine the thoughts of other people and moves among them warily. He cannot forget the accidental possibilities of every step, the crossroads in every minute, the potential disasters that lie in wait. Nothing sinister, no bogey man calling his name, just the world and its indifference. All the unknown lives colliding. It's scary enough.

Today he is outside the train station again, and sniffs the air as if he can smell another beginning here. Inside, the station is like a cathedral, but modern. High vaulted glass ceiling, blinding white everywhere, clean, bright, no wonder it is his favourite place. In the beginning he used to come inside only for a few seconds, like some shy creature checking out the risks of a nibble. Dart in, dart out; dart in a bit further next time, a bit longer, then out, back to the city centre, Union Street, Black Friars Row, St Gabe's Park, where he knows how to be invisible.

Today he takes one step further, a giant step further. He takes a deep breath and holds it until he is on a train, actually inside a carriage. Ticket-less, but not unprepared. He has given this a great deal of thought, staring into space while sitting on kerbs and benches, pews and gravestones, and mostly while walking his lop-sided rolling gait around the city.

He has already picked up a Press & Journal from a station bin, flattened it, and now sits down and pretends to read. Forces a look of preoccupation. The train leaves the station, and he conceals the deep wondrous thrill of illicit motion. Illicit for him, anyway. The ticket collector can be heard moving up the carriage towards him, chanting, Tickets from Aberdeen, tickets from Aberdeen. Jamie yawns, shakes his paper, focuses on the print, the shapes that make no sense to him but look familiar. Plays a game in his head. Find the letters of his name in one sentence, rearrange them. Sense begins to waver and emerge. He knew all this long ago, words and things.

Tickets from Aberdeen voice comes nearer.

He holds himself still now, wills himself into the background, the worn vaguely striped seat, the smeared window. Outside, tall dark granite buildings swish by, then a lush green cut away, then back gardens full of washing and barking dogs, stout women in floral housecoats blooming in the winter sun, young men in black leather under car bonnets. The collector passes, goes on up the carriage.

Victory! And he still has the two other train tricks up his sleeve. Oh, he is rich, life is fine. But where is the train going? He hadn't thought to look, getting somewhere had never been the point. Enough to be sitting here, unmolested, rolling away. But now he wonders. What next?

Kate Gets a Big Surprise

This is it, Kate, insisted big Murdo, slamming her table with his hat, while Kate tried not to notice several small insects springing off it. Forget the tea, what we're needing here are a few drams. Get out the glasses, woman, I'll fetch the bottle down. Oh, wheesht, I know where old girls like you keep your bottles.

He heaved his obese self up on her creakiest chair and found the whisky on top of the dresser. He was a far removed cousin and bore a similarity to her in his sallow skin (Spanish Armada?) and sharp dark eyes with undernourished lashes. Though his eyes were not squint like hers. He was the kind of worker who was only hired in times of dire need, like late lambing in desperate weather, and even then reluctantly. The rest of the time he appeared very busy, walking from house to house, bearing tidings, emptying tea-pots and sometimes bottles. Wee Murdo was his silent cohort. Another relation of some kind. People generally ignored him and assumed he was simple. Why else would anyone spend time with big Murdo?

As usual, she felt trapped by her own good manners, or the habit of manners she reserved for the Murdos, and got out the glasses. They were her tribe after all; corrupted post-incomer-wave locals. A tribe so diffuse they were hardly a tribe. It wasn't as simple as locals and non-locals any more. And yet. Liking or not liking each other seemed to be irrelevant. They were connected. Hybrid Highlanders.

Now what are you on about, Murdo? Have you got a proper job? Are you moving away? That would be good news.

Big Murdo laughed, revealing his yellowed teeth. A deep-chested affectionate roar. Now, Kate, what would you do if I went away? You would curl up and die. No. This is real news.

He waited, finishing his dram and pouring another.

Oh, get on with it! Do you think I have nothing better to do than listen to you swallowing my whisky all day?

Another grunt of a laugh. Wee Murdo slouched against the kitchen door, smiling at the air. He never drank, a good thing too.

Alright, if you really need to know, although I'm surprised, so I am, that you've not heard the news already. Seeing as how it's to do with your nearest and dearest.

Don't tell me, then.

Course I'm going to tell, and you'll listen too, you bluffer. It's about your Mhairi. But surely you'll have guessed.

Kate's brain received less oxygen, and she perceived the air in the kitchen turning pale, shimmering. Peripheral objects lost their focus. What? What about Mhairi? And you'll tell me right quick and straight now, Murdo, or you're out of here.

Get ready with your glass for a toast, then.

She's never getting married?

No.

Thank God for that.

He paused, finished his.

She is married. (Poured another.) Now Kate, don't go on like that. Please. Put your head down and breathe deep a few times, there you go, old girl. Drink this up. It's not the end of the world. It's good news, so it is.

And who, may I ask, is her husband, not Euan who walks funny, from Culmoran?

No, no, Kate, don't be daft, she has more sense than that, your Mhairi. No. She married a nice young man she met at the Tech.

I don't believe you, Murdo. Put that bottle back up where it belongs for real occasions.

Ah, Kate, I was only coming along to tell you out of the goodness of my heart. To prepare you. It's true. I heard it down at Shelagh's last night, you know her sister-in-law works at that place in the multi-storey car park in Inverness. The marriage registry place.

The room stopped tilting and resumed normal colour as these words settled around Kate. Mhairi with a husband? Her baby. Baby.

Why wouldn't she be telling me, then? Why is it a secret?

Well, Kate, think on it now. She has a pretty fair idea what you think of early marriages, don't you think?

She'd at least tell me, still. She wouldn't keep it from me. She said she'd be home tonight, she never said anything was out of the ordinary. She'll be on the eight o'clock bus. I don't understand it. She looked at wee Murdo, who shrugged and mimed her bewilderment.

Come and sit down, you. I'll put the kettle on for you and me at least. She pulled out a chair for his gaunt behind and he slumped into it. A little cloud of body odour settled with him.

Filling the kettle, she looked out of the window at the bare hills of stone and whin. They stared back, useless.

Well, we'll see what Mhairi has to say for herself tonight, then.

Jesus, Kate, I was only wanting to prepare you. I'd hardly go around spreading lies about her. The girl's married.

So you keep saying, Murdo. And I'm not saying you're lying, only you might have got the information wrong. Happens easily enough.

But clearly as everything around her, she suddenly saw the belly and breasts, swollen and blue veined, and Mhairi's long hennaed hair swirling around them. Surely it was only seconds ago she'd had the same body herself? All of her organs recalled it vividly, though at the time she'd felt quite detached and dreamy. Doomed to live life only in memory or anticipation, always a veil between herself and what was actually happening.

But it didn't matter. It was only the way she had always been. Maybe everyone was built that way. Looking at the two Murdos, she doubted it, but you never knew what was inside other people. You just never knew.

The kettle whistled, the belly and breasts vanished. Wee Murdo smeared a flea dead on the table, and big Murdo tsked and said the place was a disgrace.

Jamie

He has heard this song before, it is an old song, not on the radio, but round and round on the black box he mustn't touch.

He slouches against the wall and closes his eyes to listen to the busker play his guitar and sing. A high voice, a Neil Young whine that somehow soars over the traffic.

He feels queasy and it's not just because he's had nothing to eat since yesterday midday or that he has been kipping rough three nights running and his clothes are beginning to chafe his skin with his own filth and his own special high perfume of fear and sweat. It is none of these things. The busker is doing this to him, killing him with his high-pitched nasal voice, his guitar's plaintive notes, he is dying, fainting, sliding down the wall, where was that black box he mustn't touch? Jimi! I told you to leave those knobs alone, now look what you've done, oh shit, now you've scratched it! You little bugger. Ah, don't cry like that, wee mannie. I'm sorry.

Silence and blackness, a pit of dark relief, an absence of nausea, blessed blessed nothing. Then, Hey man, you alright? (The busker, a slightly foreign accent — Dutch? Unshaven and a smell to match his own.) Can you hear me, man? Say something. Do you want me to get a doctor?

No. No doctor. He opens his eyes, sits up, lets the busker rearrange his bag so he's sitting against it instead of the cold stone wall. No doctor. I'm fine, he whispers. I'm alright now. Just felt a bittie, a bittie . . .

Hey, you want a piece of chocolate, man? You look like you could use something.

The busker breaks off a piece of Cadbury's and inserts it into the boy's mouth, since he's gone limp and can't seem to lift his hands to feed himself.

At first the boy wants to retch, his mouth is dry, the chocolate gags him. But then it works. Saliva spurts out of nowhere and the sugar hits his bloodstream like an amphetamine. Thanks, he says, and he shakes his head to clear it. Smiles.

Look, fellow, why don't you and me get ourselves a cuppa at the wee café down Stewart Crescent? They never mind how you look in there, come on now, I could use something warm and wet myself.

He lets himself be helped up, makes sure he still has his holdall (which literally holds his all) and ventures down the street with his new friend.

The song recedes, as does the woman's scolding voice, painfully mysteriously familiar, and the black spinning discs and forbidden knobs.

The next morning when he wakes in the old van the busker had discovered unlocked, he is alone again. Not surprised, he unfolds his stiff body from the back, stretches and yawns on the pavement of an unknown road, and sets himself the first task of the day. To find a place to pee. Wonders if this could be another train day.

Kate Makes Porridge

Eight thirty and Kate was in the kitchen again, marvelling that despite the previous four tense headachy hours, she was not exhausted. A familiar sensation, since she was frequently amazed she was not dead yet. Still here, and not even old, really, just times of feeling that life was considerably longer than she kept expecting, like a wave she sometimes rode, and other times felt dragged along by. She could feel her sap rise to meet the presence of her daughter who was sitting nonchalantly in her old chair at the kitchen table.

Mhairi, on the other hand, wore the face of indifference she habitually kept for home. It was extra horrible being an only child, now there was just Kate. Why was she hovering, smiling, staring? How she longed for a preoccupied mother and the distractions of siblings. Everyone else had hordes of them.

A mess had already accumulated around her: shoes kicked off under the table, her jacket across the armchair, her bag on the floor, spilling contents, a tissue already blowing towards the hall on an up-draught. She'd been the kind of child who created a little nest of clutter no matter how briefly she alighted. The floor of the house had been a continuous map of her whereabouts and activities. An only child who perhaps made up for it with multiple childish messes.

Mhairi, will you not eat something? You must be hungry.

Kate stood at the cooker, not minding the mess any more than she ever had, which was very little. The sight of Mhairi melted her, too slender and pale, not in the least pregnant-looking. She was a tall girl with green blue eyes. She wasn't what anyone would call pretty, but there was something about her – skin that was naked-looking, not olive like Kate's but moist cream. And the sharp angle of her face bones, half hidden in long baby-fine hair. When she spoke, Kate noticed that people tended to listen, perhaps just to hear what her voice would sound like. She never said anything much.

You know what I wouldn't mind, Mum? Just a bowl of porridge. Milky. And a cup of tea. That'll do me fine. I had some chips waiting for the bus so I'm not all that hungry.

Kate started the porridge and waited for Mhairi to tell her. But her daughter's silence seemed the kind that wasn't waiting to say anything at all, so she had to talk herself.

I had the miserable Murdos up this afternoon.

Poor you, Mum. Could you not pretend you were sick in bed or something?

Do you think for one minute that would stop them? No, I had to bear it. They stayed maybe an hour, and I had to leave the windows open all evening to get rid of the stench.

Oh aye?

Mhairi did not wish to have a conversation. But there was Kate, hungry for talk. Oh, the weariness of daughterhood! Well, and what did they have to say for themselves this time? Or rather what did big Murdo say?

Well, they, he had some funny news. Not funny ha ha, more . . . odd.

Oh aye. And what would that be?

Kate turned from stirring the pot, looked at Mhairi, then back to the porridge. He said you'd married. A fellow from the Tech.

Mhairi sighed. Did he now? Well, he was right and wrong.

What do you mean, girl? You're either married or you're not.

Not necessarily, Mother. She looked irritated, a crease between her eyes. I might as well tell you now, though there's no real need for you to know, that I did marry a friend, an American called Brendan, so he could stay here.

Kate took the saucepan off the burner, burned her finger — shit! — and sat down.

He's started a computer course, but his visa expired last month. It's just a marriage of convenience. We'll get a divorce. Don't look like that, Mum, it's nothing really. Lots of people do it. Why shouldn't he be allowed to stay here if he wants to? Brendan loves Scotland.

It's alright, Mhairi, I think that's fine. It's only relief I'm feeling. I thought you'd really married without telling me. I thought . . .

You thought I was pregnant?

Yes, she said, and burst out laughing.

Well, I'm that as well.

Aye, I really had myself in a state imagining you with morning sickness and a stupid shotgun-wedding type husband tagging along with you here.

I am pregnant, Mum, she said simply, as if it was unimportant, a mere detail she needed to correct. You were right about that. Only I don't get morning sickness, I'm getting afternoon sickness.

Kate's swallow of tea took for ever to get down. It seemed at once inevitable, old news, and shockingly fresh. The clock's tick slowed.

Wait a minute, Mhairi. Let me get this straight. You are married to Brendan, but he's not a real husband. And you are pregnant and it is a real baby. Right?

Right. Can I have that porridge now? It'll be thick as cement.

Hold on just a small second. Tell me, is your not-real husband the father of your real baby?

Not a chance, Mum, don't be silly! He's already got a girlfriend called Isabel.

And why didn't she marry him?

Because she's already married. (Obviously!) But she'll marry him when her divorce comes through. And our divorce too. It's okay, Mum. They live together, they're as good as married now anyway.

A pause, quiet but for Mhairi slurping her tea.

So who is the father?

A blush at last, and the words rushed and shaky. A lovely man named Roddy that you haven't met. He's from Livingston. Now, can I please have the porridge? Thank you.

Mhairi stuck into her porridge like she always had. Pig-like, shovelling great honey-laden spoonfuls into her mouth. But, like everything she did, her greed was laced with grace and was not revolting. Kate, who was beginning to be aware of her own decreasing ability to get away with looking anything but middle-aged unkempt, usually watched in wonder touched with envy. But tonight she turned and stood by the uncurtained window and looked out at the night and stars. Saw the swollen breasts and belly again. Felt her own stomach juices churn in sympathy with her galloping heartbeat, the blood whooshing in her ears. Was it possible to get seasick in your own kitchen?

Mhairi, Mhairi. She sighed, then she turned back to the cooker. Look, have the rest that's in the pot. How far along are you? Have you seen a doctor? Are you still not taking sugar in your tea?

No, I'm back to that, Mum. No point in slimming now. I'm about four months. At the clinic they gave me a pink card to keep track of things. Like pees and pounds, she said, proud of her own cleverness with words.

Is that what they do these days? (Eyes vague, forehead frowning.) That's nice. Good.

She brought her cup to the table and sat down. The baby that was not quite real to either of them yet wheeled around in the air, doing little somersaults and cartwheels. Kate batted it away, a survival technique, concentrated on another issue till she was ready for it.

Now, what are we going to do about big Murdo telling the whole wide world you're married?

Ah. That could be a problem, Mum. It's illegal, what I've done. Even if it is a stupid law.

Listen, Mhairi, I won't pretend it was wise, but I think we'll just have to deny it. Say his information is wrong. That it was another lassie with your name. After all, there are more than a few Mhairi McKinnons in Inverness, I'm sure.

But not more than one who would marry as a favour, get

pregnant by another, and calmly drink tea as if it was all in the natural order of things.

But maybe it was the natural order of things.

The baby, a wee boy who was to be called Patrick, swung closer and closer to the two women who hardly believed in him yet. To him, everything that happened was absolutely the only way things could happen. He pirouetted and spun out a gossamer shawl to settle about their heads and shoulders, to further persuade them that nothing could be simpler than himself.

But you're so young.

Mum. Jesus, Mum.

So . . .

So what?

So. When will I be meeting this lovely Roddy?

When he comes back, he'll come here straight away. He can't wait to meet you. And see this place. I told him all about it.

Comes back from where?

Oh, from Poland. He's got some fantastic building job lined up. He isn't exactly hired yet, but he will be. He's a very persuasive man.

Kate said nothing for a full fifteen seconds.

Is he now? I can believe that. I can well believe that.

Ah, don't be like that, Mum. Roddy's a good man. You'll love him. The baby is a bit of a surprise and he'd already planned this trip. But he'll be back.

When?

Later this spring sometime. Maybe early summer.

Kate could think of so many wise things to say. About men, about babies, about life. Then, poof, they were all gone and she was empty, skimming along the surface, too saturated by surprise for coherence. A chant had started up inside, silencing all else.

Me a widow granny, Mhairi a teenage single mum.

Me a widow granny, Mhairi a teenage single mum.

A dozen maternity scenes sketched themselves quickly, even a second's vision of buying bootees in Boots, one of those fancy German pushchairs from a catalogue, a coat for Mhairi to encompass her belly. She could hear her mother asking if this meant they'd all go on the social now, with *that* look on her face. Suddenly, an overload switch in her brain clicked down, and she wished only for oblivion. She yawned, stretching her arms.

It's incredible. You having a baby, Mhairi. How did it happen? No, you don't need to answer that. You're happy about it? You don't want to consider other alternatives? It's early days yet.

No way, Mum, said Mhairi with disgust. Don't be sad. You're soft.

Just checking. It wasn't such a shocking alternative in my day. I don't know how you'll manage, I can't imagine at all. What about your college course?

It's not the end of the world, Mum. Sorry I didn't tell you earlier. One of those daft things that's so hard to bring up, I guess. It just never seemed the right time and, well, it didn't seem to concern you. She giggled, as if she'd told a funny joke or been caught doing something only slightly naughty. Tears seemed to be in the air, but neither knew whose.

Anyway I'm off to bed, Mum. I'm wiped.

As they kissed goodnight, the baby boy, Patrick, floated between them, wavering first towards Kate, then finally to Mhairi, whom he followed upstairs to bed.

In the night the wind howled and scoured the sky of clouds. The hens gave up their plum-tree roost and flapped down to the shed where they perched awkwardly on hay bales and bike handlebars. Two tea-towels, forgotten on the line, whipped into the field where some mice would later find them and shred them into nests. The sea lost its rhythm and roared and crashed. Every living beast, from the otters in the tide pools to the sheep in the lee of the stone wall, cowered and breathed slow till the wind finally, near dawn, died down to a mere chilling icy whistle. Ha, said winter. I'm back.

Patrick listened to the wind and the sea and liked them. Mhairi and Kate heard nothing and slept, dreamt of men.

Mhairi had Roddy in her arms, but he kept dissolving and reappearing in another part of her flat. First the kitchen, then the sitting room. Every time she found him and folded her aching arms around him and felt about to melt into his extraordinary soft hardness, he would suddenly not be there. It was like fainting into a cloud. She had begun to feel more than a little anxious about this when she remembered the baby. Where had she left her? In the lift? She ran out to check and she wasn't there. Was she still in her pram in the hall? If the baby was lost, it was Daddy's fault, it was all Jack's fault. He should be helping her. She felt herself shaking and sweating, almost urinating with all the worry of it, then before she reached the hall, managed to drag herself half awake and convince herself she was home. She had no baby yet and she had no father and she had no Roddy either. She had Kate.

This was not sufficient. She fell back into sleep warily.

Kate, sleeping, had Jack again. Not specifically, so to speak, but he was in the background. She was aware of his presence, unintrusive but distinctive. Safe and simple, he was just there adding himself to the air and to her feeling about herself, while she made a pie. As usual in this dream, it was a good pie, and all the ingredients she'd been unable to lay her hands on in her waking day magically appeared. The pastry was unbroken, and laying it on top of the dish was like putting the fruit to bed. Jack was somewhere in the house doing something. The feeling of Jack being there was so exactly how it had always been before his death that when she woke at dawn, she tried without success to sink back into the same dream. The trouble with normality was that it was too normal to notice till it was gone.

She was cold. She pulled on a jumper over her nightie and stared out of the window at the monotone day, the better to fret about Mhairi and her new grandchild growing right this minute. In fact, during the night while the wind howled and the women dreamed, the tiny cells that were building Patrick increased their production speed. Working their complex magic like a good team should – every cell doing its bit for the good of the whole. Silently sending messages of co-operation and good will to each other, little pulse beats like fire-flies. While, over it all, a kind of foreman or conductor kept the rhythm going and the morale up. Pour that blood, heave that nerve-ending, plant that hair root, excellent men! Keep it up, no slacking, let's build this boy good and strong.

During Mhairi's dream, his heartbeat had quickened as well as hers and it had become a rushing, throbbing roar. In his well of red warmth he rocked and thrust his little feet until she woke and slept again, peacefully this time. He woke again and again towards dawn, but not when the cockerel squawked just outside the window. Not when his mother rose.

In his world of no day or night, no division of time whatsoever, he simply swung from one event to another, dipping in and out of profound sleep, and only now and again popping out to see what was what.

What he understood of what he saw was both more and less than we would. Unhindered by interpretation, or even by the restricting knowledge of his own physical limitations, he viewed the world as shapes. Moving shapes whose colours, sounds and smells were interesting but not as LOUD as the general pulse that emanated from each. The uncertain, half-formed, erratic beat of his mother was overwhelming most of the time. But drawn by new voices, he simply homed in on them. More whim than will. He was fluid. Which was to be expected, given his habitat.

Kate's voice had drawn him like a flash. She called to him without knowing it.

Gairloch Gets the News

On the tail end of a conversation, as old Betty and fat Izzy part in front of the post office:

Were you hearing about Kate's Mhairi?

Her getting hitched to an American millionaire? Oh, aye, that's old news, Betty. Tommy told me, we were checking out our books in the mobile and he whispered it in my ear, as if it was fresh news, and I was to keep it entirely to myself, he said. You know how he gets — full of importance, that man, he's a right joke really. As if it wasn't around the whole village, and I had to hear it a dozen times that afternoon.

Oh, aye, but did you hear it's not a real marriage?

Izzy shifted her bulk to stand more comfortably and leant forward to hear more. What do you mean, not a real marriage, Betty? Do you not mean not a real millionaire? You know how stories get exaggerated, I never believed that bittie. As if every American is a millionaire. They're all rich, right enough, but they can't all be millionaires, can they? I mean, it would ruin the meaning of the word, and they'd be inventing something else to be rare.

Betty squinted her rheumy eyes with the effort of concealing the joyous fact that she knew something, finally, that her friend did not. Oh, the triumph! She paused a second longer to savour the untold words – like a gift, it was; she was about to impart a gift, and the giver always won.

No, Izzy. Listen, I'm not knowing if he is a real millionaire or not, but the thing is, it doesn't matter.

What are you meaning, Betty? (Forehead furrowed, alarm beginning to register.)

It doesn't matter because he's not her real husband.

Oh, I think you're wrong there. Everyone knows, we've all known since the day they did it – you know Shelagh's sister-in-law works at the marriage, death and baby place, in the multi-storey.

No, interrupted Betty gleefully. I know they got married, but it's not a real marriage. It's one of those marriage-of-convenience thingies. Her face shone, a cackle just held in.

No.

Oh, aye.

You mean like in *Green Card*, where that froggie mannie marries the lassie who was later in *Four Weddings and a Funeral*, the one with the boy's name. Andie.

Aye, that's right. You mustn't tell anyone, though, Izzy. Mhairi could get into real trouble.

Oh, I would never breathe a word. It's serious, I can see that. I had no idea. How did you find out?

Betty looked both ways down the road, empty but for some gulls fighting over a crisp packet and a sleeping ewe, then leant close enough to whisper, Oh, I better not tell, she said to keep it quiet, so I'll not tell you who told me. It wouldn't be right. She wouldn't trust me again.

Oh, I understand, dear. I completely understand. Confidentiality, and all that. Well, I'll not tell anyone, it's safe with me. Poor Kate, do you think she knows? (Kate had become poor Kate since Jack's death; achieved a popularity she'd be needing.)

Oh, I never know with Kate. She won't let on if she does, but I think Mhairi will have told her. They must be that close, after losing Jack.

Oh, poor Jack, he was a lovely man, so he was.

Aye. Remember the time he fixed my fence after a storm?

Both women let their eyes fill, enjoyed the moment of grief, for the contrast to the sunny day and the fact they had eluded death themselves. They searched for and found cotton hankies, blew their noses.

Ach, well, I'd best be getting on my way, Betty.

Oh, aye. Myself as well, Izzy. There's a mountain of ironing.

Oh, stop, don't talk to me about ironing. It never ends. I've got a mountain range of ironing.

And mind, not a word, Izzy.

Oh, never worry about that. Shocking.

Aye, terrible shame to be breaking laws like that.

Still, not our business, is it, I mean?

Oh, exactly.

Old Betty and fat Izzy toddled off in opposite directions: Betty, depleted for having given away her secret, and Izzy bursting with untold news, wondering who to shock discreetly. Her hubby? That wouldn't be telling anyone, would it? But would he really appreciate the honour, the seriousness? No, it was too big to find release in telling just him. His response would be so unsatisfying. Perhaps Ellie, down the shore . . .

But wait, here came Ian McTod, her old dancing partner and the perfect recipient. She could feel the news rising, eager to be away and implanted in another. She increased her pace towards him, mouth already parted, eyes merry.

Jamie

Fit's a loon like ye doin in here? Awa and dinna come back. Now.

The park-keeper makes as if to use his brush on the boy, so he scuttles quickly down the path, shoving his things into his bag as he goes. One sock remains on the ground under the bush, and the keeper picks it up with his gloved hands as if it is contaminated and drops it into his bin.

I dinna ken fit the word's coomin tae, a young mannie thinkin he can kip in a private park like this'en, he later tells his fellow worker, as they drink their flasks of sweet tea.

Aye, but imagine havin nae place to put your heid doon but the wet grun. It's sad, ken? I mean, he must've had a hame someplace.

Who kens? He's maybe on the run. Maybe he's taken the drugs. I just dinna want onyone kippin in my park at a'. It's mankie. There's nae public toilets, ken. He should find the shelter the back side of Littlejohn Street.

By the time they finish their tea, the boy, or man, is crossing Union Street and heading down to the harbour where he can feel unseen for a while and watch the boats till he feels too hungry to stand about any more. Once he got a day's work on the docks, unloading fish crates, and this event still imbues the docks with a lucky texture. He stands and watches and is as happy as he gets these days.

Things That Eat Kate's Life

Duncan, Jack's old bachelor friend. And here he was again.

He'd taken to looking at Kate just that way, lately. Kept popping by and doing small jobs about the place, as if they were married. Hanging about the kitchen, sitting in Jack's chair, going on about the animals, the guttering, the window-frames, the weather.

Have you phoned the plumber yet about the pipes, Kate? Shall I do for you? I know a fine plumber over the hill. Or, That cat's needing wormed, I'll bring some tablets by with me tomorrow, look at the way it's acting, starved-like.

She'd found his presence comforting at first, he was a bit of continuity from the old life, but lately she'd been unnerved by the way Mhairi and her own mother talked about Duncan. Oblique references to his future with herself. On New Year, he'd given her a log for good luck and an open-mouthed kiss that tasted of Colgate and Old Holborn. She'd waited till it wouldn't seem rude to stop kissing, then politely disengaged her lips. Blushing, not from arousal, but confusion. Of course, Duncan would be a logical replacement husband, if such a thing was essential. Perfect, in fact. The devil she knew. He would move in and everyone would come to the wedding and think,

Well, that's Kate taken care of, no worries there, and don't things always work out for the best? He was lonely, she was lonely, *voilà*!

Now, with Mhairi's belly on the horizon like a distant but approaching storm, Duncan annoyed her even more; he interrupted her fretting. She'd been fretting hard for two months, and had pretty much perfected it. As if he sensed this, he perversely visited more.

She did not have time for this. No time. Today she stood on her doorstep and said, for the first time ever: I'm sorry, Duncan, but I'm busy just now, could you come back another time?

He sucked in his breath but managed a smile.

Alright, that's fine, Kate. I'll be back tomorrow. I got some paint for the window-frames.

Casual words, but his pale eyes flinched and she felt bad.

Thanks, Duncan.

Right, then, I'll be off.

But phone tomorrow, just in case. Will you? I may be out. I'm so busy these days, I hate it, but ...

He left her to her quiet house and she instantly slumped into a chair, exhausted. What was she so busy doing? Time slipped unheeded, speeded up and spiralled into the ether whenever she carelessly looked the other way. What, besides Duncan, was eating up her life?

Her pub job at the Sea View Hotel. The getting ready, the getting there, the getting home, the getting over it.

Her column. The wee bit of nonsense she had to write for the *West Coaster* every week, for money and the scrap of self-respect it gave her.

Her house, of course. It was very time-consuming and

33

tethered her to her life more strongly than even Jack had. (Which made her wonder if she'd actually married Jack's house, not Jack. It would explain a lot.) Not that she actually did much to the house. The window-sills were peeling, one gable end had a growing crack, and four slates lay on the ground where they had fallen months ago. Inside was messy, but she had certain standards: the kitchen table was usually wiped, the floor usually clear. She was proud of the fact she had never *intentionally* Hoovered up something that looked remotely like something that shouldn't be Hoovered, though she had been tempted. Occasionally, though never in spring, she would wash all the windows, paint walls, scrub tiles, then feel discouraged by how little difference it all made and lapse into domestic lethargy again. Anyway, aside from somehow eating a sizeable portion of her life, her house gave her the most joy of any material object she knew. In return for this adoration, she felt the house could not begrudge her the peeling paint or dusty stairs. If it had its priorities right.

The animals. The dog, called Dog. The three cats and the hens, all unnamed. The free-ranging sheep, two dozen last time she saw them all together; but she did nothing for them. They were Jack leftovers, the ones who'd eluded the final auction. She'd twice written *find and sell sheep* on lists of things to do, and subsequently lost the lists.

Her friends. But, come to think of it, they didn't take up much time these days. She'd lost the habit of close female friendships after marriage, and only briefly resumed it while Mhairi was very young and sanity seemed to depend on frequent contact with other mothers. Now, most of these women were working full-time, or had divorced and moved to Alness, a depressingly common solution to marital unhappiness. If she was to have a party, there were probably twenty people she could invite, consider them all dear old friends. They were the fabric of her entire life so far; she *knew* them and they her. But day to day, aside from passing each other on the road, she hardly saw them. So friends, somehow, didn't count.

Her mother. A major life-eater. Frequently on the phone to her, or in her house, cleaning windows and blethering away about bargains or her newest WRI flower arrangement. On the scale of emotional tension, about equal to Mhairi.

Suddenly, right on cue, as she was slumped in her chair imagining her mother eating up her life, there was her mother.

Hello, Mum, come on in.

I am in, darling. Were you having a snooze?

No. Aye, well, maybe a little one.

I saw Duncan down the road, he said you might be out. He said you were busy.

I am. Just having a little sit-down first. Cup of tea?

He's a lovely man, that Duncan. I love the way he always stops and chats to me. Most young men couldn't be bothered.

Mum, Duncan is nearly fifty.

Still.

They went into the kitchen, Kate filled the kettle.

Kate, why on earth have you bought that washing-up liquid? I told you about the special offer in the Mace, were you not listening? Maybe you've money to spare, I don't know.

No, Mum, I just forgot.

And will you not bin that old man's shirt, hey? You look enough like a scarecrow. Will I get you one in Marks'? I'm away in later today. They have some lovely ones, so they do.

Wrinkle resistant and pastel colours. You wouldn't need to bother ironing, Kate.

Ironing? Here's your cup of tea. What are you frowning at?

Is that chicken poo on the floor? Are you letting the hens into the kitchen again? I'm not fussy, but that is just unhygienic, Kate.

Aye, would you have a word with them, Mum? They've no respect for me.

Her mother was called Margaret, of course, and she was secretly despised by her peers in the village for her superior competence in most things. These days Kate found herself protective of her perfect unlovable mother, rarely had the heart to tell her to shut up and piss off, but did a lot of sighing in her presence. She was just an old dear, after all. Physically out of the traditional Highland mould – short and big-bosomed, pink-cheeked and blue-eyed. A knitter of cardies, baker of uniformly bland scones, builder of inoffensive flower arrangements to be raffled off at sales, finder of bargains. Her creations always won first prizes for their perfection and economy, but she'd made the mistake of being proud. Not pretending she was undeserving. She didn't *get it* and her framed awards hung immodestly over the sideboard to be admired by nobody, for visitors rarely came.

As if that wasn't bad enough, she had a very unHighland grasp of punctuality and was always the first to arrive everywhere. Community council meetings, church services, children's birthday parties, the local pensioners' club teas. She was always first in and had the advantage over every person who sensibly arrived later. Gave them her unflustered greeting from the best seat, and was far too accustomed to her unpopularity to recognise it.

As a child, Kate used to pray for her mother to be late. Late meeting her after school, late with the tea, late at anything. She would daydream of her mum arriving at the shop only to discover she'd forgotten it was half-day. Even once would make her more human. And if she could now and then look even a tiny bit dishevelled, as if she had a life in the same world as everyone else. Her house was so spotless it made people nervous. Kate did her best, even now, but her messes vanished as she made them, she left no mark anywhere.

But poor Margaret, she could not help being the arch enemy of all dust and clutter, an alien to unpunctuality with an unerring instinct for frugality. It was the way she was born, the fault of a recessive efficiency gene from three generations back, from her very unpopular great-grandmother who used to brag about a flagged floor so clean you could eat porridge off it.

Margaret's husband, Kate's father, married her for her impeccable sense of order, but objected to the way she would never let him fill his ashtray. Kept putting a clean one in front of him between roll-ups. And fussing about the way the shreds of Old Holborn floated on to the carpet and chair. She fussed, he frowned, and one day, when Kate was seven, he left. His letter later explained. Apparently the new woman was a hotel cleaner, but he didn't remark on the irony. The letter had stains on it, maybe tea stains, and Margaret held it at a distance, with clear distaste, then threw it quickly into the bin and washed her hands.

Well, lassie, she'd said to a puzzled Kate, who sat watching her. Your dad, well, he's away on a work trip and won't be back for a wee while. He sends his love, and says he's sorry to miss your sports day, but we'll take some photies, will we? And send them. He may have to work on there a bit.

Kate recalled her mother sighing and briskly rubbing her hands together, as she tidied this messy truth into a fib, then getting out the Hoover. The absence of any dust or dirt whatsoever seemed glaringly hurtful to Kate, and she considered putting on her wellies and going out in the mud for a while, just to traipse back into the house with some of the world on her feet. Give her mum the satisfaction of real particles to suck up into her machine. It seemed the least she could do.

Her father did turn up occasionally after that, but only to touch base. She used to think he only visited to comment on her new height. He never seemed to know what to say. Once the woman came with him, but she sat in the car and wouldn't come in.

Bring her away in, her mum had said, she can have a cup of tea, I'll not bite her.

No, Margaret, she won't. Just leave it, woman, I'm not staying long anyway. Just came to see how the wee lassie was getting on, and see you're managing fine.

And that was it. He sent cheques and life was able to continue more or less the same without him. New dresses for her Christmas dances and parties, the same toys the other kiddies got over the years, a new bike when she needed one. Margaret did volunteer work, organised Brownies, arranged church fairs, took over the WRI rota for teas. She did not date, not caring to risk another messy involvement. Life was smooth, simple and, well, clean.

As the years went by, Kate had less and less curiosity about her father. Guessed her own untidiness was his gift in her bloodstream, but he was a stranger, incidental to her life. An inarticulate man who held a blurred shape in her mind, and none in her heart. He came to her and Jack's wedding, but not to Jack's funeral. By then, they'd lost all contact, and both Margaret and Kate gradually erased every visual reminder of his existence. He was a ghost.

But he was a ghost who helped her love her mother. Kate loved her especially because she had been abandoned. Because she was alone and proud, and that seemed a most poignant combination. Besides, there was always that mother-daughter similarity thing, which worried her, so perhaps it was only herself she was protecting after all. A charm against being treated badly by Mhairi. A good agnostic, she believed in hedging all her bets.

Well, Kate, said her mother now. Are you sure you're not needing anything in Inverness?

Aye, Mum, thanks anyway.

I'll pop in to Mhairi while I'm there, see how she's getting on. Poor thing, she must be feeling it. I remember when I was carrying you. Six months is when your energy goes.

Aye. Well. Energy.

Margaret left, and ten minutes later the Murdos came.

The Murdos ate her life for breakfast, lunch and dinner.

They got a cup of tea and an offhand denial of the wedding rumours.

Ah, you'd believe anything now, wouldn't you, Murdo? If it was juicy enough.

Well, it does look like certain other rumours might be correct.

39

Go on, you'll not keep such good tidings as a baby from your cousin now, would you?

Kate paused, gauging his sincerity, then plunged in. Absolutely not. I would've told you first, had you a phone. Mhairi's expecting early June. We're both dead pleased about it.

Wee Murdo beamed, but big Murdo's response took the cake. He threw his bulky arms around Kate and squeezed, tears rolling from his eyes. He'll be a beautiful wee boy, now you wait and see. And Mhairi's looking right bonny on it, I saw her in town. It suits her.

He went on and on, and for the first time in a long time, Kate brought down the bottle herself and poured herself and Murdo a dram. Wee Murdo got more tea.

And another day was filled and tumbled down the hill of time to join other forgotten days, a massive messy heap of them, bits of long afternoons and early winter mornings sticking out for no apparent reason.

Like the cards Jack used to shuffle in preparation for another game of rummy. Dovetailing into each other, randomly, kings sliding up to threes, diamonds to clubs, quicker and closer till the two decks were one, but for the few corners of cards sticking out. He was a clumsy shuffler, and the cards were imperfect, no tidy clean pack in Kate's house. Then she'd perform the crucial ritual, presumably to stop cheating and any kind of real excitement, and cut them by lifting off the top half. He'd put the rest of the cards on top, and that would be that. Another deck ready to be dealt.

Patrick's Current State

Six and a half months old. Favourite position: upside down, arms and legs crossed. Sucking his thumb. All his cells were still humming and chortling, busy growing more hair, longer toenails and fingernails, increasingly efficient lungs, strong white bones and mysterious cerebral compartments. He ingested, hiccuped, burped and farted, all the time it took his mother to drink a cup of tea. While she watched one episode of *Heartbreak High*, he swallowed amniotic fluid, peed it out again, and accumulated meconium for his first bowel movement.

His hobby was dreaming, and he smiled frequently. Features like his lips were proportionally huge and his smile was beatific; would sadly never be seen outside the womb in quite this way. He was moody, and sometimes he felt irritable with an itch he could not scratch. He would frown then, an ugly old man. The itch was merely growing pains. He was no longer at his peak acceleration, but was still growing faster than he ever would again. He could no longer fling out all his limbs and dance quite so freely, and missed it without knowing what missing was.

Jamie

He is trying to sleep, but it is not easy. If he moves an inch, cold air will penetrate, find a gap in his carefully arranged bedding. And yet his leg itches, torments him, feels like there are ants crawling up it. No, not ants, spiders. Spider eggs have hatched in his trouser cuff and now baby spiders, millions of them, are crawling up his leg, tickling his hairs, towards his crotch. He forces himself to lie still, not to expend more energy shivering, moving, scratching, but suddenly it is too much and he erupts. Bags and newspaper blankets go fluttering over on to the ground, and he is tearing madly at his leg, both joyously relieved and freezing. Fuck fuck fuck, he mutters, and begins rearranging the layers.

A squat three-quarter moon comes out from behind some clouds, offers some light to see by.

Mhairi Keeps Things

Like her mother's columns. What are you cutting? Kate would ask, if she saw Mhairi with the scissors.

Nothing, she'd say, and wait till later to cut out and keep the column.

Today she cut out the column without having to hide it, as she was not at home. She was in her flat in Inverness. Her room mates were watching *EastEnders*. She cut it out and taped it into the scrapbook she kept at the bottom of her desk drawer.

Her head felt heavy and stupid, as if the baby was lodged up there, blocking the flow of thoughts. She flicked back through the pages.

WEST COAST CRACK

I may as well tell you my husband died two weeks ago. I have to tell you because now when I try to write any other words I don't recognise my voice. Gus was always here before and then I knew who I was. He was Gus and I was Eilidh and we were husband and wife and everything else sprang from there. Our daughter, the house, all our outings and jobs and friends.

Now he's gone I have to invent myself. I am Eilidh who has no husband. Eilidh and not Gus. I write this slowly, after hours of sitting here. I have moved to another country and the language is difficult to grasp.

When I was eighteen I went to a dance in Fingall town hall and a boy with curly brown hair and pimples asked me to dance.

43

I don't remember what song it was. I do remember that as soon as he could, he wanted to stop dancing. He was not a dancer, he said, and it touched me that he'd done something he didn't like just to be near me. It was the seventies but Fingall town hall was still in the fifties, and all we did later was hold hands. After a dance ended we just let two of our hands remain entangled. As if by accident. It was enough.

And that, readers, was my husband Gus. We were very different, but he was my husband and he was always there. He danced just to be near me.

Meanwhile, the world, Gusless, continues to spin. Or so I am told.

The first lambs have been born up the hill and totter about after their mothers, who pretend not to know them. Old Mac finally got his hull repaired and will put to sea again as soon as Easter. Could be his last season and everyone wants to crew for him.

The Free Church is getting their new roof after all, despite a very poor turnout at the fundraising tea last week. A mysterious benefactor was hinted at, and by the way a certain local merchant is strutting around with everything but a halo pinned to his scalp, I have a pretty good idea who.

Lochinellie High School is getting ready for their next term, and pre-exam anxiety is palpable in the air as I drive by. I try not to inhale too deeply. Too tragic, all those tender young minds unable to frolic this spring.

Have I told you about the light here on a winter afternoon, the sun under the clouds, how it turns the sea to a blinding sheet of metal, opaque as mercury, and the sky a bruised plum purple over it? Stones stand stark, cast sharp shadows. Can you see it?

The air tastes of cold wet strawberries and breathing gets mixed up with drinking.

Snowdrops have been spotted, but not by me. It all goes on and on, regardless of who no longer witnesses it. Gus is gone.

Funny how Mum lied about their names, but nothing else, as if names mattered the most. A kind of irrational modesty. Names gave away nothing, and protected nothing. Like hiding her face behind a scarf, while standing perfectly naked. It was stories that exposed, never names.

She rubbed her hard belly though her T-shirt. (Seven months now, Patrick arched his back when she rubbed. He could use a good rubbing all over, his muscles ached with wanting this.) Incredible how the time flew, the baby grew, and she still felt asleep. Every time she thought of the baby, she came hard up against the fact of her father and his remarkable absence. How could he go and do that dying thing? *Dying*, for God's sake. It was just too melodramatic and fucking final. As if she didn't have enough problems as it was. Who was she supposed to get mad at? When she figured out what to say, who was she going to say it to? For fuck's sake, even after all these months, it was still a pain.

I mean, *come on, Dad*. A joke's a joke.

The Love Interest

Brendan had always been a problem. Why couldn't he be like the others and stay put? He'd had exactly the same upbringing, yet here he was again, not doing what he was programmed to do at twenty-one. Six thousand miles from home, married illegally to a girl called Mhairi, who was about to have a baby by another man. Meanwhile, Brendan was living with the apparently perfect Isabel. Complicated, but typical.

Michael tried to read his newspaper on the train up from Glasgow, but it was impossible. Whenever he thought of his son it put a brake on everything else. He was hurtling towards Inverness when he'd much rather, with every atom of his heart, be at home having a bottle of beer on the deck, the barbecue quietly sizzling away and his daughter Beth making noises with plates. He closed his eyes for a moment, so painfully vivid was his longing. Oh! Why did people like to travel? It was excruciating and full of discomfort. He felt so exposed. But Beth was probably not home anyway. She was spending more and more time over at Tim's, was probably shifting most of her stuff over there now. His last birdie flown.

The communal nest had broken up five years ago, and the children had had two homes to choose from. Both sons had stayed with Marcia, just visiting him at weekends. But Beth had chosen to move out with him, to his minuscule apartment in Fairfax. Quiet sweet Beth, he was not much company for her, but she had been the saving of him. He needed the presence of other people. Not to think about them or do things with them, but just to know they shared the same physical space. Were breathing the same air. If Beth was gone, he knew he would have moments of feeling invisible. Gone. When he had intimations of this state, he always headed for the kitchen. Poured a beer and filled a plate with bread, cheese, nuts, anything really, though he'd cut out the junk food lately as simply suicide food. And then he would eat. Watch a trashy movie on television while filling his mouth till he felt his jeans pinching and drowsiness obliterating his fear. Not that he ever thought of it as fear, or thought about things much at all. He was a builder of fine furniture, a tactile man, who responded to feelings without analysing them.

Well, of course, the time would come. Beth was twenty, almost finished at college, would certainly leave him and he would have to be glad for her. Not cling.

Meanwhile, he was here to sort out Brendan.

Marcia, his elegant ex-common-law-wife, on the phone: Look, Michael, it's not like I can go. Is it? I mean someone has to work full-time. Beth says you're not working at all at the moment. I would pay your air fare, you have no excuse. If he's in trouble, bring him home. Kicking and screaming if you have to.

Brendan? Do something because I order him to?

You have to try, Michael. God, don't be such a wimp. You've always spoiled him, just let him do what he wanted.

True, in a way, but then he'd always understood Brendan's desires, couldn't see the harm in fulfilling them.

Alright, Marcia. I said I would go, didn't I?

No, actually. I never did hear those words. All I've heard are sulky reasons why you shouldn't need to.

True again. As usual, she created a weak and stupid Michael to turn around and despise. She was bright and successful. He was not. These were obvious facts and he was used to living with them. His shoulders rounded over his paunchy belly in defence against her sharpness.

But it hardly mattered these days. He could not sustain the intensity of such habitual hurt and it had passed quickly. No spare energy at forty-eight to waste.

He looked out of the train window. He was here on a mission, sent as an ambassador from his family, to see what Brendan was really up to now. Possibly persuade him to come back home to California. To try to impose his dubious will. Seemed the story of his history with Brendan, and the very familiarity of it all finally sent him to sleep. It had been a long trip, his first overseas flight. While his exhausted body slept through the deer-dotted Cairngorms, somewhere in his mind his perception of place slipped, so when he woke in Inverness, California seemed very far away indeed. Not quite real, in fact. His mind could not simultaneously contain both places. California was on the back-burner, he couldn't even hear it simmering.

The train-station air was crystal clear and everything was sharply detailed, with high glass dome and piercing cold draughts and somewhere just out of sight a busker's tin whistle, shrill but pure. The cold felt clean. He felt completely awake and alert and young. One of those times when a glimpse in a mirror would've shocked him, for he looked more like sixty.

Of course, Brendan was not there. He had never been on time in his life. His mind always leapt, saw no insurmountable problems, rushed at life, and basically never allowed for traffic. Michael supposed he would come in about ten minutes, so he walked outside and leant against the freezing stone wall of the station. Good to be standing, though he thought he could hear the wall sucking out his body heat. Like the noise a straw makes when the drink is almost gone.

California might be unreal, but hard as he tried, he failed to absorb the fact that he was in Scotland. It was a fairy-tale land of antiquity. Everything looked so charmingly drab and picturesque compared to the strip malls and suburbs of home. Like entering a period drama on Alistair Cooke's *Masterpiece Theatre*, channel nine. Was his LL Bean costume appropriate? Would the wardrobe police blow the whistle on him? He couldn't take it seriously, believe that these people, these rather undernourished-looking people dressed mostly in dark colours and rushing around with downturned faces while clutching plastic carrier-bags, were as real as himself and his family. Not possible that they had houses and jobs and gardens and aches and pains and believed this was the centre of the universe in the way Californians believed California was. He raised his eyes to some stone cornices on the building opposite. Carved angels reclining on Grecian urns over a Victorian market. Give me just a little break, he thought.

On to this stage of quaint unreality he saw his son coming from away off down the road. His heart quickened and his diaphragm lifted and tingled. That old unbearable almost painful pleasure in his lower chest.

Here was Brendan at last, the child who affected him the most, and that was the irony. Caused him the most grief, never took the easy obvious routes in life, grating, abrasive, stubborn, yet Brendan alone truly interested and excited him. He called his name aloud, startling himself. First word he'd spoken all day: Brendan!

Dad. Sorry I'm late, Dad, I was about—

Oh, shut up, Brendan and let's go get a drink. Goddamn cold place you choose to live.

They laughed and hugged quickly. They had the same kind of laugh. A noise that seemed to erupt against the wishes of the owner. Their light eyes always shone long before their mouths gave in, and the final gust of air and sound was always genuine pleasure. Physical contact was brief and awkward. Both tall, Brendan slightly taller and less broad than his father. Identical foreheads – high and pale and square. They looked intelligent, but not glaringly so. More than a hint of under-achiever about them both, and self-mockery. Something in the way they smiled, and walked without strong purpose. Ambled.

In the end, they bought some beer from Safeway and went to Isabel's flat up on Crown Circus. It was tiny, more a cave, but Isabel had draped tartan and floral covers over the furniture. There were red tulips in a blue vase on the kitchen table. There was no television, but a computer was set up in a cupboard space, with the door taken off the hinges. Everything managed to be shoddy and cheerful at the same time.

Isabel was tiny and bright, like a pretty little boy, with her pea-green eyes and head nearly shaved of hair. Each petite ear had three gold stars piercing the pink clean flesh. She wore black jeans and one of Brendan's shirts bought by Michael last Christmas. She smelt of baby powder and joss sticks and something else quite alien.

When Michael offered his huge cold hand, she smiled and slipped her warm one into it.

Sit down, you must be worn out. Coffee alright? I got some fresh ground in.

He sat and listened to Brendan and Isabel chatter in low voices in the kitchen. Their voices overlapped, halted simultaneously and united in a giggle. By the time they emerged with the coffees, Michael knew it had been a wasted trip. Isabel was a surprise, a waif with grace, and Brendan was besotted.

Why couldn't it have been a girl in California? His mind ran through the golden girls in Brendan's high school. Spoiled, perhaps, but wholesome, familiar. But it could never have been one of them for his son. Brendan was not drawn to the known. So, was this to be his home now? How would he fit? Did he want to fit? Is that why he liked it here, the impossibility of ever belonging?

They went out to an Italian restaurant for dinner. He had heard Indian restaurants were the only places to eat, but things had changed, his son informed him. Some excellent Italian and French restaurants had opened and he was forced to alter his view of the Highlands slightly, add the word cosmopolitan.

They drank wine, shared dishes of pasta.

So tell me, Brendan, have you sorted out your visa problems?

Oh, yeah, got my permanent visa last week. Had a little interview with someone from Immigration and Mhairi was brilliant. I'm all set now.

Will I get to meet this wife of yours, then?

Of course, Dad, we'd planned to spend a week there. Her mom's got an amazing place over on the west, you'll love it.

And her mother knows all about it? The marriage, and everything?

Oh, yeah. She's cool, you'll like Kate.

And you'll just get divorced?

Eventually. Neither of us has any plans to marry anyone else for a while. Isabel's divorce will be through in September, but I don't think she'll be wanting to get married again.

Michael raised his eyebrows at Isabel, who laughed softly. No, definitely not. I'll not be making the same mistake again.

Michael remembered his own courtship. Marcia, known as Mercury then, had moved into his apartment. There had been sex, great sex, then babies, pets, mortgages. No wedding, though he always thought of her as his wife. It had been the early seventies in San Francisco. They had a party with some friends, got stoned and walked to the beach and announced to the Pacific they were now a couple for ever and ever. Someone had even thrown rose petals on the frothing waves. They had all been barefoot, of course. Her hair had been long. His longer.

Later, he couldn't pin down the exact time, Mercury had shed all the hippie stuff, including her name, declared it a phase, became Marcia again and took a course in accountancy. Built up a business. Ambition flaring from her nostrils, while he had continued the same carpentry jobs, pottering along from job to job, quickly overtaken in earning power by Marcia. In the end it had made more sense for him to stay at home raising the kids. And when they were all in their teens, it ground to a halt. A scene etched into him, the final confirmation of his incompetence.

You turn me into a bitch, I hate the me I am with you.

But you still love me, he'd protested weakly.

This is nothing to do with love, Michael, for Christ's sake. Look, I need to be able to like myself. I hate the way I treat you, but I can't help it. It's a destructive pattern.

Well, just stop it.

I wish I could, Michael. I wish you could make me. But you can't. I want a divorce.

But we're not married.

You know what I mean. You never could talk about serious things without making stupid little jokes.

He hadn't meant it as a joke, it had felt like a loophole he might use to trap her into staying. He had felt he was falling through space, grabbing hold of anything. He had been very much afraid of crying in front of her, further disgusting her.

But now his stomach was full of fettuccini and red wine, and his son was sitting close to a girl who always turned towards him but had no wish for ties. He wished for a moment he still smoked, to dull the almost painfully exquisite sense of repletion. And a yearning for something forgotten, perhaps never possessed. He hurt, but couldn't discount happiness as the cause.

They walked back home through damp yellow-lit streets and he was given two hot-water bottles for the sofa-bed. When he woke very early to the gulls crying he felt strange. Neither here nor there. Both California and Scotland were just lumps of land protruding from the sea and he had flown from one to the other to see and do ... what? What was he but another lump, only of flesh and blood and bones, and he moved through life with the illusion of purpose until he filled a hole in the ground. Empty, empty, meaningless and absurd. He glanced at his watch. Three o'clock. Of course. He smiled, closed his eyes, slipped his head under the duvet and let sleep drown him.

Jamie

His life has not always been this way, but he doesn't remember that other self. Or rather he remembers, but it feels like remembering some distant relation. An acquaintance he has known casually, been slightly envious of, perhaps not liked hugely. His self in the before-time hadn't lived lightly, yet left few ridges, only smooth forgettable surfaces. Like flicking through a stranger's photo album. Not that his own mum had ever bothered with taking photos, or the other mums either.

That other person was not him. He is only now, in the rain, waiting for the doors to open so he can fill his stomach with some lukewarm watery soup against the winter chill that in Aberdeen is more wicked than anywhere in the world. A penetrating bone-cramping head-cracking damp.

His turn comes and he nods to the familiar woman's face — a round blandness of flesh that says, Yes here you are again and so am I let's get on with it.

He sits down with his soup and plate with two slices of dry white bread spread with Stork. He wishes he could hold his spoon steadier and not slop any, but it is fine. Another familiar face looms up to his table. A man who smiles broadly, revealing four missing teeth.

Fit like, old man, sit doon, sit doon, fit's the crack?

Ah, it's the same old same old, you ken. Just chavin awa. The old man laughs as if he has told a big joke, and the boy, or young man, laughs too.

They slurp their soup till it's gone, and they leave together to walk up the hill. It is another hour before the shelter opens, but there'll be a queue already, with this rain. And what else is there to do anyway? Just keep putting one step in front of another. The boy bows his head against the drizzle and walks in the lee of the larger man.

Hours later, he is woken up by many sounds. There are eleven men in the room, and by the sounds of it, not many are sleeping soundly. Several are choking on their phlegm, in great heaving hawking spasms, sitting up in bed. One is masturbating, regardless of the lack of privacy, or he is asleep and lucky enough to be in the arms of a dream lover. The bedsprings wheeze away, as does his breathing till it is over. The man on his left lies on his back, muttering away to someone called Eunice, about how he's going to fucking kill her if she doesn't shut her big fat ugly trap. Eunice-hater's eyes are wide open and he is staring at the ceiling, now and then slamming the heels of his hands together. The man on the other side snores and the exhalations are exactly like a rubber ball bouncing down an empty wet street. Three beds away, but loudest of all, is an old man praying, eyes shut, and rocking back and forth. Lord is the answer, the light, the everlasting mercy, have mercy mercy mercy on me, praise the Lord, Lord loves a sinner, take me, Lord, please ...

Until someone throws a shoe at him and hollers, I'll fucking take ye if ye don't shut the fuck up, ye fucking wanker.

Mhairi Comes Home

The days had lengthened, against their will, lashing out protests of hail and even snow. We will go down fighting, cried the Highland winter days. Never let it be said we gave in easily to the turn of a season.

Kate, on a freezing pink May evening, waited for the Westerbus. Thought she had lived a sizeable portion of her life doing just this – waiting in her car for her daughter to appear. She closed her eyes and tried to savour the moments before her arrival. Especially this arrival – the final one. There'd been a time not too long ago when she would've defined her maternal success as her child's true independence. But now. Somehow the edges were blurred.

A second's flash of memory – proudly taking an excited, albeit newly fatherless, Mhairi to college; the kind of event that validated a parent's lifestyle and sacrifices. Installing her in her student flat, buying all those little things a flat needs, a desk lamp, toilet brush, etc. The strangeness of coming home again to an empty house, but strangeness had been her familiar since Jack's illness was first diagnosed. Loneliness came into it, but mostly just a sensation of running on empty.

The bus came, the moment ended, as usual without inspiration or clarity, except for her awareness that another era had ended without her fully understanding it, and before she felt ready for the next one. The wheel was turning, regardless. She took the bags from her daughter, who thrust her belly out and seemed on the verge of toppling over backwards. She put the bags in the boot, then went back for the boxes the driver was removing from the back of the bus.

I'm home, Gairloch! said Mhairi, joylessly. Lucky me! Lucky you!

Kate said nothing. Gairloch had been fine for Mhairi's growing up, but how could she become an adult in the place that had witnessed all her tantrums and puddles of pee? It was hard not to see this return as a defeat. Mhairi was dense with need, Kate felt the car sink into the road with the load and her heart sank too. They headed home.

How is the bump, Mhairi?

She's kicking all the time, mum. Wakes me up. Feel.

I'm driving, darling. Later.

But Mhairi dragged one of her mother's hands off the steering-wheel and placed it on her belly. Kate sucked in a breath. The strong punch and kick, the insistent I'm-alive-in-here signal. She laughed out loud at the sheer electric strangeness of it.

Wow, that is some kick. She laughed again.

Mhairi took Kate's hand off and sighed. Pain in the backside, it is, don't know what's so funny. I hate it. It's like a – a parasite or something. A leech.

Patrick heard her words as a series of deep vibrations, with erratic stops and starts. The words were mostly orange and red, with cool violet streaks streaming through them. Meaningless.

He was himself, every cell was Patrick; he was not Mhairi or Kate, and he knew none of their versions of the world. He was not expecting a powder-blue room with teddy-bear borders, or a father who might cherish him, or a mature settled mother. Nor did he know the clouds held acid rain some days, or that the Chinese might be hatching plots to eliminate his own race, or that scientists were at this very minute developing a pesticide that would result in a rash of cancers affecting his own generation forty years hence. He had no expectations of order and calm, he was chaos and wilderness personified.

Asleep or awake, he was increasingly alert to his internal world and had less curiosity about the world outside his sphere, preferring just to wallow in his briny home. Only Kate's voice still drew him out. He was compelled by her, in the purest definition of the word.

Kate's hand crept back to her daughter's belly, despite the hairpin turns. Just rested there, to feel a being who had no thoughts with words, but managed to kick and wave just the same.

Michael Phones His Daughter

Bethie, yeah, I got here fine. The land of haggis.

What's that? You don't want to know.

Yeah, Brendan's fine, and you would love Isabel. She's not at all like you thought she would be. No, she's so sweet and pretty, and she hasn't cast a spell to steal Brendan from us. Brendan's the one — he's in love up to his eyeballs.

No, I mean it.

Her? I'm not so sure, she seems pretty together by comparison. It'll end in tears, as your mother would say!

No, you're right, it was a little weird at first actually being here but, yeah, I'm getting used to it.

Not much.

I have to remember not to call them English, or even British. Yeah, total inferiority complex.

Oh, some real weird habits.

Like what? Well, for lunch the first day, we had baked beans from a can poured on to white toast.

I know, well I almost did, right on the table. And get this — they never ever eat breakfast out, can you imagine? They eat their pancakes cold, spread with jam in the afternoon! Gross, huh? And they fry tomatoes in fat, scramble eggs with milk in a pot, and the portions of meat you get in a sandwich are a joke. No, not cheap. Not by a long shot.

My fave place? So far it's an amazing second-hand bookshop in an old church, with a café upstairs, you'd love that.

Well, save your pennies, Bethie. Or ask your mom.

No, no, I think they like the hard life, honestly.

No, listen. There are so many obvious ways they could make life simpler.

Like what?

Oh, loads of things, little things that would drive me crazy. Like the fact most Scotchtapes are sold without that little plastic dispenser thing, so you spend hours trying to find the stupid end bit. And phone numbers – sometimes you have to look up two numbers, the codes are in another part of the phone book.

I know.

Oh, yeah, and they hang their clothes up to dry in the rain. I am not joking. Everywhere you look, clothes are dripping on clothes-lines.

Why don't they have clothes dryers? I do not know.

I know, Beth, it does all seem a bit strange and hopeless, but when I mention it, Brendan just looks at me in disgust. And he hates it if I point out the fact that anything is cheaper, bigger and better in California. Hates it.

I've been here five days now and I've been aware of a waiting feeling, but couldn't put my finger on what I was waiting for – you know?

Yeah, like that.

Then this morning the sky cleared for a minute and I realised I've been waiting for it to stop raining. You know how you do.

When it begins raining, you automatically just start waiting for it to stop. IT DOESN'T STOP HERE.

It's raining right now, a steady grey drizzle.

No, I don't think summer means that here. I'll ask Brendan.

Inverness is sitting smack dab in the middle of a raincloud, and the whole shebang is sticking out into the sea.

Oh, no, no. Much worse than the fog, really.

And what is more bizarre, you won't believe this, Beth — THEY DON'T ADMIT IT! They walk around in the pouring rain with hardly any clothes on and say things like, Nicer day today, isn't it? Oh, aye, much. Nae so much frost in the air.

Of course he doesn't. He never agrees with anything I say. He says the weather is always changing, that every day has several climate changes in it, that rainbows are common as muck.

Muck, I said. His expression, not mine. I don't even know what muck is, probably a kind of mud, which is coming out of the woodwork.

Yeah, my boots work fine. You were right about getting them sealed.

Don't phone here next week, we're going to a place called Gareluck to visit his illegal wife Varey and her mom.

Which reminds me, I'd better make sure this lady knows we're coming, you know your brother, assuming he's welcome everywhere.

Yeah, okay, I'll look out for a piece of white heather for you. Hey, don't forget to pay the paper boy. And tell your mom Brendan will be writing her himself, and I've done my best. What?

Oh, I've only seen three guys in kilts, two with shaved heads and nose-rings, and one old guy with a runny nose who looked lost. All their knees were red and sore-looking.

Yeah, they're all midgets.

Probably inbred.

Jamie

He is hanging his socks over the gorse bush to dry, for all the world like an old wifey, carefully arranging them to get the maximum benefit of the little breeze blowing from the coast. Then the shirt, arms flung out, and the underpants, grey but odourless, now they've had a scrub in the burn.

He stands back, bare-chested and barefoot, hands on narrow hips, to admire his handiwork. His black trousers are held up with a piece of bungy cord, knotted at the waist. The sight of his clean clothes gives him satisfaction. The thought of putting the clean clothes on later gives him satisfaction. He whistles and looks around for a place to bide the time till his clothes are as dry as the day can make them. A nice hidden hollow to curl up in, his jacket over his chest, and dream away the hours. Lie so still the birds will forget he is there and sing closer and closer.

Then he will get dressed and move on. He never stays in one place very long. He is Aberdonian and keeps returning to it, but only for short spells now. He likes to think he is a travelling man. Only a real travelling man would think of doing his laundry in a field.

Certainly no job has ever held him for long. A girl has once. That was a few years ago, but still, when he says her name to himself it hurts. He wants to hurt sometimes, because at least then he feels something, so he says her name out loud now, picks the old scab. Catriona. There. Catriona Catriona.

It cuts like a dull knife, jagged and sore, and his closed eyes flinch as he lies in his nest in the hollow.

She shouldn't have done that. But then maybe he shouldn't have done what he did either. It is not clear.

Her da had said Jamie was bad news. Probably her da had been right about lot of things. Like after the miscarriage, he talked Catriona into using the inheritance from her gran to buy a house in her own name.

Jamie used to go off to jobs and not come back for weeks, sometimes months. Working up in Fraserburgh on the boats, or in the fish factories. Stayed in digs then, or in a workmate's house, eating some wifey's cooking and chipping in a few pounds. Living in the here and now, forgetting half the time he had a wife himself at home.

Then going home one day unexpectedly to find Catriona red-eyed and blotch-faced, saying she didn't want him any more at all, she was better off without him and never knowing where he was or when he'd be coming home. There were far better men waiting for her to be free. Or was it one man? She had started divorce proceedings. His belongings were in two cardboard boxes in the entrance hall.

I dinna need this, Jamie. I dinna need ye any more.

And he couldn't persuade her either with his stammering soft words or pleading and he wasn't the type to try brute strength. Her da came over that night, and he was out on the streets of his own town. He stashed the boxes in the shed, where did she think he could carry them? He couldn't think what to do, where to go. Headed towards Union Street. A few pounds in his pocket and the August sun shining away like it didn't know there was a tragedy and it should be cold and grey rain falling on his shoulders, not sun making his eyes squint and his confused feet stumble away down the road.

Jamie, fecksake, fit wey are ye coomin back here?

His last mother, the one who had him till his eighteenth birthday, scowling at him. He'd turned up on her doorstep after spending a couple hours down the pub, where he'd failed to meet up with any mates or befriend any new ones. When he told her he had no place to sleep, she only stubbed out her cigarette and sighed and said, Well, ye canne have a hame here again, there's nae room. You'd best be on your way again afore it gets dark. Coom back when you've something to show for yourself, like.

Even as a bairn, he'd only caused his mothers grief, never doing well in school, always losing his jacket or dinner money or door key. They'd never felt anything for him but a grudging obligation to keep him alive till he was old enough not to be their legal responsibility. God knows, they had enough problems of their own, this string of well-meaning but hard women who took the ones nobody wanted, the ones too old for adoption, the bed-wetters and petty thieves and vandalisers.

Of course Jamie had started out with a mother and father. The three of them had lived off King's Gate in a basement flat, and he'd attended the local primary. When he was in class two, during a lesson on geography, his mother and father combusted themselves in an amateur drug cooking experiment. They'd been hippies, bordering on would-be junkies. Heroin seemed so much more the real thing than smoking dope. If they'd been less naïve, they might have eventually gone back to more moderate drugs, might have married, mortgaged, had more babies, joined exercise classes, gone on package holidays. Instead they'd been careless with the gas jets and Jamie was orphaned, looking at a climatic map of Europe and daydreaming of a skateboard, and that was that. No relative could be traced and he was taken into care.

School records showed no change in his behaviour (dreamy, easily distracted) or ability (very poor, possibly dyslexic), so it was difficult for social workers and teachers to tell how this drastic change affected him. He was given a photograph of his parents and was told they had died in an accidental fire and were never coming back, but he didn't seem interested in either the photo, which was repeatedly found just lying on his floor, or the death story, to which he listened with a glazed expression.

They were wrong, telling him lies. The photograph was not his mum and dad. He carried them for a long time in his head, their voices and their smell when they held him, the feel of their favourite shirts and jackets, a snatch of song. And as for the fire story, anyone could tell it was a complete nonsense. If his flat had been on fire, and even that was pretty impossible given there was no fireplace, *if* there had been a fire, his parents would have left. Walked out. Phoned the fire brigade. They weren't stupid. Who would stay in a burning house? It was all rubbish.

The social workers didn't even know his name was Jimi (after Jimi Hendrix, his mum's hero) and kept calling him James, and eventually Jamie.

He hung on to the shirt he'd been wearing that fateful day, washed and ironed by his mum the night before, until it was just rag and one of the mothers took it from his sleeping hand and threw it away.

When he asked for it the next morning and was told it had gone to the bin men, and it was no good looking in the bin because the day was Tuesday and that was the day the bin men came at dawn and took everything to the tip and burned it, he just shrugged and said: Oh. Doesna matter.

Nothing else, no tears, nothing anyone could see.

Jimi and his shirt were gone for ever, but there were worse things to contemplate.

After leaving the last mum's house, still smarting from her words and wondering how long this trend of females ejecting him would go on, if it was to be his fate for ever, he walked all the way up to Barley Lane, to his old mate Rick's house. Him and Rick, they'd done a few gigs together, jobs and that. It had been a while, but he'd known him since school days.

Hey, Jamie, fit's new? Come awa in.

Wow, fit's happened here, boy. Jesus fuck, the place looks amazin. New carpet and a'. Even the wallpaper. Fit gives?

Ah. (A secret embarrassed smile, then a shuffling of perfumed fluff behind him.) Jamie, this is Shirley.

A blonde girl wearing Next office gear extended a manicured hand with red nails. Nice tae meet you, Jamie. Will you tak a cup?

Great, cheers.

Have a seat. Sugar? Milk?

Aye, both. Ta.

He sat on the new green leather settee, so did Rick. Who is she? he whispered to Rick, when she could be heard clattering in the kitchen.

She bides here now, whispered Rick back.

Oh. Ah.

Jamie pointed to his ring finger, eyebrows up.

Rick laughed. Shouted through to Shirley, Hey, alright if I give him the big news?

Aye, go on then, might as well now. He'll have guessed.

Right. September third's the big day, man, ken?

Your weddin day?

You got it!

His heart sank as Shirley brought the tea through. He was used to drinking tea from chipped mugs set on the mucky floor by Rick, but here they were, the matching teacups and saucers on a tray. Even a few dry Jammie Dodgers on a wee dish.

Ta, that's great. Just what I needed, ken.

Where do ye bide, Jamie? Shirley's pinky floated in the air above her cup as she raised it to her mouth.

Oh, closer tae town centre, ken. About a mile's walk.

Oh, that's nice. Convenient for the shops and that.

Aye.

Silence. The phone rang and Shirley said, Ooh, it'll be me mum again, sorry, boys, I'll not be long.

High-pitched giggles from the hall.

Hey, Rick, I don't suppose I can kip here tonight?

Rick looked crushed. His mouth grimaced, a parody of a man in pain.

Aye, he said.

No, forget it, that's okay, man, I can see how 'tis. She's a smashin lassie, really, I'm pleased for you.

Rick smiled again, relieved.

It was two o'clock in the morning by the time he got back to Catriona, to the house. There was a light on upstairs and he knocked, but she didn't open the door. He sat on the stoop till dawn, cold and stiff. In the morning, when she came out of the door on her way to work, she nearly tripped over him. For heaven's sake, Jamie, can ye not get it through your thick skull? Piss off, will ye, and leave me in peace. Go your own way. Ye always did anyway.

She stepped around him fastidiously.

Trina, to her retreating back.

She paused and looked at him. He didn't know what to say. Catriona. I need tae get in. I'm needin the toilet. And a bath. I need tae get the rest of my things. Please.

She looked at her watch, sighed. She plunged her hand into her bag and threw the door key at him. Mind you lock up when ye go. And leave the key under the pot, ken.

She trotted away down the pavement, then tossed over her padded shoulder, And dinna bother coomin back. You'll no get in again. You've had your last chance.

He sat a while longer, watching her disappear. Then he went inside. He was her husband and this was his house, did he not have a right to be here? But it had always felt like her place, not his. And he was not welcome now. It felt like Rick's house now: foreign territory. Not home. Sooner or later he always blew it.

He stood quietly in the hall. Then he went into the tiny kitchen to make himself a cup of tea and think what to do next. He'd done something wrong, been bad, but he couldn't think how, beyond the usual not phoning or coming home when he said he was or sending money. Yes, money was probably it, it always was. His head felt heavy and ached. He went into the sitting room and turned the television on. A talk show. Women discussing the benefits of breast-feeding. He took off his boots and put his feet up. Fell asleep. Never even heard her come in.

Whit the bloody hell? Get up. Get oot. You've some nerve. Shoes on the table!

He sat up, flinched. Christ, Trina. Nearly gave me a heart-attack.

Look at this, telly blaring, mess everywhere.

But the edge was gone. He had to go, but she could not do it right now. His instincts, still marginally functioning, told him to try again. Can I just bide the night, Trina? I dinna ken where tae go. Tae stay. He didn't look at her, kept watching the news.

She didn't say anything. All her fire drained away into the screen and she too sat, hypnotised by his helplessness and simplicity. She lit a cigarette, took deep drags, flicked the ashes into the ashtray. Had the urge to light another the second it was out. The very things that had drawn her to him now shot her through with repulsion and yet and yet. It was still something not to be afraid of a man. Whatever else he was he never made the old panic fear drench her blood and quiver her muscles. And she knew fine he had no real friends, people he actually knew the last names of, no family. He had never really connected with people. And no wonder, look at him.

Look. Jamie. You can stay a week. (Staring at the television, and in a flat voice.) That should be long enough, ken. For even someone like ye tae organise another place. Then ye have tae stay oot of my life. Understand? You canna be coomin back here after that. This has come tae an end. Completely.

Jamie went limp with relief. Thanks, Trina. I'll be awa fae

71

here in a few days. I'll sort somethin out. Dinna worry about that. And you willna be tellin your da, will you?

She sighed with the unfairness of it all. She hated being responsible for him. But, No, Jamie. I'll no be tellin Da about ye stayin on here the week. Ye can rest in peace.

Then, without looking at him, she got up and left the room to make tea. They ate bacon, egg and chips silently, wiping their plates with thick white slices, and washing it all down with strong tea. He cleared the table and washed up, just as if they were still an ordinary married couple. He even let himself forget, it was so easy to pretend nothing had happened. He'd never risk losing this again, this lovely precious safe ordinariness. But then Catriona left the kitchen, tossing some words over her frozen shoulder: Mind, you'll be kippin on the settee.

And he heard the bedroom door close with a decisive click.

When he woke it was to the black sky pressing on him and choking him. He rolled off the settee, gasping for a breath, squinting painfully into nothing. A hissing somewhere. Like coal well lit. Then a roar and she came tumbling down the stairs, the flames on her nightie illuminating the room, her mouth a dark cavern open in a thin wail. Jamie closed his eyes and rolled away from her. He closed down his lungs and his brain, squelched eerie echoes of memory. He rolled through the kitchen to the back door and, not breathing yet, plunged down the steps to the garden. He lay for a minute panting, then got up and ran. He ran and ran. When the sun came up, he was at the beach. In the sea, flailing.

Later a policeman walking on the promenade stopped to look at a strange sight. Jamie had no shoes on. He was wearing a T-shirt and underpants. His skin looked blue and black. He was sitting on some driftwood, his head sunk on his arms across his knees. Huddled into himself. Soaking wet and shaking violently. Not an old man, maybe an alky. Maybe the victim of some so-called friend's practical joke. Like the pre-nuptial tar and feathering that still went on. You found half-naked fellows chained to phone boxes in the strangest places. He almost went over to see if he could be of assistance and give him a lift back home and a blanket, but changed his mind. Instead he used his mobile. Almost phoned an ambulance, then phoned the shelter instead, said he had a sorry-looking one on the beach. His shift was over in ten minutes and he was hungry. He went home to his sausage and eggs.

That was the wrench. The beginning and the end.

That first few nights had been a nightmare. Walking and walking, feeling conspicuous and scruffy. In the shoes and clothes from some charity box, or somewhere, he didn't remember. Socks seemed to be missing, but were not an issue. Night was only a space of time without natural light, that's all it was. But it had to be passed under a roof or something horrendous would happen. That was the superstition he had to fight. Everyone he had ever known seemed to pass beyond a veil to an unreachable world full of fiancées and families, washing-machines and toasters, all equally forbidden to the likes of himself.

He slept fitfully under bridge arches, in parks, in car parks and shop doorways. Anywhere out of sight and the weather. Then came the day, waking up to see the respectably shod feet of strangers passing by yards from his face, when he was no longer disoriented or shocked. It had become normal.

He tried to work again. He tried hitching to Arbroath, Perth,

Peterhead, any place he thought there might be work. But his fear wafted off him, more offputting than his unwashed body, and rides were not forthcoming. Neither was work. Neither was help of the social-service variety because he never asked for it. Officials of any kind made him feel paranoid and he shuffled incognito, willing himself into his own shadow.

There was a spot in him now that needed oblivion daily, a painful dot, he could feel in his gut, and it only stopped hurting when he poured drink down his throat. He couldn't always afford it and those times were bad. He always shook, and the shaking got worse then. Like an earthquake, his teeth would rattle and his hands were incapable of tying his bootlace. Bundling into all his clothes at once and not caring if he lived or died. The kindness of others had pulled him through a few rough times. He couldn't recall who they were at all. Only knew that by the time he regained consciousness of who he was, he'd be lying in bed somewhere, sometimes a hospital, warm and not hungry.

He is two years older now — twenty-four — and he doesn't drink any more. The need just passed through him, and now the smell of alcohol shivers him. He rarely thinks about the past and doesn't imagine women at all. He hardly feels male, it would take too much energy. He is simply Jamie, a being who needs very little to live and doesn't like to stay in one place too long. This is the way things have worked out. Surviving from day to day is his main goal and he does not waste thoughts.

When he wakes in the morning, there are always, but always, a few seconds when he doesn't know where he is, when he cannot tell the season of the year or his name. He floats inside his body, eliminating possibilities, till he comes to — first of all — his name. Jamie, Jimi, Jamie. Then the correct locality —

perhaps the lot behind the supermarket, the shelter on Bonnie Brae Street, the park. Then the time of year, hard to judge if no greenery is visible, it is always cold. Finally, what he ate last night, his current financial state. The inferno image of his Catriona lies buried inside him, along with his parents' mythological fiery demise, only emerging in dreams he wakes from but can't remember. Saying Catriona's name is a prick of pain, but there is pleasure too, and sometimes he inserts her name in little songs he sings.

Since he stopped drinking, he has been organised. Socks have regained their status as useful items. He has his plastic holdall with two pairs of underwear and socks, only slightly dirty; he has a strict rota for underwear, and turns them inside out several times before deeming them in need of a wash. He even has a toothbrush and a bar of soap wrapped in a flannel, his shaving gear, a pocket knife, a box of matches. Some crockery, an old pan, cutlery. A jumper, an anorak and a cap.

He is a pared-down man. Odd-looking — his clothes have that permanent slept-in look, his teeth have aged prematurely, and he has a periodic stammer and tremor. Except when he forgets everything and stares limply at nothing. He cannot hide his own self-knowledge, his zero social status, and he frequently lowers his eyes to passers-by. A man, or boy, who knows his place. Catriona, if she is alive (and she might be), would hardly recognise him.

But it is increasingly unlikely she will ever see him because Jamie has discovered the most civilised way to live rough is to keep on the move and get out of the city. Little things, like hanging up his socks to dry and finding a spot to relieve himself, are much easier to accomplish in the countryside. Jamie likes to travel and it is something, maybe the only thing, he is good at.

Michael Sees Some Sights
by Himself

Excuse me, miss. Excuse me, could I ask you a question? No? Oh, okay, be like that.

Pardon me, sir, do you have a minute, I just ... well, hey, I only ... be like that then.

Hello, do *you* work here? Could I ask you a question?

Work here? This is a church. Do I look like a minister?

Sorry, of course not, no. I'm a visitor, and I just wondered something.

From America, are you, then? Or should I say Canada, in case you feel insulted? Made that mistake too many times. Always assume they're Canadian, then you can't go wrong.

No, uh, I am American.

Not Canadian?

Well, actually, no.

You could have fooled me. You don't need to let on you're American. I'd never have guessed.

But I'm not Canadian.

But you could be.

Ah.

If you wanted.

I'll keep that in mind. I was just wondering about this sign.

Aye, what are you needing to know about it? Do you maybe want me to take your photie beside it? Were your ancestors buried here or something? Are you a roots person?

No, no. I'm just here to visit my son, and I wondered what on earth the sign meant by Free Church. Do some churches charge money?

Do you not have Free Churches where you live, then? Where is it you come from, anyway? Seeing as how you're determined to be shameless about being American.

Near San Francisco.

A lovely place, lovely. You'll be knowing my cousin, maybe. A Robert McAllister. About my age, but no hair.

No, uh, no, I haven't met your cousin.

Ah, but then it's a big state, San Francisco, is it not?

Oh, yeah. Huge. So, about this Free Church business.

Ach, you'll not be wanting to bother with all that. It's called that because it is, and no one cares a toss why any more.

Hmm.

I think you'd better let me buy you a drink, seeing as your seeing the sights all by yourself, like.

Do you? Oh, okay. That's nice of you.

My pleasure, I was just away off to the pub for my lunch anyway. Look at this weather! You brought the summer with you. You must be melting, with your jacket and jumper. Take them off.

Nope.

Go on.

No no no.

Typical bloody American. Can no one tell you anything?

77

Mhairi Fantasises

She knew that no one in the world was like herself, but she could not conceive of this being a universal fact for everyone her age. It was her shameful secret, and clearest and hardest to hide when she was high. After that bad trip at the King's Hill rave, she'd stopped taking anything at all, except the occasional e or joint with Roddy.

It was a fact that everyone else fitted in fine, but she didn't. Her external self was a façade, a layer miming her peers for survival, while underneath, grumbling and cringing in embarrassment, were all the thoughts and sentiments of an outcast. The pregnancy intensified this, severed her last tenuous ties with her friends.

The only place where this didn't matter was here at home, with her mum, who was such a pariah herself that she was incapable of judging her daughter. A house of misfit women. At least she was not as overtly weird as her mum.

Mhairi napped on and off most afternoons, and on her third day home she had her usual fantasy to get herself off to sleep with. It began with her own consciousness of her new voluptuousness, her tender nipples and the novelty of cleavage. A dreamy eroticism would plant Roddy in her mind, but instead of recalling their afternoon passion, she would curl up and play this scene. She would be thin again and blooming. On her lap would be an angel of a wee girl, with curly blonde hair and a floral Monsoon frock. They would be sitting on a rock down by the shore, and perhaps she would be reading. Yes, reading a book. And be unaware of the man's soft approach. The little girl would look up first and laugh delightfully and raise wee chubby arms. Dimples in her elbows. She would at last look up and there would be Roddy, his pack on his back, three days' stubble on his face and eyes that ate her.

About there, she gave herself the needed strokes to slip deliciously into a river of sensual sleep, hoping to be carried off into a continuation of the scene. The baby's name was Chloë and she was always smiling. Or if she was crying, she stopped immediately when put to her breast. It would feel like a kitten nuzzling her.

Later she took a bath; she and her belly were a drifting boat. She watched, slightly bored, as tiny feet and hands distended her skin. She had remained unstretchmarked, which gratified her vanity. She lay in the bath and greatly admired her own beauty. Such a waste Roddy could not see her now. He hadn't thought she was strange. He had loved her. Her skin, her breasts. Her nipples stood up just remembering, and he had loved it when she pulled off her T-shirt slowly and peeled down her tight jeans. Afternoons with the curtains drawn, and the roomies away at class; getting stoned and listening to Blur. God, he'd never tired of doing it. Sometimes she'd wanted to go out, to the movies, or even just for a walk, hold hands, but he'd always dragged her back to the rumpled sheets, and turned her on her belly or thrust her against the wall for a kiss that never ended until they'd done the whole deed again. No wonder the stupid diaphragm hadn't worked.

Poor Mum. No way had she ever had sex even once that was that good. Probably frigid. Probably only did it once or twice. Poor Dad, married to such an unsexy woman. No wonder he got sick and died. Probably died of frustration.

When she'd been about seven, eight, nine, they used to fetch the Sunday paper together. Just the two of them. They would walk down the brae and take the short cut across the drainage pipe over the burn. They would come out on the beach and walk up the sands to the shop. Even in summer, these mornings on the beach were cold, but she would always kick off her shoes and frisk in the surf. He usually carried her shoes and walked alone. But one August morning, when the tide was turning and the water was still, he sat down and took off his boots. His big feet were winter white and his ankles had black hairs. She took his hand and coaxed him down to the water. The second the surf washed over his toes, he yelped. Fucking freezing, he said, and she felt grown up and close to him because he'd used a swear in front of her and not seen the need to apologise. Fucking freezing, he'd said, and laughed and ran, kicking through the water, dragging her shrieking with laughter behind him.

That memory was one of her secrets. She'd never told her mother about the swear and she noticed quite carefully that he never swore around her mother. And that was the irony, because her mother swore all the time in front of them, though not in front of her own mother. Had he been a non-swearer by nature, or a suppressed swearer? Why was he unable to say fuck around his wife, but could, at least once, in front of his daughter?

They had both lived their lives reacting to Kate. Kate had always been the conductor, foul-mouthed, squint-eyed, tartan-shirted, grey-haired boss, waving her baton to run the show. Bitch. Mum. Mummy.

Kate Wastes Wrinkles
While Patrick Floats

Kate pacing, Mhairi sleeping, almost midnight. The house was wrapped round with a sea haar, but inside it was cosy and warm.

Under a quilt and his mother's skin and his own membrane, eight-month-old Patrick was now firmly ensconced in Mhairi's belly and never ventured forth. His brain did not retain images in memory, but the things he had experienced, the thousands of sounds, movements, climate changes, digestion troubles, acrobatic feats learnt and forgotten, his flights to see Kate — all these were incorporated into his personality, which had a substantially solid core at conception. Patrick had always been Patrick. But now he was seven pounds and except when Mhairi had a too-hot bath and he kicked out of irritation, he was sluggish and biding his time. For what, he had no idea. Like his mother, he was in a dreamy limbo.

His crop of red hair floated in amniotic fluid. His eyes stayed mostly closed, but through his lids he took in the shades of darkness — sometimes black, but mostly a reddish pulsing shade that was his own and his mother's blood and the sun shining or electric lights burning. His hands curled tight and his legs crossed at the ankle. He had a calm life, riding the waves.

Now and then music roused him and he tried to stretch out his legs and arms and caused Mhairi to pause in whatever she was doing, to lay her hands on her belly and wonder. Oh, yes, she thought each time. I haven't forgotten. I know you're in there.

But she didn't, really. It felt like she'd been pregnant for years and she did not, in her heart, believe it would ever end in a real baby. The tiny clothes she had accumulated – the sleepers and vests and knitted caps and mittens – might as well have been for a doll she was going to get at Christmas, a long way away. There was no reality to it. The bump was permanent.

If mother and infant were unconcerned about the future, lived as if nothing would ever change, Kate had grown more anxious in the few days since Mhairi moved home. She took on the role of mother cat, frantically searching for places to birth; she cleaned and ruthlessly filled bags to take to the charity shop and imagined every possible birth emergency and how she would cope with it. One morning in the bath she caught herself doing breathing exercises and knew she had to stop. That the baby was not her responsibility, and at her age stress would only bring on ugliness. More wrinkles and grey hairs. There was absolutely no point to it.

Of course this knowledge failed to stop her. Worry coloured every minute of her day, and now, in the middle of the night, she fretted with frustration, knowing the futility of it. Far better to worry with the illusion of purpose.

Patrick woke and started to stretch in his elastic tent, skin tight now. He wiggled his bum, thrust his right arm, frowned.

Hard to get comfy when your hostess was lying sideways leaving you squished down one side. Then he lay quiet, perfectly alert, and heard: his own heartbeat, quick, light, tiptoeing; his mother's heart, regular and heavy; his mother's breathing, like a wind whistling in and whooshing out, like the sea, which was another sound he heard. The waves were always there, surging and crashing or placidly licking the sand. He liked the waves. They were not just sounds, they were shapes – full and frothy, then thin and drawn out, like breaths. The fluid in his own body reacted to the same lunar forces, he felt this too, and the sound of the waves was an accompaniment to his own tidal motion. He floated and rode rhythm, wide awake, did not fight it yet, absorbed it. Beyond the continent of his mother lay nothing but air and water, and the occasional sounds of visiting continents. He was not afraid.

PART TWO

By all accounts, 'tis very fine,
But where d'ye sleep and where d'ye dine?
I find by all you have been telling
That 'tis a house, but not a dwelling.

Jonathan Swift (1667–1745)

Architecture is an extension of the psyche,
with floors and rooms acting as containers of personality.

Carl Jung (1875–1961)

Not the kiss, but the seconds before
Not the kiss.

public toilet graffiti, Ullapool

Jamie

He has turned down the wrong street, and now he doesn't remember which way to get back. The houses are large, set well off the road, some with private gates and drives. Traffic has dwindled down to nothing. The only sounds are a mower and a dog barking. Where is he? Jamie feels like he is growing enormous; he is so obviously out of place, he will soon hear sirens and be swooped on by a dozen policemen. This is forbidden territory. The houses regard him with deep suspicion; their respectable lawns and well bred rhododendrons shudder when he approaches on his silent scuffed shoes. Go away, they whisper, in affronted green voices.

He turns again, goes around another block, only to find he is back where he started. A Jaguar drives past slowly. He does not look, he keeps his eyes on the pavement, concentrates on not tripping. This is a nightmare, a maze of nightmares.

But then, right in front of him, inches from his feet, lies a gold watch, sparkling in the gutter where it has slipped off some harried wealthy man's wrist. Fear momentarily forgotten, he scoops it swiftly into his pocket, fails to suppress a smile. God, what a lucky man he is.

Jamie was luckier than most of his race because he had a way about him, even through all the grime. Large-house owners might feel threatened by him, landlords might not rent to him, but employers did occasionally give him work, after his drinking phase had ended. He did not look like he had the wits to be dishonest. He was slow but he was cheap. And so he went the rounds of the chip shops and factories in and around Aberdeen, and they told their friends, and he got by. A day unloading boxes, a week packing fish, an evening sweeping out the factory floors, a few hours selling the *Big Issue* magazine on the street corners. An enormous man called Luigi was always good for a few hours peeling tatties, and gave him the fish from yesterday as well, but his shifts were erratic and Jamie couldn't count on him.

He kept his money in an old kiddie's purse found at the park, slipped down inside one of the socks he was wearing. When he slept, if he removed his shoes, he put the money deep in his trouser pocket. He always, no matter what the weather or where he was, slept with his trousers on. Never again would he find himself on a beach in his underpants.

He avoided other homeless. He didn't know their stories and felt confused when they started to tell them, as they frequently did. He was aware of the camaraderie they offered, could see the temptation to belong to a group, any group of humanity. Only they drank, most of them, formed masculine huddles around bottles and fires leaping out of old oil drums and this combination never failed to terrify him. He kept himself to himself.

Winter was hardest and aged him. Nights in shelters were only marginally better than nights rough, and sometimes not even that. The noises and scrutinising warden's eyes. No privacy. And men so much worse off than himself, having the delirium tremors, puking and peeing and worse in their sleep. The smell gagged him. These men, if they caught him looking at them, would always smirk, as if to say, Whit're you lookin at? It'll be ye one day and soon, so whit're are you lookin at?

Jamie didn't think it would be him one day. For one thing, he did not drink. For another, he told himself that if he was going that way he would just find an icy loch someplace, take his clothes off but not his boots and get in.

He never thought, I will never have a home. It was always a day-to-day thing, though less and less could he imagine another kind of existence. In his memory was the experience of having a home, many homes in fact, and taking them completely for granted. Then there was no memory for a while, only the detached knowledge that his wife had not wanted him any more and that thing had happened to her, the mothers had never wanted him either, and the irony that landlords did not rent to someone who looked like they had no home. Even if he had the deposit, which would be miracle enough. Then a short time when sleeping rough had been a new shock every night, a nightmare, a panic filled ellipse of time when the setting of the sun brought him out in hives and bizarre strangers seemed to stare at him. Frightening noises and insufficient sleep in jerks and starts, sitting up, cuddled into himself.

The time he was in now was a time of habit, of routine. Of knowing where all the public toilets were, and if they were locked or broken, of knowing which pubs and restaurants and sometimes parks and empty car parks he could use. Of knowing all the exit routes from the city, which roads to take to empty wild places, the train and bus tricks, the best places to try hitching, the short cuts for walking. Of using the hair-cutting college where, if he managed to have a wash first, he could get his hair cut for free. Of always keeping a bit of toilet roll in his pocket. Of not talking to himself too loudly in public places. Of always looking like he had a place to go when police were walking by. Of having regular safe spots to pass the night, familiarity with the care workers and the shelters and not noticing normal people's reaction to him.

Jamie thought of them as the homefulls. He was labelled homeless, and homelessness had become his entire identity and reality. So the opposite must be true and everyone with a home must be full of home and homefull. Their whole world started and ended with having a home and they could not exist as they did without it. Home – even just four walls and a roof of the grottiest kind – was wealth, credibility, luck, privilege. A jumping board, without which they would only be able to tread water, never spring and dive.

Being homeless was often hell but he'd learnt to do it well. He didn't expect to live a long time, and sometimes on winter's nights when he fell into sleep so deeply he didn't wake till the sun was high and the rest of the world was on their lunch-break, he didn't care if he never woke up. Being alive these times was painful. Sleep was like delicious death to him then and he could not get enough of it.

The travelling had begun by accident. Falling asleep on a bus; missing his stop and waking up and getting shoved out by a disgusted driver, at the end of some rural line, in the middle of nowhere. Somewhere in Perthshire, late September. Rolling hills, late evening, cows lying down under oaks, their breath pluming out. He'd stood watching the bus roll away, scratching himself, and patting his pockets and socks to make sure he had it all.

A farmhouse not too far away, but he headed away from it, hating by now the suspicion in people's eyes. Headed instead for a copse of beeches up a hill. It began to rain, but soft, and he was well sheltered. No wind. After Aberdeen, the air was a tonic, an elixir of wet grass and trees and manure.

But it felt too open and exposed, without buildings, and he hid himself well under the dark trees. And the noises – at first it felt too quiet and he could hear his own heart beating, blood pulsing through his ears. Then came the wood pigeons (five oooos, he counted) and the owls and the night insects and occasional rook rustling and cow grunting. It came to seem like a racket.

At the shelters and soup kitchens, restaurant skips and bakery bins, he always squirrelled away something before eating. Tucked it into his pocket for later, and never finished it until he'd found another bit to tuck away. Now he found his piece and ate some of it. It was a dry ham roll and it tasted fine. He shook out his bedding, took off his shoes and climbed in before he lost too much body heat. He felt lonely and strange, and after a while, his mood felt like a companion and he talked to it.

Since he didn't have a building to call home, to be himself in and roam the rooms at will, compartmentalise himself – a room for relaxing, a room for satisfying hunger, a room for sleep and sex, a room for emptying his bladder and bowels – since he had none of these, he had shrunk up his perimeters and his body had quite literally become his home. He sat right now in his version of a sitting room, and had a wee chat with himself about the current state of affairs, the possibility of spiders and bats.

(Simultaneously, the entire world was Jamie's home. His kitchens were the Sally Army, the shelters; his bedrooms were dozens of safe hidden spots, derelict houses and building sites and parks; his toilets were innumerable, and his clothes cupboard was a holdall hanging off the end of his hand.)

In Jamie's case, because he liked to imagine he was a traveller, rather than ordinary homeless, his body had become something of a tent instead of a bungalow, and he inhabited several parts of it every day. He dwelt in his stomach when the pangs grew monotonous and crowded out thought, or when some warm stodgy food found its way down his gullet. He lived in his feet when they were cold and sore or, quite rarely, when they were his friends and carried him away from bad places towards better places.

When he wanted to be private, he went upstairs in the tent. It was an orange canvas tent and the light filtered through it like a torch pressed against a child's thin hand. There he huddled or dreamt or mumbled and no one saw him. He was at home in every inch of his body-tent, but mostly he was snug at home upstairs. When he was there, from the outside he simply looked vacant.

Jamie chattered away, his first night roughing it out of Aberdeen, then drifted off to his own lullaby. An owl's sudden screeching woke him and he had to start the lullaby all over again.

Fuckin go back tae sleep then, right, Jamie? Well, just shut up, ken, and do it then, just close your eyes and forget the boogie men out tae get ye, just fuckin get some sleep and tomorra try and see where ye are, get back some way, just shut up now and go tae sleep. Right. I'm doin it, I'm doin it, get off my back, ye fucker.

He was not an angry boy and his swearing was soft and meaningless. He liked the hard-soft sound of fuck.

He obeyed himself and slept again. He snored and several small rodents and birds were curious enough to come quite close to him. When he woke he was dazzled by sun. He rubbed his hands on the dew and rubbed it into his face, to wash. He urinated. Had another bite of the ham roll. Walked around to stretch his legs. Spotted some brambles in the hedge at the side of the wood. Sweet, perfect. He filled his stomach with fruit, then washed it all down with bramble juice, strained through his teeth. Found a warm dip in the field, recently vacated by a cow, napped a little, then went back and ate brambles again. Couldn't remember ever tasting anything so good. Watched the cows lumbering along, vaguely wondered about the mechanics of getting milk.

That was how it began, his travelling.

And if he ever approached the feeling of belonging some-where, it was on the road or with countryside around him. It had purpose and more dignity than kipping in the same old closes and parks and shelters. He was not part of a group when he travelled. He did not imagine anyone looking at him and saying, There goes another hopeless homeless. He was simply Jamie, going somewhere. A travelling man.

A big house can make a man think he is big, a small house may make a man feel small, and no house has the power to make a man feel non-existent. But a man may slip the noose of all these, if he can travel. If he can stop thinking of houses that way. A travelling man is free.

He has found the way out. He is back in the stream of humanity he knows, swimming in his own current of invisibility, away from the watchful eyes of the big silent curiously empty houses. The watch, which used to live in one of these big houses, seems content enough in Jamie's pocket. It ticks, anyway, and no sirens chase him. Probably it is not real gold after all, but still — it will come in handy when he's on the road.

What Michael Makes of Kate and What Kate Makes of Him

Isabel had to work and didn't come. On you go, boys, you'll have more fun without me, anyway.

Brendan kept fiddling with the radio, which had ceased to receive any stations except a fuzzy one playing accordion music. They'd already gone through market town Dingwall (now more Tesco than cattle), Victorian Strathpeffer in the shadow of the Cat's Back (where no one appeared to be under the age of ninety, except a small group of trendy young mothers with push-chairs), damp wooded Contin, then up the glen to Rogie Falls and Garve. Turned left on a single-track road for Gairloch and five minutes later they were in another world. Barren stone mountains, sheep on the road, clumps of yellow gorse, scattered old man's beard. Peaty rivers and lochs, like black coffee. They stopped at Achnasheen, at the petrol station. Drank from a flask of tea, listened to the bees hum in some wild rose bushes. Conversation died, it was like being in a church. Spoken words seemed garish.

Then back on the road again, curving by still lochs, spied by occasional grand old houses and derelict cottages and caravans with washing hanging out.

Up a long incline, curved between two wedges of stone, then teetered on the top. Far below them, laid out like a strand of silver silk, was a loch. Beyond, more grey mountains with unlikely peaks and asymmetrical summits. And on the horizon, the sea.

For Michael, the sight was like a physical blow. He had a sudden sense of the size of Scotland. He was straddling the place. Had seen the east coast half an hour ago, and here he was, glimpsing the west coast. Domesticity on one side, wilderness on the other. No green here, no trees, no crop fields or small towns. No clutter. Hard land, soft air, luminous light.

Jesus, Brendan, you could have warned me.

Impossible to articulate. He felt his chest expand with the kind of feeling he associated with hope, though what he would be hoping for he had no idea. He was only on a run west so his son could further show off his chosen home to him, and meet the mother of his daughter-in-law-of-convenience. A girl called Mhairi, who was expecting a baby, but not Brendan's.

What did any of it matter to him? His life was elsewhere, suspended and waiting. He had come to fetch back a straying fragment of that life, one whose departure had left a gaping hole. Gaping now, but he could see it closing up without too much damage to his life as a whole. He had moved from New York to California in his twenties, and his great-grandfather had sailed from Ireland to New York. Children were forever stretching away from their parents and scattering family seeds in foreign soils. Mongrels made the healthiest dogs. Or so they said.

What's that? he asked his son, as they began the steep descent.

Loch Maree.

Name of a pretty girl.

Actually, it means priest in Gaelic.

But the sound of the word was still as romantic as the image. A loch that kept sliding out of view as their car wound down the road, till it lay long and calm to their right, the bare mountains mirrored in it. They drove by a small tree-filled islet and Michael had to look away; so much beauty made him feel sad, almost nauseated him.

He rolled the window down and pulled the air into his lungs. Soon he was yawning.

Tired, Dad? It's the west. It always knocks me out too.

Must be the air.

Yeah, must be the air. Sea and mountain air molecules all mixed up. Heated by the Gulf Stream. Heady stuff, Dad. Don't breathe too deep.

What did you say? (Another yawn.)

Michael sank into himself, and by the time they were overlooking Gairloch's sandy beach and the old Free Church with its lumpy graveyard he was as disorientated as if he'd had a bottle of wine. Something had happened while he catnapped between Loch Maree and Gairloch. The umbilical cord that tied him to his country, his house, all the objects he had accumulated to provide a sense of continuity, of identity — this cord, which had a wonderful elasticity, which had begun stretching the minute he boarded the aeroplane — quietly, between breaths, snapped. First he was still marginally who he had always been, then snap! He was not.

He giggled. So tell me Brendan, why is that church free? Do the others have admission prices? Why would anyone pay if you could go for free and have a view of a beach to boot?

* * *

Mhairi had never, not even during the ceremony, thought of Brendan as her husband. The ceremony had moved her unexpectedly – it told her she wanted love and commitment, the words promise and for ever and I do. A real wedding was definitely on her dream list, but Roddy was her man. Brendan was just not her type, she could never fancy him – too American, for one thing.

Kate, however, could not get the connection out of her mind. She had already envisaged too many future scenarios of romance and domesticity for her daughter. When he came occasionally to visit with his girlfriend Isabel, she always made an effort not to feel slighted on her daughter's behalf. And now that Brendan was due with his father, she was cleaning the house as if it was an in-law coming she had to impress.

They arrived earlier than expected and caught her with the mop in her hand. Her face was flushed with exertion and embarrassment. Oh, it's you. You're early, she said stupidly. Come in. Mhairi's just hanging the washing out.

You mean we're not late for once. My dad's influence. Won't happen again, I promise. Dad, meet Kate. Kate, my dad, Michael.

She began to reach for his outstretched hand, then withdrew. No, I'm all wet and cold.

Michael didn't know what to do, so he took his hand back and smiled inanely. Real nice to meet you, you've got a real nice place here. (Cringing at the sound of his own accent, which he had never noticed, not even talking to Isabel, but which now suddenly jarred. Bull-in-a-china-shop voice.)

Thank you. Come in, please.

She looked out of the door past them with a yearning expression, as if she'd rather be leaving. It was a glorious day, the sea like turquoise gel and the sky clear of clouds. Birds just everywhere.

Time went into slow warp for Michael. He met Mhairi. A tall girl, thin but for her bump. A little unfocused, he thought. Kate, a different story. Thin and sharp. A squint in her left eye, occasionally noticeable, startling the first time. She made quick darts around the kitchen till they were all settled with cups of tea — coffee for himself, she'd assumed he'd prefer it — and when she sat across from him she seemed ready for flight, back straight, head up and eyes flickering.

These men are so big, she was thinking. They looked out of proportion in her kitchen. Dwarfed it and herself. She felt small — a novel sensation, for she was tall by Highland standards, had been as tall as Jack. There was a fraction of a second of enjoying it, of letting a wave of femininity pass through her. This must be how petite women feel, protected, fragile. Then back to seeing their size as ostentatious and mildly threatening.

This tastes great, he said. Thanks.

Is it alright? It's only instant. I always thought Americans were fussy about their coffee.

Not me. I mean, I drink instant at home a lot, I even drink tea.

Do you now? Well, that's good. Instant's all I've got at the moment. And you'll get a nice cup of tea next time, see what you think of it.

Friendly but dismissive. He felt unliked by her. Appalled that it seemed to matter. It couldn't be personal, she'd only known him ten minutes. He felt humbled.

He drank his coffee and listened. Everyone seemed to be able to converse quickly, with no difficulty, but him. Awkward and self-conscious, he watched Kate. A woman his own age, maybe a few years younger, unwrinkled but loose-skinned enough to foretell the way the sags would lie one day. Surprisingly full-bosomed, considering her general wiriness. Very dark hooded eyes, receding chin sporting a few hairs, a mole on her forehead, yet the sum total was oddly attractive. Frizzy grey and black hair tied up in a hairband. Strands kept escaping on to her forehead and she flicked these back with long bony fingers. She wore a black skirt to her calves and a man's tartan workshirt, with a gaudy brooch pinned on the pocket. Black ankle boots, grey socks and unshaven legs, which slightly disturbed him. He thought of Marcia's well-groomed body – smooth tan legs, short hair, permed and dyed, nails rounded and painted. High heels clickety-clicking out of the door and down the stairs, off to work. All her movements had been purposeful and smooth. Michael could not imagine Kate going off to work.

What do you do?

What?

Everyone stopped talking.

Sorry, did I interrupt? I was just curious. About what you did.

She still looked puzzled.

Dad means, what is your job and how much do you make at it? Us Americans always ask that. Sorry, Kate.

Michael shot his son a reprimand look, Brendan shrugged his usual unapologetic apology.

Oh, I don't mind at all. I just didn't understand. You mean what do I do for money. Well, the answer is not much, and there isn't much. We used to run this place as a croft, when my husband was alive. Mainly sheep, but I don't bother now. I work behind the bar in the hotel.

Do you? I came to the right place then, he said, laughing loudly.

No one laughed.

This place is like paradise, he continued, diving into sheer gushing. It's the most beautiful place I've ever seen. Brendan never sent any photos, it really is incredible. You are so lucky to live here.

Us and the midges, laughed Mhairi.

What's a midge?

Finally he'd said something right, and they all roared, though they seemed to be laughing at him. Again, he ached to be home. Beth, barbecue, sun.

The kettle whistled and the pot was refilled. Kate did not speak to him directly again that night.

Kate Hates Americans but Cleans Her House for Them Anyway

Kate sat down to write her column. Everyone – Mhairi, Michael, Brendan – was in bed and the house, though quiet, felt full.

Kate could write whatever she wanted in her column. No one in Gairloch knew she was Eilidh McKay, columnist writing about rural life in Lochinellie. Not that many of them bothered with newspapers anyway.

It was easy, the main challenge being the word count. Four hundred words, give or take five. It was a bit like packing for a camping trip. You had to keep taking inessentials out of the boot, till it all fitted.

WEST COAST CRACK

I know I shouldn't say this, but I have never much liked Americans. They're full of themselves and have more money than is fair and have ridiculously large bodies which must cost a fortune to run. But I don't think those are my main reasons. They have no subtlety. They're like children, literal, too open, trusting. They talk with huge gaps in their sentences, slow, stupid. And I find that unappealing. There, I said it, and that means I am a terrible person, mean and unkind. Not very nice at all. When I see them and they are warm towards me, and they always are very friendly, I am friendly back. But inside I am waiting for them to go away.

They make me feel old and not fond of myself.

Perhaps it is just age, after all. Perhaps America is a spoiled teenager and our country is a batty pensioner. We are dried up and they are new and we resent it like hell. But it's hard. They're so damned nice.

Lochinellie is heaving with tourists already, and the school holidays haven't even begun. Germans, French, English, Japanese, and they all spend money here and we are grateful enough to ignore their mess and noise, but I have a hard time ignoring the American accent when I hear it in the shops and café. They speak and laugh loudly, happily, with the assumption that no one will mind hearing them – the assumption that everyone will like them as much as they like themselves.

Well, as you know, I don't like them half as much as they like themselves. They don't need my liking, anyway. Does this mean I only like people who need my liking? How patronising that sounds. I hope it isn't true, but admit the possibility. Self-loathing is never far away.

I saw two otters on the beach this morning, the first I've seen in years. I was sitting on the machair, still and quiet, and they were like giant sleek rats, tumbling over each other. Mating? Or perhaps siblings, less afraid of open spaces than their parents. Round and round they played, long tails splashing in the tide pools, making little sounds I wanted to believe were giggles. I wasn't far away, but they didn't notice me. Or perhaps they did, but were too young to sense danger. I watched them for about ten minutes. Then my dog barked up at the house, and the sound, though distant, scattered them back to the rocks. Their shiny dark pelts became instantly invisible.

And I went home feeling honoured and that this day was special, even though I had intended to spend most of it cleaning my messy house for visitors coming. Who are here now. Who are, you guessed it, Americans. But they'll never read this and you'll never tell. Will you?

Meanwhile, grandbaby is weeks from arrival, and the house is holding its breath in anticipation. As are we all.

Brendan snored away on the sitting-room settee, but Michael was not asleep. He lay upstairs, under the pink coombs of a box room. He listened to a muted tapping noise that he at last translated into a computer. Must be Kate. Kate at a computer?

Across an ocean and a continent, perched on the far coast, was a white house with a redwood deck, and inside was an apartment with all his things in it. His own computer, his high-school yearbooks, his CD player, his Pete's coffee, photos of his parents and his children. As Michael lay in bed still awake at midnight, the rain streaming inches from his head, the sun was beating his plants to death and two cats chased each other over the roof. His daughter Beth was stepping outside to go for her afternoon jog. She stopped to tighten her laces and squint at the sun.

Tap tap, went Kate's fingers, matching the rain in rhythm. His breathing slowed, deepened.

Mhairi was not asleep, she'd had too many naps lately, and she lay awake counting the times she and Roddy had done it. She'd get to twenty-four and have to begin again. If all the counting hadn't been having such a soporific effect, she would've got out of bed to write it down so she wouldn't get so mixed up. The minute she dropped off, on number seventeen again, the doggie-style experiment, Patrick opened his eyes and began to hiccup.

Jamie

He watches the other hitch-hikers for a while. Studies them. Thumbing used to be easy, but he has lost the knack, hardly anyone stops for him now, and he is watching them to see what he has forgotten. The boy now, for instance. He looks about twenty and he stands on the roadside with his hand flung out, his thumb wriggling at particularly likely cars and lorries, hanging limp while unlikely vehicles pass, the Renault Espaces and taxis. A kind of communication seems to be going on even though the traffic flows by. Yes, he could copy that. Easy. But what else?

A fish lorry pulls up and the boy grabs his backpack, a new blue one with a matching sleeping-bag tied to the bottom, and runs up to the cab. First the shouted questions through the open window. Where are you headed? Can you drop me off in Ellon? Then the open door and the pack thrown in, followed by the boy's long legs propelling him up into the cab and the door slams. The lorry revs and rolls off.

He stands and watches, telling himself what he must to do to duplicate this skill. It used to work for him, it used to work! But maybe he looked different then, aye, that was no doubt the problem, and a driver could ken a mile off if he'd slept in a bed the night before, or just a bittie ground in the park.

He is about to walk up to the place to stand for rides when a girl walks up and steps one foot off the kerb and has her try. He stands back in the shadow of the bus shelter and watches her.

She has long hair that sails behind her like a flag, and only a small canvas bag, the kind he's seen in army-surplus shops, slung over one shoulder. Not like the boy then, not a well-off student, but a light traveller.

He indulges in a moment of imagined kinship. Like me, he thinks. A lassie traveller. And he saunters over to her, nods acknowledgement, and though his heart is hammering, he calmly takes up a place just in front of her and stretches out his thumb to the traffic.

Excuse me, she says.

(Uh oh, he thinks.) Aye?

I was here first. Do you mind?

She jerks her head back to indicate where he should stand.

Sorry. Right.

He walks just beyond her, the better to admire her hair, sort of golden in the sun. He feels dizzy watching the light on it.

She smiles, he smiles, all is right in the world.

A Ford Escort van stops. For her, of course, and she leans over to speak to the driver.

And then the miracle happens. She says: Hey! You! (Just as if he was one of them.) There's room in the back if you don't mind sitting with tools.

He stares.

You do want a lift, don't you?

In he gets, amongst plumber's bits and pieces, the thick smell of grease and old dog, though there is no dog.

The driver does not encourage talk, which is fine. He sits in the back, letting the vibrations on the wall numb his skull. He almost sleeps, he is so empty and relaxed.

Then it is over. The driver is turning off, and putting himself and the girl out.

The girl takes a good look at him now, as they stand alone on the verge. Takes him in, his holdall with the safety-pinned zip, his three-day growth, his odour, the truth in his eyes. He can feel it, and she begins to walk away, her bag slung over her shoulder again, saying, Good luck with the rest of your trip.

Words that whip past him, get carried away so quickly he cannot even recall her accent, the texture of her voice. She is walking fast and is beyond sight within minutes.

He doesn't know where he is, he was too happy in the van to take any notice of road signs. Somewhere about forty miles north, near the Broch maybe, he guesses, but not the main road. He crouches on his haunches, stares out at the road and doesn't move for a long time. He tries to work out what happened. How he felt alright for a little while and now he doesn't again. How to get it back. The wind blows straight from the North Sea, keens straight through him.

A woman passing in her Volvo full of screaming kids slows down, gives him a worried maternal look, but does not stop. Drugs, she thinks. Pity, but what could you do? She speeds up, decides that if he's still there in half an hour when she returns, looking like that, she'll phone someone. This is a nice place, there are young children playing on trim lawns, riding new bikes. Nice families.

Kate Laughs, Maybe

They were to stay five days, see all the west-coast sights. The first day, like all first days, was endless. The weather held and a long walk to the lighthouse was organised. Michael felt in a daze most of the time. He ate huge amounts of picnic and followed the rest passively. Once Kate startled him by asking, And what do *you* do, if I can ask?

Oh, a bit of this, a bit of that. I used to be a carpenter, but stopped to look after the kids when they were young. Now I just freelance. Cabinets, mostly, to order. Nothing much at the moment.

So you were a stay-at-home dad.

Kate seemed to find this amusing. When he looked back at those years of tedium – monotonous housework, toddler tantrums in supermarkets, being the only dad at PTA meetings – he couldn't see the joke. He'd loved his children, but raising them had mostly been like living in a dark tunnel with only the tiniest speck of light at the end. When he'd stopped looking for it, he was alone, but for Beth. They were suddenly grown-up and he stood in the glaring light, weak and unfit for anything. He'd considered getting a dog, but the apartment had rules about animals. Recently he'd bought a very good camera. Something to carry with him and frame the world. Without the kids and their demands, he felt too light. Floating. And here he was, on a beach explaining himself to a woman who seemed to think he was a moron.

It helped to think of his house – the redwood deck, the wind chimes, the kitchen cupboards. This was done with great difficulty, and his stupor was such that he didn't even feel surprise that a place he had left so recently might feel so unreal. Almost all his resources were used to convey an impression of normality, to give no clue to his new inner state, his disintegrating self. Rather like having too much to drink at the house of a mere acquaintance who didn't appear to be intoxicated at all. Was he fooling her? Did she believe he was a serious legitimate person? Her dark eyes, deep and fathomless, going this way and that, yielded nothing; merely took him in. It was like talking to someone wearing dark glasses.

My wife wore the trousers, he blurted. I wore Laura Ashley if I was going out, but mostly just plain skirts like yours.

Kate froze, then smiled vaguely, turned away. Walked away from him and in a second he heard her laugh. Or what sounded very like a laugh.

Margaret Tries the Soup

What's the soup today, Kate?

Oh, Mum, I didn't hear you come in. She was drying beer glasses behind the bar, which was mostly empty but for the two Ians in their wellies and Hamish from up by Flowerdale, playing the fruit machine. They sat in their usual cloud of whisky fumes and cigarette smoke.

Ach, well, do I not usually come in on a Tuesday? I thought to myself I'd skip the prawn Marie Rose sandwiches today and just have soup. Home-made, am I right? Did Fiona make it this morning, or is it from the deep freeze?

Split pea, Mum. And I've no idea how old it is. Will I ask? She finished drying the glasses and came round to her mother, who was sitting at the table closest to the bar. She refused to sit at the bar, said it wasn't ladylike, but if her daughter had to work behind a bar, she was glad at least it was in a nice hotel that did home-made soups.

No, don't bother. I don't really mind either way. A bowl of the soup then, with some bread. White, mind. I can't stand that wholewheat with the bitties in. I was still finding bits in my teeth the next day, last time. You're looking very well, Kate. Pretty.

Am I?

Aye, what's different?

Nothing. In fact, I'm tired, I shouldn't be looking well at all.

Ah, but you do, you look grand. Something is different, I don't know what, but a mother notices these things.

Great. Hm. I'll just tell the kitchen about your soup. You boys alright? she called to the Ians and Gary. Are you wanting anything through the kitchen?

No, you're alright, Kate. We're having our liquid lunch today.

That's no true, said one Ian. I'm eating cheese and onion crisps, that's vegetables, right. Potatoes, onions, cheese. Two veg and a protein. He held up three fingers, a roll-up pinched between one of them and his thumb.

Kate laughed. Went and shouted the soup order through to the kitchen.

So tell me, Kate. I hear you've got some visitors. Americans.

Aye, one or two. Well, two, I guess. Mhairi's friend from college, Brendan, and his dad.

And?

And what? They're just there, they're fine, clean, house-trained, you know.

Not loud, funny-dressed, full of bragging and money?

Well, that too, of course.

But nice.

Aye. Well, I hardly know them. And I think they're only here for a day or two. They didn't say, but.

Well, I'll probably stop by to meet them, if they're still here tomorrow. And Mhairi, how is she? Any word at all from that fellow, what's his name? Robert?

His name is Roddy and I would forget about him for now, alright? He's not on the scene at all, and it's not a huge scandal for a girl to have a baby without a husband. It is pretty unusual, in fact, these days to have one with a husband.

Aye, but no need to get snappy, I was only asking.

Sorry, look, it's just that disapproving but pretending to be approving tone I keep hearing. Oh, look, I'll have a bowl of soup with you. It's quiet enough.

She went and fetched two soups and sat down with her mother. Out of the window they could see the bay, shining grey and green, with two bright wind-surfers skating over the surface. Beyond them, the beach curved around to where the old church perched, ancient gravestones crumbling into the sea.

Nice enough day they're getting anyway, said her mum, back on neutral ground – you had to be so careful what you said, when your daughter was probably pre-menopausal and also probably going through a stage of delayed grieving that thoroughly concealed grief.

Aye, it's not rained for at least half an hour, it's a good day. Should've worn my shorts.

Now, Kate, sarcasm doesn't suit you, and the soup's lovely, so it is, I must ask Fiona for her recipe. Stock cubes, I suppose?

I don't know, Mum. Probably. She makes an awful big pot, anyway. I thought sarcasm did suit me. Haven't I always been like this? It's you it doesn't suit, Mum.

I'm ignoring you, you're just crabbit. What's that you're reading, Kate? You've always got a book on the go, I don't know when you find the time.

Well, there's plenty time to kill in here, most afternoons. All the touristy types go to the Old Byre. More authentic, they probably think. All those low ceilings to bash their thick heads on.

Aye, well, this place is good enough for me, anyway, her mother said loyally, and also because she approved of new buildings, with their easy-to-clean floors and absence of queer corners and cubby-holes. There's not too many dust collectors in this place, I like it.

Do you? I can't say I really even notice it. She looked around as if to confirm her eyes were incapable of taking in the room. The shiny brass fittings, the upside-down bottles of spirits, the beer mats and ashtrays, the stag antlers, the fishing prints. No, none of it was visible, all cancelled by familiarity. Even the smell – whisky, beer and tobacco. Mostly beer.

Anyway, is the book good?

Wuthering Heights? Aye, I think it's the best book I've read in years, actually.

Looks different from the books you usually read, Kate. Is it not too serious?

It's not about the usual domestic dramas and suburban love affairs, anyway. I've sworn off all the bestseller stuff for a while. On a diet of literature. Births, marriages, deaths, you know. Life.

You are so daft, Kate. That's what all books are about. Even telly is like that. Is that not just a posh old-fashioned version of Barbara Cartland? I wonder if it'll be on my *Reader's Digest* list this year. They do proper stories too, you know.

Aye, well. Listen, Mum, about Mhairi.

Yes?

She seems withdrawn, spacey. I think it's just the pregnancy, and she's always been quiet, but, well.

What?

I worry, Mum. Was I like that when I was pregnant? Is it normal? She doesn't want to talk about the baby, or the future, or anything.

Oh, my, this soup's so filling, I don't think I can eat another spoonful. I don't remember much about your pregnancy, my dear. I think you were just normal. You sewed that wee quilt, remember? And I had to unpick all the stitches and do it right.

You did?

Ach, did I never tell you? Now that just shows my age, I've been keeping that secret for, oh what, eighteen years? And here I've just spilled the beans. She giggled.

I can't believe it. That wee one I made? The one I got framed and hung in the hall, with her name and birthdate, the one I tell everyone I made myself?

Aye, oh, Kate, don't get angry now. It was all squint, love, you were only young then and, let's face it, you never were much of a hand at sewing. I took it home one night and you never noticed. I just brought it back the next day and slipped it back in your basket.

Kate stared at her mother. Then laughed. Well, a belated thank-you. I never noticed. To think I've been taking credit for that all these years. What will I tell Mhairi? She thinks her mum's a needlework genius.

No need to tell her anything, dear. It was the thought that counts, and you so wanted to make something lovely to wrap her in.

If I loved her so, and you loved me so, why did we each have only one baby? Kate thought but did not say.

Jamie

He wishes sometimes. It is a game and it is not a game, because he would not be surprised to find his wishes come true. He creates rituals for himself and enacts them, in the proper order. Tonight he is in the mood, has nothing to lose, so goes around the block three times without stopping, almost gets hit by a delivery van coming over the pavement, and he keeps his paces steady, he counts his footsteps. When he completes his circuit it must be on an even number, and no cheating. He marks his starting point so there can be no mistake. He completes this successfully, counting aloud to keep track, and then he reaches into his pocket and removes the salt packet he'd found in a discarded McDonald's bag. He rips it open with his teeth, then with his right hand, eyes squeezed shut, he flings the salt over his left shoulder while wishing his wish.

I wish, he says aloud, with a long whoosh at the end of wish, indifferent to people's stares.

I wish.

But what is he wishing for? One older man, who has paused to watch him, thinks the words are: I wish I wasna. I wish I wasna.

But it's hard to say, with the noise of the traffic. And in any case, when he opens his eyes he simply drifts off down the pavement, shuffling his feet, and the older man carries on home, disappointed. As street theatre it was a little flat.

Poor Duncan Keeps Trying

Kate only believed in fate when it reinforced her desires. So when she found herself, by sheer coincidence, alone on the beach with Duncan the third day of the Americans' visit, she did not surrender and say to herself, Ah, well, it was meant to be, and fall into his arms. No. She stood straighter, pursed her lips, and fought fate.

Duncan, what are you doing here? she asked — no, demanded, as if this was her private beach and his presence an intrusion.

His face dropped. I'm taking a walk, same as you, Kate. His face up again, smile creeping out. Great minds think alike, hey?

Rubbish, you never take walks.

(But this was worse, because she was scolding him as if he was already her husband. Bad. Some distance was required here.)

Sorry, Duncan. *Do* you take walks? I never knew that. Well, it certainly is a lovely day. (As rain began to spit down her face.)

Well, truth is, I was driving out to your place, but spotted your dog running down here, and thought I'd join you.

(Not good, he was being endearingly disarming.)

Oh, that's nice, Duncan. But it's starting to rain now, shall we head back? Don't you have a job on today?

They turned and walked back, his body continually closing in on hers, and hers swerving from it, so their course was diagonal, rather than straight. They headed straight for the waves.

Aye, but I have to let the first coat dry and it's only up the road so I just thought – nice cuppa would do.

Mhairi would've put the kettle on for you, Duncan, you know the house is always open, even if I'm not there.

She stumbled in the shingle, her feet trying to change their seaward course, and he, ecstatic at the opportunity for contact, made as if to lift her entire body off the beach.

I'm fine, Duncan, thank you, you can let go now, I'm steady. It's just such an incline and the stones are so tumbly. (And you were forcing me into the water, you great ass.)

Take my arm, Kate, you're not wanting to sprain an ankle.

Where's the dog? (to avoid answering). Dog! Dog! There you are, good girl, stop it, don't shake all over Duncan, oh dear, what a mess, you bad girl.

That's alright (wiping dog saliva and sea water from his face and hands). It's only water. Good girl. Dog growled at his outstretched hand.

I hear the mobile cinema is coming, Kate.

Is it now? I heard it might be.

Fancy seeing a film?

Yes, I think me and Mhairi will definitely be going. She loves films.

Ah.

Will you be going, Duncan?

I expect. (Guilt tugged at her, he was so transparently woebegone. Jack's ghost seemed to be pushing her towards him – *Be nice to my friend*, it said.)

Come with us, Duncan. I could make some popcorn.

Then guilt raced away, chased by revulsion again, as his face filled with eagerness and hope.

But what about those American men you've got staying, Kate, will they be around very long? Are they just here for a few days or what?

Ah, Mhairi's friends. I'm not sure, but I guess they'll be bored soon. Bound to be. No decent coffee, you see.

Duncan laughed, Kate did not join him.

Mhairi watched them from the kitchen window, holding her belly with both hands to give her stomach muscles a break. It felt like far more than a baby in there. It felt like a television and video-player stacked up.

The sight of Duncan and her mother was, on the whole, pleasing to her, and this surprised her. She'd expected to feel torn loyalties and confused jealousies. Her mother attached to another man would set her daughter free, and that could only be a good thing.

Michael and Brendan sat behind her in the sitting room, reading books; both of them stretched out, legs crossed, books propped on chests – identical as twins in their absorption.

Patrick was dreaming his dream of being exactly what he was when he was awake, and his thumb completely filled a space that seemed to fit it like a glove – his mouth.

The Very Very Big Day

Patrick listened to his mother brush her teeth and wash her face. Loud and vigorous swishing and splashing. Then, on her way up the stairs to bed, Mhairi's glands released a minute fluid substance that, by the time they were in bed, had signalled to her uterus. It was time to eject the alien.

For weeks now, Mhairi had been noticing her belly hardening, then loosening. Had been told by the midwife who came every fortnight that it had a name and was not the real thing, but a rehearsal for it. No pain, and there was none now as she lay on her back absolutely still, trying to catch the sound of the surf, her lullaby to sleep. Just a rock hard belly and a minute later a soft belly. She closed her eyes and drifted off to the rhythm of both seas.

Patrick, on the other hand, could not sleep a wink. He was in a tropical storm, being squeezed and pushed and his little heart fluttered erratically. He tried to stretch and could not. He had not flown out to see what was happening for a while now and was solidly wedged into his body and his warm dark red sack. This was life for ever, as far as Patrick was concerned. Already, not even nine months old, he showed signs of being averse to change. He blocked messages to squirm his way into light. He went completely limp. Earlier Mhairi had noticed his absolute stillness, and wondered unemotionally if he were alive or dead.

Another odd night in the box room. (Queer name for it — it was just a big closet with a window. Surely its purpose could encompass more than storing boxes?) Michael kept waking and having to re-identify his surroundings. And a few times, even his self. Re-orientation had become a habit. I am Michael, I am in a box room belonging to a lady called Kate, a secret word processor, and my home is in a wooden structure over to the left about six thousand miles. I have a green table by the kitchen window and when it's open on summer evenings like this, I can hear water sprinklers and frogs and crickets. A blond man is sleeping in this house too and he was once my blond baby whose belly I used to nuzzle with my chin.

But all this felt a lie. Again. Interesting, perhaps even true, but it did not feel true.

He told himself he might as well give up and just stay awake till morning, but instead fell into an unpleasantly deep sleep. His mouth went slack and open, and his breath stank. He made strange muted noises, half-way between a dog whimper and a sigh.

Kate slept on her back inhaling the salt air drifting through her open window. She did not dream or stir. Downstairs on the sofa, Brendan also slept. As did the dog, but not the cats or mice.

Mhairi's uterus continued to tighten, but so slowly there was no pain, only a hardening. Enough to wake her, but not enough to keep her awake past its slackening. All night she contracted at intervals of between eight and fifteen minutes. Each mini-nap refreshed her, like a drink of good water down a parched throat. Patrick was squeezed slowly into a tighter and tighter space. He continued limp and calm, perhaps hoping that if he held himself still nothing would happen. An infant animal playing dead, hoping catastrophe might pass it over.

It was daylight, but only four in the morning, when Mhairi woke to a gushing out between her legs. Her fright and movement brought on stronger contractions and within minutes they were longer and more frequent than the spaces of time uncontracted. Mindful of the house full of sleeping guests, she did not shout out for her mother. She rose, pulled a dressing-gown over her doubled self and hobbled quickly down the stairs to the toilet, then back up to her mother's bedroom.

Patrick, suddenly finding himself upside down and bumping up and down stairs, let gravity take over. The neck of her womb, already dilated eight centimetres, widened now to ease the pressure of Patrick's descending head. On the top step, Mhairi stopped, held her breath. She opened her mouth and called, Mum! Help! but no sound, only wheezing, a nightmare of sweat and slow-motion pain.

She braced herself against the banister and slid to the floor. Her mouth framed her mother's name again and opened, and although only a guttural noise erupted, Kate was out of bed in a flash, stumbling towards her daughter. What are you doing on the floor? Oh, my God, fuck! This is it, okay, calm down, lass, can we get you back to bed? No? Listen, let's just stretch you out here, then. You want to stay upright? That's fine, that's a good girl.

And she swivelled and slid her daughter's body till it was on the landing carpet, safely away from the top of the stairs. Then she got the torch, because the landing had poor light and she needed to see how things were.

Jesus, Mhairi, why didn't you call me earlier? Alright sweetie, it's alright, just breathe slow, or puff — oh, what is it you're supposed to do? In through your nose, out through your mouth. Just concentrate. Watch me. In. Out.

Wait here (as if Mhairi was not glued to the carpet, writhing around the banister). I'm phoning the ambulance and midwife.

She flew down the stairs, into the kitchen for the phone. A second's panic as her mind completely refused to divulge the emergency number. Then she watched her fingers in grateful amazement as they dialled anyway, no cerebral help at all. Got through, garbled all the relevant information. Yes, yes, come quick! Raced back up the stairs.

Mhairi, her eternally familiar unknowable daughter, was not there. She was in another land, of drowning seas and lost men, of frightened animals and puddles of blood. She was a poor thing being wrenched in half, twisting her contorted body from side to side, rocking and moaning, but not shouting. The muffled cry of a creature who instinctively knew that loudness could alert a predator.

Brendan half woke, heard Mhairi and Kate, but interpreted it as some variation on the sexual noises he and Isabel had been developing as they lost their inhibitions and, without questioning the source, fell back into sleep. Michael, exhausted, heard nothing.

Kate, ears alerted for the sound of the ambulance or midwife, got a damp cloth from the bathroom, mopped her daughter's forehead, stroked her belly, muttered nonsense: There you go, girl, what a clever girl, it'll soon be over, and all gone, all gone, what a good girl, Mhairi, you are doing so well.

Mhairi heard not one word of this. Her ears were roaring and rushing and she swam towards things that seemed like salvation but always dissolved when she reached them. Over and over and over and, oh, it wasn't fair. The pain was like a being outside her; a solid entity, a wave of metallic pressure, but not her. She had never imagined such sensations.

Then it changed, the pitch pulled taut, the tempo tightened, till Mhairi stopped making any noise but a thin squeak and the sweat poured out of her.

Kate was sweating too, frightened, was this her daughter's death she was watching? It certainly resembled it. What should she be doing?

Hold on to me, lass, here's my hands, squeeze them, I've got you, don't worry, hold tight.

I need to, panted Mhairi, I need to I need to, oh, help I need to . . .

What is it sweetheart, what is it you need?

I need to shit, oh fuck oh help, help, here it comes, I'm shitting, fuck off, fuck it!

Kate pulled the nightie right up, and shone the torch with one hand, while Mhairi almost ate her other hand, and then Mhairi stopped breathing. Just stopped breathing altogether, looked like she was about to submerge underwater and she held her breath for dear life and turned bright pink and gave out an unearthly grunt that lasted and lasted. Kate listened for the midwife, the siren of the ambulance. Willed them to hurry, but only the sea, only the wind.

She peeked when Mhairi sucked in her breath on a wail. Nothing, just wet hair and swollen pudenda. Then another big intake of air, the inner concentration and push. This time she thought Mhairi might pass out, it was so long. She peeked again, nothing yet.

You're doing just great there, girl, just what you should be doing, go on, now breathe before you faint, you're almost there, just think.

Another explosion of breath and weeping, then, Here it comes, Mum, oh!

This time when Mhairi was in the throes of thrusting out what she was convinced was an enormous bowel movement, Kate was rewarded by a dark hairy head emerging in her torchlight.

I see him! I see his head, oh, Mhairi, he's coming.

Another burst of exhalation. What? Who? Not he, Mum. A she. She, oh shit, here it comes again.

The final squeeze seemed to do it, Mhairi's muscles were strong and wanted rid of this obstruction, and out shot Patrick. Whoosh!

Kate tried to catch him, but he was like a fish and he landed on the landing carpet, dog hair and fluff already adhering to his wet skin. Kate took the sheet she had grabbed from the airing cupboard, wrapped and lifted his surprisingly solid and muscular body to her daughter. Mhairi pushed him away, legs quivering, awash with the euphoric relief of just having had the world's biggest dump. Then they both heard the ambulance outside.

The next half-hour was a blur. The ambulance men did their this-is-an-emergency routine, all very important and intimidating, severing the cord with sterile instruments, pumping up blood-pressure instruments on Mhairi's arm, loving all the excitement. Then in came the midwife and spoiled their fun, shooed them away, delivered the placenta, helped Mhairi on to her own bed, and convinced the ambulance men she'd be better off here than taken all the way to Inverness. Now the baby was here, and both he and Mhairi were sound, what would be the point? It was her hey-day too. Not enough home births these days, in her opinion.

She asked for a bowl for the placenta, said that would need checking later, and then her bleeper went and she said she'd be back in a while, just had to check her other lady over in Poolewe. The ambulance men departed, deflated.

Patrick lay trembling on Mhairi's chest, not quite crying, but breathing fine and giving the room and his mother dark little glances. Kate lowered Mhairi's nightgown and led Patrick's mouth to the nipple, which seemed enormous but did not daunt him. He opened his petal mouth and latched on quickly. His first sucks were vigorous and Mhairi cried out at the sharp contraction they caused. Then stroked the warm peach fuzz of his head and cupped him to her. All over, but especially in his nostrils, where the air blew in and out with little moth-wing puffs, he experienced a tingling, a tightening. Patrick's skin dried out at a rapid rate, about equal to the speed with which his stomach filled with the thin sweet colostrum. The world had become a faintly familiar but strange place full of undiluted noises, lights, smells and powerful, warm beings touching him. But I've been here before, he thought in non-words. Overwhelmed, he fainted into sleep, nipple in mouth.

After Kate cleaned her up and she was settled, sore but incredibly not in pain, Mhairi dozed. Listened for the sound of the midwife's car returning and heard instead the beat of the sea. She thought of her father. This is your grandson, Dad. Not a girl, not who I had imagined. A son. Will you just look at him? Not much to look at, is he? But, oh, will you just look at him?

Outside the sun shone and the world busied itself using it. Kate's white house looked secretive and smug.

Jamie

He is a bit like a magpie, really. He is drawn to shiny objects, discarded in odd places, small things he can fit easily into his bag. He has several eating utensils, found on beaches; he has a lighter, still working; the watch he found in the big-houses place; he has a metal brooch, broken, a large safety-pin and a penknife with one blade; and he has an empty Golden Virginia tin. They are his treasures and he is convinced they will all have their uses one day.

He walks up the hill because he believes the sea will be on the other side of it. He left the A92 what seems like hours ago, just started heading over the fields, following his train of thought and letting his feet make the destination decisions. It is early evening, late spring, and he feels young. His body has no aches, his bowels are neither constipated nor loose, his muscles are co-ordinated and his socks are clean. Or feel clean, anyway.

At the brow of the hill, he gets a little surprise — the sea is not straight ahead, but up to the left and quite a way off still. He sighs, and keeps trudging. No people in sight now, must be a big farm, a thousand acres of barley, one big house somewhere. He keeps to the tractor tracks, mindful of leaving a trail of crushed crop. A gentle breeze has turned the field into a sea, the green heads of barley undulate and flow. He runs his fingers absentmindedly along their feathery tips, and it reminds him of something — somebody's hair?

By the time he comes to the coast, it is getting dark and he is beginning to wonder if this is a smart place to be after all. Does he have enough food, will he freeze, get chased by stray dogs, get lost? He arrives at the beach and it is empty. The shore stretches north and south, rocks and small dunes. The sun has set and he moves back into the dunes to find shelter, settle for the night. A slight haar is already beginning to rise, he can taste it and his clothes feel damp.

He hums. Coughs. Sings in snatches. No wind, and the waves are calm, polite little breaths. Splash, suck in, splash, suck in, splash. He eats his dinner. Two Safeway Scotch eggs, past their sell-by date but fine, drinks his water from an old squash container filled from the sink in the toilet at the petrol station where the driver left him.

When he is finished, he stretches, watches a sliver of moon in the royal blue night sky. Then has one of his inspirations. Yes! God, he is a fucking genius. But will it work?

He finds the apple, only slightly bruised, then gets out his Golden Virginia tin and lighter. Scrabbles about for some kindling — dried seaweed, twigs off a blown whin bush, small soft bits of driftwood. Finds some old newspaper in his bag, originally squirrelled away for bog roll.

Lights his tiny fire in a sheltered pit, cups his hands around it till it glows, then places two stones three inches apart at either side of the flames and puts the open tin on top of them. It is clean, he has wiped it with his shirt tail. He slices the apple with the old penknife and pours a few drops of water into the tin to help soften the fruit. Semi-covers it with the lid. Jesus, he can taste it already. Stewed apple, cooked by himself, the genius travelling man.

Patrick's First Day And Michael's Extraordinary Behaviour

Michael woke to the sounds of a house well awake already. Footsteps, radio, dog barking, voices, water running. He got up and stumbled down to the bathroom. In the bathtub was a bowl of what looked like liver. He knew this had been a small farm and guessed that things like raw meat were stored just anywhere and decided to pretend he wasn't shocked. Sure, of course that's where liver goes. But what a massive streaky bit of liver it was, and was it meant for tonight's dinner and did it come from one of the sheep who had died in the night of a mysterious disease? Or been hit by a car and lain fly-covered for days by the roadside, like he'd seen on his way there? He looked away and washed his face. Out of the window he could see the hen run, a long narrow enclosure alongside the veg patch, which was choked with docks.

Someone knocked on the door.

I'm just finished, he said, and opened the door to a uniformed woman.

This is the midwife, Michael, Kate informed him. She needs to check the placenta.

He looked stupidly but politely at her.

Did you not hear any of the commotion? Mhairi delivered early this morning. A wee boy. Patrick, after her grandfather, bless his heart.

The midwife, fresh in blue, lifted the bowl and prodded it with a plastic gloved hand.

It looks to be all there and fine, Mrs McKinnon, but I'll have to take it back with me to check more thoroughly. You did well, both of you did, and the bairn's a good weight considering he was near three weeks early. If her bleeding doesn't increase, everything should be fine. But I'll be back again tomorrow, see how she's getting on.

Michael continued feeling stupid but was waking up fast, and time did one of those somersaults, where suddenly he felt he'd been in this house far longer than three days, and the wallpaper of the bathroom zapped into the most familiar pattern he'd ever known. Purple daisies embedded permanently, displacing all previous wallpaper patterns.

He tried to be useful. It was a momentous day, the beginning of Patrick's non-aquatic existence, and yet there seemed to be long spells of time that yawned. Mhairi slept a lot. Patrick cried a few times, not a proper cry, but a weak kitten noise. Kate gave Michael chores to do – put the rubbish bags down to the corner, feed the hens. But wouldn't let him do anything else.

Get your son to take you down the beach or the hotel. Have a dram to Patrick.

And to Brendan: You'll entertain your dad now, will you, while we get on with things?

Brendan began to feel a queasiness he attributed to the distance between himself and Isabel, but which might have been simply boredom now that an infant was centre stage. Actually, I think we'll be heading back to Inverness now. When everyone stared at him, he laughed and said, Well, come on, guys, it's not exactly brilliant timing, is it? You'll want a little peace and quiet now. Michael's heart quite surprised him by sinking at these words. He shrank from returning to Inverness, to Brendan and Isabel's intimacy. He hadn't known he minded. Or was it a reluctance to leave this place?

He lifted an eyebrow to Brendan's plan, eyes sad. Kate, hyper-perceptive through lack of sleep and excitement, jumped in with, But you can leave your old man here a few days, surely. He hasn't even really seen the place yet. That's if he wants to stay, he may be thinking we have babies born here every night.

What do you think, Dad? I can come fetch you anytime, and there's always the Westerbus.

Well, if you're sure I won't be in your way, I'd like that. Thanks.

And so his reprieve came and the long day ended with Brendan being waved off. Michael watched his car disappear with detachment, till it was out of sight, then gasped quietly, full of regret. Why had he wanted to stay here? These people were strangers.

He held Patrick. Nervous at first, then remembered. Held Patrick's head close to his heart, in the crook of his arm. Forgot to be anxious, forgot to be puzzled. Here, my turn now. And looking, saw that Kate also had this hunger. To lose herself for a minute. The sweet immediacy of an infant.

In Kate's arms Patrick watched the window, then her hair, and finally her dark eyes looking into his own. There he fixed his stare until he drifted off to sleep again.

Mhairi, who had watched both Michael and her mother with something like dismay – was that how you were supposed to do it, to feel? – lifted him and took her deflated belly and engorged breasts off to bed. She felt dizzy and drunk, as if she'd had all those painkillers after all and they were only now beginning to wear off. The initial euphoria forgotten.

Michael dipped into and out of dreams, this fourth night. Both states were strange. So much of the physical side of life was in the open here. Bowls of placenta in the bath, dead ewes in ditches, hens in the kitchen. Mhairi's breasts hanging out, dripping bluish milk. Patrick's entry into the world, quietly in the dark hallway, charged the house with importance. He could not imagine ever walking past that stain on the carpet without remembering today. If he lived here, of course, which he did not. In fact, what was he doing here without his son at all? Had he already abandoned his task to fetch Brendan back? Reasons were not forthcoming, but the fact remained that he wanted to be here, was glad, albeit bewildered, to find himself in this single bed under pink coombs.

He felt his blood and muscles and bones all as separate arrangements of fluid and substance. And to the brim with life. The air pulling into his lungs and out again, bringing sea and mountain oxygen to his blood. His skin and sinews, all his fibres cried out to be touched.

He woke from a short feverish dream and without thought of rejection or offence, went down the corridor to Kate's room. He'd not done something like this before, but then away from his home, he was hardly himself any more. And here he was, following a sexual impulse as if he'd spent his life following sexual impulses towards women acquaintances.

Mhairi? Kate whispered, but when there was no reply, knew.

And could not speak. He was in her bed and her senses seemed to have clear memory of male contact, because they responded as if sex had been a nightly occurrence. But she watched from afar as if her own limbs were not her own. Then, all too soon, he was rolling over and saying, I'm sorry. Sorry, Kate.

Shusht, whatever for? I could've said get out.

But embarrassment was surging through him. And not just for the intrusion. The lack of prowess.

He raised himself on one elbow and tried to see her in the shadows. Her face was above his, on the pillows, one eye looking at him, the other at the wall. He focused on the one looking at him, and the other eye joined to listen.

Kate. I'm sorry. I don't do much of this.

He felt undone, unconnected to his words, actions. It seemed a marvel that the thoughts in his head could turn into comprehensible speech.

Well, and neither do I. But it's been one of those days. We can act out of character now and then. Can't we? (Thinking, Christ, he's hating me now, I'm too skinny, my boobs are too saggy, he felt my chin fuzz.)

Yeah, I suppose. Still. God, I can't believe what we've done. This is so weird. Do you mind if I ...

He reached for his clothes, and she pulled her nightie back over her head.

He sat on her bed a few minutes, trying to make sense. He

was a stranger, a guest. She was a widow. Well, that didn't mean anything. They were a similar age. Why did it feel as if the air might break if he moved too quickly. He had intruded, slipped through her defences the one night in her widowhood they were down. Had the wit to realise his fortune, sensed something of the rarity of it. But his incompetence and undeservedness. Like the court jester, instead of the prince, who wakes Snow White with a kiss. She must hate him.

Go ahead and go back to your own bed, if you want, Michael.

Yeah. I'm sorry, Kate, don't worry about it ever happening again. This was an aberration, okay?

Short sentences in little bursts of wind, his eyes searching for her good one. If he moved too close to her, they went cross-eyed. If she had to turn her head to look at him, they went opposite ways for a second. It didn't repulse him. Made him feel protective in a way. No, something else, something more.

Don't worry about it. It's not a big deal.

Exactly. Thanks a lot.

You know what I mean.

Yeah. Sure, look, I'll go now.

Goodnight then. See you in the morning.

And he stumbled back to his room with his very slightly lighter body. He felt he was walking on felt and the house was like a cave. That all the separate stones had been put into place by brawny red-faced men who didn't wear shoes and ate oat bannocks and warm watery milk when they were tired, and had to rub mutton fat into their roughened hands at night before their women would let them near with their virile animal urges.

The house was too vivid and he was crazy. He fell into bed and a sleep like dark fudge.

Kate lay awake and took inventory of her body. Like checking a room for broken glass and dangerous wiring after an unexpected tornado has charged through it. He'd not been rough, but there were imprints nevertheless. His body had entered where no man since Jack had been, and because of his illness, that had been at least three years ago. Virginity had reclaimed her, and she'd just lost it again.

Why had she allowed him, after turning down all those other post-widowhood suitors? They'd mostly been married, and to her friends usually, but Duncan had been suitable and she'd not even considered sex and him in the same thought. What had come over her? Must have been the baby. The shock of Patrick coming into their lives so sudden.

The sex had not been earth-shattering, not even memorable, but after all this time it felt, well, let's face it, she thought, it felt great. Like waking up when she'd not known she'd been asleep.

She inhaled the after-smell of sex and found it more arousing than the event, but maybe that was par for the course. Several possible outcomes spun themselves in great detail in her head. Snatches of conversation, different embraces, loaded glances, the design on the icing of the twenty-fifth anniversary cake.

Jamie

The two-year-old boy goes up and down the train, trying to catch people's eyes. He is bored and restless. His mother sits with his three brothers at the far end, nodding over her cold tea. The boy gets a few smiles, but not many. His clothes are nice, but they are dirty and his face is grubby. This is a neglected child — loved probably, but unwashed and unsupervised. Other mothers glance with pity, but distract their own toddlers, firmly sitting down, from being influenced by the wandering child. At the end of the carriage is someone different, who has been watching the child mesmerised, whose face lights up when the boy smiles at him. For a minute, they smile at each other. Madly, surprised and excited, as if each has discovered his long-lost twin. The small boy approaches the man and lifts his arms to be picked up. The man takes a while to understand, then lifts the child. He is light, lighter than he expects, and he swings him higher than needed to come to the seat. Ends up sitting the boy on the table top. This child is the first person he has touched in a long time. The contact is sending sparkly exploding signals, and the smiling continues. But his smiling face looks funny to the boy, who laughs. A real toddler chuckle, like he is being tickled. Other passengers notice and look. Some smile too, it is infectious. Others tsk and sigh, What on earth is that mother thinking, allowing her child to sit with the likes of him? To let him be touched by a strange man.

The toddler climbs to his chubby legs, so he is standing on the table, and his hands are held by the man, and he dances and laughs, this is the best fun. The man's feet tap in sympathy. Eventually, the mother comes to retrieve her son, wearily, it has been a long day. In a second she sees what this man or boy is and is afraid. He is one of them. But when she reaches for her son, the boy clings to his new friend and threatens to throw a screaming tantrum. He is capable of this, and she knows well that the signals, the ones he is emitting now, mean business. She knows the probable duration of the screams while she is hauling him back, while passengers glare at her. Her head hurts. She looks back at her older children — all busily reading comics or drawing. Considers the options, and she sits down with them. Lets her son remain, but in her sight. Anything for peace.

When they reach Aberdeen, she is suddenly so grateful to this man for keeping her child entertained, and so sorry for him, so ashamed of her earlier aversion, she gives him the box of Black Magic she'd bought to give her mum. Then gathers her children and gets off the train. In the station, greeting her relatives, she looks around for him, guiltily hoping he'll be gone, make no claim on her in her safe world.

He has disappeared. She holds her small son and kisses him on the back of his neck. Lucky, lucky, she thinks.

Gairloch Is Psychic

The two men threw their gear aboard the fishing boat in the grey light of dawn.

Hey, Ian, you mind that big American fellow who's biding up at Kate's?

Mhairi's fake hubby?

No, he's gone, he left yesterday, after the bairn was born. No, this is the older man he brought with him. Could be his dad, maybe.

Hey, watch how you throw that, Ian, it's got my new mug in it.

Oh, our mugs aren't good enough for you, hey, Ian?

That's right. I prefer my tea without the layer of scum, thank you very much.

Oooh, fancy fisher-boy, hey?

You fancy me, then?

Like a shot, mate.

I'll let you use my mug, then.

Fuck off, you. Listen, you know the big American, not Mhairi's fake hubby?

Aye. The sort of fat one?

That's the one.

Aye?

Well, I have a notion there's something going on between him and Kate.

Wink, wink, nudge, nudge, say no more, hey? Ooh, you scandal-monger, you.

Ach, it's only a notion. Something about the two of them. I noticed them walking together.

Oh, that's a sure sign of sex, aye, you're right enough there, Ian.

That's exactly what I thought, Ian.

Well, more luck to them. Wish I could say the same for myself.

But you can, Ian, you're a married man, are you not?

Oh, aye, and what's that supposed to be when it's home?

WEST COAST CRACK

Things that happen to a house when a baby is born: the inhabitants grow antennae that hear the baby's thin wail as a siren, drop everything till someone quietens him. It is not only our Annie who has had a baby. Now I sleep in spurts, walk about with a dazed look, wear a cloth nappy over my shoulder and inhale milky vomit. Our American guest finds reawakening memories when he holds Joe, as well as a premonition of his own grandparenthood, probably not too far down the road.

We all, including the house, know without discussion that the baby is all that matters. The world has always revolved around and for newborns, and only trivia-induced amnesia has blinded us to this startling fact. We go about our days, accomplishing whatever is necessary for another day's comfort, but we know we are mere satellites, fading planets, and one whimper from Joe halts us all in our tracks.

Of course, myself and the American feel this more keenly than Annie, since she is so close to the event. Like a wound reopened or a lesson relearnt, it is more vivid than the original sensation.

I do regular breathing checks, I test his body temperature, lift blankets off or lay them on. I can hardly take my eyes off him, the sight of him could never tire me. It is lucky my camera is broken, for I've saved myself a fortune already.

The cats, of course, want to sleep curled up next to him. They purr loudly, and then growl in protest when I remove them, for I do not want them raising Joe's body heat. I have read the stories of cot deaths and overheated babies. Not to mention the way cat hairs float and stick to blankets. The thought of even one small hair near his nose gives me palpitations.

The house is warmer, the stove being lit continually despite the season, and some old bar-heaters are consuming electricity at an alarming rate. The dog does not get so many walks, and the hens do not get a song along with their hastily thrown scraps. It is a quieter muffled house, but louder too, as different sounds fill it. The walls have not absorbed a newborn's cry since Annie's birth. The air is very partially altered, as some of it now contains air that has been filtered through the lungs of a newborn. It might conceivably taste sweeter.

The house shelters us and we shelter Joe. He is a stranger, has been evicted from his own home with no warning or explanation, and we are giving him all the shelter we can, to protect him until he builds his own house.

I want to drape soft cottons and old crushed velvets around every hard surface. I want to cover all the lamps with orange and yellow silk. I yearn, most of all, in the middle of summer, for a snowstorm that will justify a very long hibernation.

Kissing Wants to Happen

Ach, no, Kate, it's them. And I only just got here, too.

So what, mum? It's only the Murdos. Aren't they your nephews or something?

Nonsense. Your uncle Sammy left that Angusina long before big Murdo was born, and as for the other Mr Skin and Bones, that was your father's side and doesn't count.

Well, give the baby to Michael and put the kettle on. I'll let them in.

Margaret, looking natty in her favourite Marks & Spencer's waisted navy daisy dress, plumped Patrick on to Michael's lap. At least you know the right way to hold him, simpered Margaret. Most men haven't a clue.

She approved of Michael – he was American, he must be rich as sin, despite the clothes.

Lots of practice. Like a bike, you never forget.

Isn't that an elephant?

No, I meant, oh, never mind.

Patrick mewed. Studied Michael's nostrils.

Well, well, full house today, Kate, hello Margaret, and hello wee man, aren't you just the stuff, hey? You must be Michael, I'm Murdo.

Michael took the outstretched hand, clasped the warm and sticky flesh.

I was just about to introduce you. Michael, these are my cousins, Murdo and Murdo.

The Murdos looked at him with such undisguised delight that Michael laughed, couldn't help himself. Great to meet you guys. So are these your great-uncles, then, Patrick? He lifted the baby so they could all admire him.

Oh, God, but Mhairi did a fine job, he's that perfect. Where is she, anyway?

Mhairi? Out somewhere, I think. Probably walking, said Kate vaguely.

Good for her, getting some fresh air.

I don't think it's good, I think that girl spends far too much time away from her baby, she's never here when I come. And when did she ever like walking before? Now, would you two like to wash your hands? Margaret poised by the table with a plate of cakes and sandwiches arranged meticulously in circles.

Now, now, Margaret, you've to stop talking to us like we're imbeciles, we like our hands this way, don't we, Murdo. (Wee Murdo smiled, nodded.) And Kate never makes us wash, do you, Kate? A bit of dirt's good for you. Anyway, these hands are clean, only stained from the peat I've been stacking for old Peggy.

A quick wash just the same, boys, make an old lady happy. Soap and towels in the bathroom, now off you go, Margaret twittered, enjoying the old routine. Men were just boys, wanting to be nagged.

Mum, you really do have a nerve. But they do what you tell them, that's something. You've got the right tone of voice.

Ah, well, I've only known the scamps for ever. Besides, it always worked with your father, until he, oh, well. Now, Michael, I know your hands will be clean, would you like a piece of fruit cake, made fresh this morning?

Later, when they were all gone, and Mhairi had not come back yet, Kate paced the kitchen with a howling Patrick over her shoulder.

Let me try, Kate.

Michael sat down with the moistly miserable baby, and placed him belly down across his crossed legs, so Patrick's cheek lay along his own knee. Then he rocked very slightly while stroking Patrick's back. So gently he was almost not touching or moving at all. At first Patrick just stiffened and screamed louder. Then, from full blast, he sighed, was silent.

You did it, whispered Kate in awe. Was unexpectedly jealous, a sharp yearning for Patrick's physical proximity to Michael. Wanted the gentle strokes to be on her own skin.

Ah, well, it'll work once. Anyway.

Peace, she mouthed the word, weak suddenly. Sat close to him, whispering, Tea?

No thanks.

Cake?

Well, okay.

She took a piece, went to put it on his plate, then noticed his hands were Patrick bound, so put it in his mouth. (God, how bold, how cliché, what if he thinks I'm making a move?) She took a pace back, aching to touch his face, bury her face between his shoulder and neck. Desperate to hide it.

He chewed the cake, Patrick closed his eyes, slobber soaking into Michael's jeans.

Kate?

Yes?

He gave her one look that lasted a second and might have said it was alright. It was alright, and the kisses they'd had that other night and not *felt* suddenly wanted to replay themselves in intense full colour and sound.

Kate, you . . .

His body arched to get a millimetre closer to her, without disturbing Patrick, and she leant towards him another millimetre, and their lips might've met in a minute, had Mhairi not chosen finally to come home.

Hi, you two. Oh, good, he's gone off to sleep. I'm starving, what's for tea? By the way, ran into Duncan, he'll be round later to finish off those sills.

Who's Duncan? asked Michael.

Oh, just a builder, keeps the place from falling apart, said Kate, frustration leaking from her pores.

Duncan's an old friend, said Mhairi possessively. He's always here, and he never wants any money for anything he does.

Oh, said Michael.

Jamie

He is hot and tired of carrying his holdall, which has a plastic handle and around which his sweaty hand is cramped. A vision of submerging himself in a bath starts to taunt him. He can't get the picture out of his head. Putting down the holdall. Peeling off his clothes, his socks, T-shirt and underwear. Feeling the water cool and cleanse him. He thinks. This could be the challenge for today. How to accomplish a bath.

He checks his pocket. Three pounds sixty from selling the Big Issue in front of Bon Accord. That would surely see him into the swimming-baths. He could have a shower instead of a bath. There used to be public baths, he remembers a mother taking him there when they'd no coal to heat water, but they are gone. He has not kept up with the general prosperity, and apparently most Aberdonians have no need of a public baths. So. A shower, then. He pictures this, walking down McNab Way. Gum glimmers on the pavement, bus exhaust fumes make the stale air fuggy. Yes. He can walk to those posh swimming-baths by the beach, save bus fare. But clothes. He has no swimming costume, and he doesn't want to put on his dirty clothes after cleaning his body. Major problem, and he has to sit to contemplate. He chooses a concrete rubbish bin for this purpose.

Thinks, thinks.

Heads to St Barts charity shop. Looks in dismay at the amount of clothes, interrupts the circle of old women who are talking about someone

in hospital who is having a life-threatening operation, as they always
always are.

Excuse me, do you ken if there's any bathing trunks?

They pause, visibly hold their breath, for the heat has only fermented his
odour, and fetch him some old trunks from a cardboard box. Hold them up
for his inspection.

Aye, they'll do fine. How much would they be?

They are only 50p, so he pays, then starts shuffling through the men's
socks and vests, for he has become obsessed with this vision of cleanliness.
The heat is too much and he wants out of his skin.

A grey cotton vest and a pair of socks cost a further 50p. He smiles
and starts his pilgrimage to the baths, which he can't remember to call the
swimming-pool. A good few miles, away down Justice Street, take those wee
streets east, then along the shore, the traffic roaring on one side, the sea on
the other. At last he is there and stands in the queue of families and young
men in sports gear. Gets to the desk.

Yes? asks the girl warily, ready to push her alarm bell.

How much is it?

For yourself? To swim?

Aye.

Three pounds eighty.

Fit? It canna be that much. Look, I give ye all I got. And I willna even
get in the pool. Just a quick shower, ken.

I'm sorry, sir, it's three pounds eighty no matter what you do.

He thinks he might cry. Even just a wee splash? I'm needing a quick
wash, ken. It's hot.

But the woman is already making eye-contact with the man behind him,
dismissing himself. He watches his vision dissolve, his shower dry up, but then
it feels inevitable; of course, he was never going to be allowed in that place.

Outside, he laughs. He is so daft, he has to laugh at himself. He'd been *walking along the beach all the way, as if that wasn't a body of water big enough for him. He crosses over the road back to the beach, finds a place to change into his new trunks and runs into the water, a galloping gait. Freezing, delicious, tingling.*

He does not think about that morning when he ran miles to the sea in his underwear, escaping the fireball of Catriona. Upstairs in the tent is a kind place and disturbing images in the daytime are forbidden.

Michael Is Shy

Michael knew he mustn't stay much longer, these were not his people. Hospitable, and more than that, there seemed to be an easy intimacy. It didn't feel forced, but then they were so polite, so shy, behind the apparent intimacy, it was hard to tell what they really felt. A kind of contagious timidity restrained him, a reluctance to break the illusion that he was more than a recent acquaintance.

In the conversations they had, there never seemed to be a natural opening in which to say, *By the way, I'll be out of your hair soon, probably tomorrow morning.* They seemed to live so much in the present it almost felt rude to mention future plans, especially ones that did not involve them or Gairloch. The words aeroplane and California seemed pretentious, sitting in the old kitchen with people who had never travelled.

In a week, he had grown as used to Kate's domestic routines as he was to his own. Even her new routines, brought about by Patrick, seeped deep into him. They were echoes of his early married years, the shared silences, the reading of newspapers over cups of tea, the companionable watching of junk television, the sweeping up of crumbs and dog hair. And the easy mindless exchange of information.

What do you want to watch?

Oh anything. It's all crap.

Well, do you want funny crap or drama crap?

and

Have you seen my blue skirt?

Look on the line in the bathroom.

How did it get in there?

It was raining. I took in the wash.

What for? They would've dried eventually.

and

Hey, what are doing with all that? she said, as he scraped the dinner plates into the bin.

Scraping the plates.

All that goes to the hens. In this bucket.

I thought that was tomorrow's dinner.

and

Your mum phoned, Kate. She said she'd phone again later.

Yippee.

Also, the Murdos came by. So did Duncan. Said he'd see you tomorrow.

Double yippee.

(Pause) Kate, tell me. Do you actually *like* anybody?

Her dog, a mangy collie whose name he first thought was Doug but was actually Dog, had attached herself to him the first day.

Don't stroke her if you don't want her following you everywhere, Kate had warned. Touch her and she's yours for life.

But he was not averse to having a little warm fur to pat, so

Dog became his shadow. Obviously deprived of affection from the two women, he wondered if Dog had been Jack's dog.

He took to walking Dog down the slope to the beach and along the shore whenever a gap appeared in the day, while the health visitor or midwife came, or Kate was cooking, or helping Mhairi bath Patrick.

Just top and tail him, watch me. He's not needing to be dunked in a bath just yet. He's hardly dirty, is he?

But, Mum, the health visitor said he needed a bath.

Never you mind all that, just you take him in the bath with yourself, if you want. Whatever, so long as he's happy.

How will I know?

Easy, he won't be crying.

He's always crying.

Michael whistled for Dog, who was never far away, and headed down the beach. Often it rained, a streaming soft summery rain, and once it hailed dramatically for a minute, and he'd run for cover in an old half-caved-in bothy.

Today was sunny, but cold. As if without the cloud covering, Gairloch shivered, naked. He zipped his fleece and dug his hands into the pockets. He thought about Brendan, about home, about Beth and his elder son, but mostly he thought about Kate. Kate and her slender shape, her olive skin, her strange tacky jewellery, her odd guarded eyes. Her behaviour to himself. As if they had never slept together, or as if they'd slept together every night and it was old hat. Their conversations were as inconsequential and trivial as those of an old married couple, and yet he had the feeling they were coded. Not as straightforward as they seemed. But what was the key to the code? If there was a deeper meaning at all.

And then there she was, half loping down the beach towards him. There was no doubt, the sight gladdened him, and his smile erupted.

Hey, thought I might find you here, she said, catching his smile and thinking – *that was it* – that was what she liked about him. Something as simple as a smile, the sound of a laugh, was all it took. Then a second's flash of Duncan doing the same thing to her, suddenly appearing on the beach while she was walking, and her own impulse to disappear – but it wasn't the same. Was it? Couldn't be, look at the smile on him.

Her arms were crossed over her chest, she wore a thin T-shirt and looked pinched. Fine summer, this, hey?

Oh, well, he said. Could think of nothing more, then: I guess it keeps the tourists away.

That and the midges. She swiped at one. Usually not many this early in the year, though they find me no matter where I go.

They began to walk across the shale, each step landsliding smooth round stones, all perfect for skimming, if you had the right arm, but awkward for walking. Ever seen a ghost around your house?, asked Michael, who suddenly wondered.

Oh, hundreds. Ghosties all over the place.

Really, though, do you ever feel the presence of people who used to live there?

She sighed. No, not really. Unless you count seeing shadows passing windows, and being gone when I look to see. It wouldn't worry me.

Dog started barking and racing back and forth along the shore.

We'd better get back before she starts rolling in seaweed.

So they turned and started back, and although they hadn't

noticed any wind, some clouds had scooted over from the east, and suddenly the beach was a darker but warmer place. She swung her arms loosely, and he took off his fleece and slung it over one shoulder. He felt light. Like whistling. But not satisfied. Edgy. Excited.

She strode ahead of him, finding a stick for Dog. Then flinging it girl-style into the sea, while Dog plunged after it. Something caught at his throat, watching her narrow shoulders, her elbows, slightly white and rough. Her bones protruded, made him feel tender. She looked like someone from the distant past, with her long dark skirt and hair pulled into a simple bun at the back. He could believe he was seeing the echo of a fisher-wife, scavenging for firewood, or seaweed to turn into soup.

She turned away from him and another moment seemed to be over, unused. They didn't speak again on the walk home.

The next day, he managed to say it. Had to blurt it because he never found the natural opening after all.

They were all sitting on the beach in the sporadic sun, Mhairi holding Patrick well wrapped on her lap, and Michael was studying their bare feet. His were rather wide and hairy, with calluses from nearly fifty years of going barefoot on hot sandy beaches. Mhairi's were slender, pink and soft. Bits of sock fluff between her toes. Patrick's, though unseen, were little models of human perfection. And Kate's, splayed out as she leant back on her elbows, were dark and long. Coarse hairs sprouting from the pad of skin below her big toenails.

Objectively, she was not a work of art and at this minute he felt no attraction. It was time to go home, and this place and Kate would become like old postcards from places visited once and forgotten. And yet, when she moved and accidentally touched his feet with hers, a jolt of arousal shot through him, which he concealed by rolling on to his side. He glanced at her, she'd gone from comical to beautiful, just like that. How did she do that?

God, at my age. Ridiculous, he told himself. Settle down there, boy.

Patrick, whose dark hair, once dried, had turned out to be ginger, was not happy in the open sunshine. Felt too exposed. Was not being held securely enough. He girned. He was way too preoccupied with his own bodily functions now to pay much attention to things like pulses from people, but he was aware of something going on between Kate and Michael, and he did not like it. It was too stimulating. How could he relax and sleep? Suck quietly? Impossible. As if the absurdly large ocean was not enough of a distraction. He girned and farted, and eventually Mhairi said, I think I'll head back, he might settle better inside. (Meaning, I can lay him down and you won't hear him screaming.)

Aye, love, it's maybe too bright for him here anyway. We'll go back in a few minutes, too.

Then they sat together in silence. Kate closed her eyes, to feel the rays. Michael thought she looked vulnerable, kissable. Leant forward and considered the sea.

I'd better be getting back, you know, Kate. To Inverness. Better see Brendan.

Aye, I thought as much. (Not opening her eyes.) When?

Tomorrow, if you can take me to the bus.

Aye, no problem. Of course, it's Brendan you're over here to see anyway.

Sighed.

He sighed, she sighed, their sighs rose up and mingled, joined previous sighs.

Mhairi Talks to Her Baby

It was that bastard Roddy, well, he can fucking well come and deal with you, I don't want you, what would I be wanting with a little shite who does nothing but puke and cry? Every time I look at you, I get the willies. Every walk I take I have to force myself to turn around and go back. Who the fuck are you and how can I make you go away? Good thing Mum's here, or you'd be in trouble, mister. Oh, I know I'm suppose to love you and all that shit, but I don't, alright, I just don't, and what's more, I don't really believe anyone else can either. What's there to love about you? You're the ugliest thing I ever set eyes on.

Hey, you, that's you I'm talking about, so you can just bloody well scream your head off, I'm having nothing to do with it. I'm turning the telly up, so there.

You're going to ruin my life. That is a fact. My life is ruined already, finished. From now on, I will have no life. That's me, finished. I should just finish you off instead, erase you, get back to how it was. Or maybe I should off myself. There's fuck all point to anything any more.

At Last

What can I do, Kate? Let me do something, you look tired.

They were in the kitchen. Mhairi and Patrick were upstairs, asleep under her childhood quilt. Kate was washing the dishes.

No, you're alright, Michael. You take it easy. It's your last night, why don't you go down to the hotel, have a drink?

I'll take the dog for another quick walk.

Aye, that's a fine idea.

Would you come with me?

Something in his voice. She looked up from the sink. Aye, alright. I'll be done in a minute.

Wiped her hands and grabbed her jacket, Jack's old imitation green Barbour. Pockets still full of his debris. A toffee, some Rizlas, some change.

They walked down the road, then up a track, keeping a good distance from each other. Talked. The weather. Airports and jet-lag. Babies and grown-up children. What it felt like to be squint-eyed. Same as it felt to be blue eyed, if you were born squint.

At one point, they stopped and stood to admire the view. The sun had gone, but the sea seemed almost phosphorescent where the waves broke. The mountains were presiding, hump-backed shadows. Standing shoulder to shoulder in the near dark, he reached out to her, clumsily stroked her cheek, then rested his hand on her shoulder, so that he was loosely encircling her. A burden shifted in her, releasing whatever it had been weighing down. She inclined her head towards his hand, then turned towards him. They touched foreheads, eyes closed. Breathed in, out. Blood roaring in their ears. And then their mouths joined, everything dropped away but that point of contact, they were two sets of lips forming an airtight seal, from which sparks flew, meteorites spun, galaxies exploded. They moved closer and remained like that until Dog began to whine with self-pity.

Later, back at the cottage, they said goodnight as usual, as if it was not their last night, as if they had not finally had a first real kiss that was completely lived and tasted and savoured. And they went to their separate beds.

While Mhairi slept and Patrick slept, and the dog and most of the animals slept, Kate and Michael lay wide awake in their beds, separated by two-hundred-year old walls, and waited for something to happen and did nothing.

At first he thought it was the baby, but it was coming from the wrong place. A crying, then screeching. Then there were a dozen babies and they were all raining down on his head somehow. He opened his eyes and sat upright. Then groaned, slumped, collapsed back against his bed in the box room. The sun was streaming in, the gulls were having a ceilidh, and it was only four thirty in the morning.

No good. Sleep wouldn't come back and now he needed the toilet, so he heaved himself up and pulled on his jeans and stumbled down the stairs to the bathroom. Glared at his traitorous face in the mirror – who had given it permission to grow so creased, so bleary-eyed? Sucked in his belly, smiled to stretch the wrinkles, and tried a sideways pose in the mirror. No. Whatever small atom of attractiveness he once had was completely flown. He frowned. He was not someone he would find pleasure in catching a glimpse of, and there was no cure for it. From now on, things would only get worse. Unbeautiful, unloved, fat.

He hadn't forgotten the kiss in the dusk. That had already been stored somewhere permanent. The memory of it filled him with longing and sadness, for there seemed to be nothing but longing and sadness in the kiss and he had no answer for it. It was not himself she was longing for, but some past intimacy. It had been the kind of kiss people bury themselves in, meld and lose each other. He had done his best, but he was a fraud nonetheless. He was not equal to that kind of kiss.

The house lay still around him, warm and full of smells – ash, milk, roses, old dog, Patrick's sweet yellow faeces, the exhalations, stale and otherwise, of four people, and ever present, the background saline scent of the sea. Not just brine, but the summation of a billion living things and a trillion decomposing things. Stewed and pulverised and sprayed into the air and carried on even the softest breeze to permeate stone walls and windows. Michael had lived by a sea his entire life, but it was a different sea – the Pacific. Altogether a different brew. Wilder, cleaner, lighter, simpler somehow. The Atlantic air was headier. The difference between Islay malt and Sonoma Chardonnay.

Now he paused in the hallway, inhaled the air of Kate's house. Wondered if a cup of tea and toast would be best. Finish his novel. Maybe take a last walk to the beach. But decided to start packing instead.

His flight home from Glasgow was in a week. His thoughts went ahead to Brendan and the futility of even broaching the subject of his returning. Instead he would let him show him more sights. Maybe the Clava Cairns or Cawdor Castle, and he would take some photographs to show Beth, maybe even Marcia if she showed any interest. The thought of himself back home, looking at photographs of places he had not yet seen, suddenly depressed him and he sighed.

He was gone already, this place did not exist, Gairloch and Kate and Kate's kiss receded as he walked back to his room. He could already hear the hum of the air-conditioning on the aeroplane, he was looking out of the tiny window at clouds below and wondering yet again how he had managed to live so long and still miss the point. Life was a sequence of manoeuvres he seemed to be able to manage, but he had a nagging feeling that everyone else did more than just manage.

But how could anything mean anything, when it could be dipped into and out of so easily? Travelling felt promiscuous. Could he go anywhere, and after two weeks stumble into a twilight kiss with someone who momentarily seemed to know him, and then return to his redwood house by the Pacific as if nothing had happened? Apparently yes, and this knowledge flattened the world. There could be no mysterious curve, no unique encounters, no irreplaceable people. Nothing that could make any permanent difference.

He tiptoed back to his room and opened the door to find Kate asleep on his bed. She was wearing the same silk kimono he had seen every morning, but now he noticed it had tiny embroidery on it, delicate flowers and swirls of lavender and red.

He froze, held his breath. She didn't open her eyes, but said, in a voice that had rusted overnight, It's alright. Isn't it?

It's perfect, he said, slipping off his jeans, glad her eyes were closed, his flab unseen.

Without preliminary, still softened by sleep and aware this was the last chance, they folded into each other on his single bed under the coombs. Twice he whacked his head on the low ceiling, and once she fell on the floor. A middle aged couple accustomed to vaginal farts and pinched pubic hairs, and two virgins discovering sex. They chatted, despite themselves.

I'd forgotten, panted Michael at one point.

I know, me too. She smiled. Fancy forgetting this.

But this is different.

Like how? (Looking up suspiciously from his armpit, then swivelling to the top.)

Oh, better, much. I don't know. New.

I know what you mean. (Sliding back and forth across his chest like a cat rubbing itself against a leg for the sheer joy of friction.)

Hey, come back, you'll fall off again. (Shifting sideways for another angle on things.)

Outside, the seagulls' ceilidh died down as the day drew on and the two re-initiated lovers finally slumbered. The whole gang of gulls flew to the harbour where some boats had begun unloading and throwing the unwanted fish overboard. Three seals with scarred heads joined in the feast. Radio One played on someone's deck, a kettle whistled, and a young woman with thick glasses jogged past the pier. One sleepy fisherman gave a half-hearted whistle, and she smiled.

Mhairi Is Not in Love and Kate Is

Patrick was dreaming. His eyelids fluttered and his mouth sucked on a dream nipple. He was dreaming of his fish days and kicked his legs a little, kicked his blanket off. The seagull racket had not penetrated his consciousness; much louder were the signals his own body gave him. One siren signalled hunger but before he cried, he began rooting around with his mouth wide open, toothless pink gums and moist tongue. Back and forth, back and forth, where was it?

Where's that nipple?

He wasn't looking for Mhairi, but the smell of Mhairi, and her milk and the taste of her flesh. All these things had yet to solidify into a single presence. Just like the sound of Kate's voice floated separate from her body. Like the way her love poured out, as thick and nourishing as cream, yet was detached from herself, for occasionally she was present and her love was not.

Patrick was partially still in womb time, when on good days he used to spirit out to see the world. Yes, there had been the orange glow of Kate's concern and the gloss of his mother's lethargy. But now a good day meant instant oral gratification and warmth.

Where's that nipple?

He rooted around while Mhairi lay asleep near him, dreaming.

It was not handsome elusive Roddy this time, nor was it her father Jack, the two men she felt had abandoned her. Instead, like her son's dreams, she dreamt of the sea and being submerged. She could see the sun on the surface of the water, and she was swimming towards it, but as soon as she got near, the light seemed to come from another direction, and she was swimming frantically another way. Her lungs were not bursting, because for some reason she could breathe under water.

She breathed and swam with both legs together, like a mermaid, and it felt exactly like flying. Then she looked at the sun shining on the surface, and she was in the air, and swimming. Below her was not the sea now, but a bed.

There's a noise trying to reach me and I'll know what it is in a minute. Oh, yes. The baby. There's a baby down here in this room and he's my baby and I must get back and feed him. If he smells, I'll have to turn on the little light and wash his bony wee bum. Okay, I'm in my body now.

I'll move in a minute and pick you up. Just wait a second. I am trying to move. My muscles feel like they've been Novocained. Numb and rubbery.

I could lie all day and all night like this. I keep thinking. Not of that baby over there. Never it. But Roddy, probably snogging right now with some tart.

Alright. I'm coming. Husht. There you are. Whoever you are.

She slipped him into her bed and lowered her breast into his mouth, rubbing her nipple softly over his lips till they found it and formed an airtight seal and he began to suck hard, ravenously. She could not ignore the similarity to a lamb, she'd seen so many do just that. And the ewe stood, sometimes even walked, oblivious to the sucking. What else was there to do? The demand was impossible to deny, and yet she had hoped for a little more enjoyment than this. More than just duty fulfilled, more than just absence of infant crying. She nuzzled his velvety head while he sucked, and inhaled his special smell, as she'd watched her mother do. Because she'd watched her mother, not because it felt especially nice. She wanted to be good at this.

I could eat him up, so I could, Kate had remarked on a few occasions, and had indeed looked as if her mouth was watering, and Patrick was in danger of being cannibalised.

Mhairi stroked and allowed her breast to be drained, which felt better than engorgement, but no other feeling than this relief. I am not a normal mother, something is wrong with me, she thought. A minute's guilt, then Patrick suddenly drew back his head and broke the suction with a popping noise. The light was grey, hard to tell, but she had the feeling he was studying her, could see her unloving thoughts, and she was afraid of him.

Christ, who the fuck are you? she asked, then scooped him back into his basket, turning him on his side away from her. Covered him up.

Bottle soon, mate.

Michael walked up the track. Headed for the shops, thinking to buy a gift or two. Found himself on the beach instead, looking for souvenir stones and shells to take home. Real talismans of the place.

Distributed them carefully throughout his clothes in his bag. Then removed one, his favourite, a small heart-shaped grey stone, placed it on the little table by his bed. Finished packing, zipped up his bag, checked under the bed for socks. Touched the heart stone again, then slipped it into the little table drawer. Wanted it unseen, but there. Sentimentality, his secret vice.

He gave her a book instead, his Nick Hornby, which she promised to consume right away. She gave him a packet of chicken sandwiches and two slices of fruit cake, which he likewise promised to gobble up.

They did not embrace at the bus, an embrace would have been both not enough and too much.

Hey, can't thank you enough, Kate. I won't forget it.

He offered his hand, which she took but didn't shake. Just held it a second, lightly squeezed it, then let it go. Have a good journey, Michael.

Thanks. Take care of yourselves, all of you. Especially Patrick.

He started towards the bus steps.

Well, have a real nice day, she said suddenly, in an American accent he hadn't heard her use before.

Hey, you have a real nice life, now, you hear? (Not to be outdone in mocking his own nationality.)

It's been real ... real ...

Hey, get a life.

I'll try.

Me too.

So fuck off then, she whispered.

You piss off first, he whispered back.

Then on the count of three, they turned from each other.

It was their one silly conversation, getting the courage to sneak out at the last moment.

*   *   *

Kate went back home and found Patrick asleep on her own bed, where Mhairi had taken to putting him in the daytime. She started to leave, then turned and, very slowly and quietly, lay down next to Patrick, as close as she could without waking him. He was lying on his back in his frog-legged I-surrender position, small arms flung up, open hands just reaching the top of his head. She drank in his milk breath, ached watching his fine eyelashes flicker as his eyes followed some aquatic dream.

Later that night, in the house quieter for one man not breathing in it, she wrote. It was not enjoyable, but she had a deadline.

WEST COAST CRACK

The Americans have left. I never told you how many were here, but I have to tell you, one is the same as many. It is an atmosphere around them, it does not enlarge or shrink with numbers. It is the air of people who breathe and speak and move as if they have a right to. I once said they had no subtlety and that repulsed me. I now have to question both their seeming simplicity and my repulsion to it. I have learnt that just because they act open does not mean they have no secrets. They hide just like us, only they have a different hiding-place. We hide in omissions and silence and sarcasm. They use the sunny spaces of apparent truth. I do not believe Americans are stupid and they do not repulse me. There. You are my witnesses. Now they are gone, will I miss them? I'll wait for the waters to close over their absence and let you know.

Meanwhile life on the west continues best. The sun dips below the horizon for just a few hours and everyone is looking weary from being active so many hours a day. Bird racket begins at three with the re-emergence of the sun. I pull my quilt over my head, try and fail to slip back into oblivion. No wonder so many drink here. The occasional urge for obliteration is strong.

Grandbaby eats continually, I can almost hear him growing, stretching his wee suits. We started off with cloth nappies, but succumbed to disposables within days. The gorgeous packaging is designed with brain-dead new mothers and grans in mind.

His first poo was announced with grand disgust to the entire world by his mother. Did she think he'd wait till he could get to a toilet? He was washed, creamed and wrapped up again in a clean cocoon of baby garments, when of course he did it again. I'd forgotten that. Never change a soiled nappy till you are sure the movement is complete. Sounds so trite, but these are words of deep wisdom. Leave the nappy. Listen for further grunts. Wait, do not rush. Otherwise you end up spending half your day washing bottoms and a fortune in nappies.

The health visitor still comes almost daily. It is very sweet the way she lets us rabbit on about his weight, his innate intelligence, the regularity of his bowels.

This morning she was asking after the American, and I wondered if he made a hit with her. He was tall, dark, very, well, American actually. Maybe he resembled some American sitcom actor I've never seen, and she's convinced we have a hot line to stardom here in the cottage.

When I told her he'd gone, her face fell, and I worried she'd come less often now. Not weigh the baby quite so meticulously. I love watching the scales prove he is growing. And, yes, I am totally aware I am becoming a real bore.

Jamie

He is walking again, glad it is evening and shade is everywhere. As bad as the rain, a heatwave. He has in mind to head for the shelter. He hasn't actually talked to anyone for a few days, and the shelter might offer a bit of conversation. Of some sort. He once had a two-hour discussion on the relative merits of milk and Christianity and the dangers of caffeine and the devil, and another time a stimulating talk about the prevalence of UFOs in north-eastern Scotland.

He is not thinking anything, just feeling alone and unseen in his body, when a familiar shape ahead alerts him. Just the back of her head, her gold cardigan, her white calves below her old floral skirt.

Catriona!

She does not look around, and he thinks he has not spoken out loud. The trouble with not speaking very often, except to yourself in your head, was that it was then tricky to tell the difference. Like dreams and waking, when you were often dreaming. So he clears his throat, leaps to catch up with her.

Catriona!

Frightened, because she might turn around and he would have to see her burn scars, melted flesh, maybe an eye missing. A monster face. Still she does not turn, and he tries to lope ahead of her. She flinches, hurries her pace.

Stop!

She is not Catriona, she is not Catriona. She turns into the doorway of a shop, alarmed.

Catriona fried. The fireball comes hurtling down the stairs and he hides, a coward, a fool, under the cloud of smoke and runs away.

In the cool evening, everything glows, everything is gone.

Michael Is Not Happy

With the first whiff of San Francisco air, Scotland evaporated. It receded like a vivid dream born of drunkenness. Lucid, but irrelevant somehow, once viewed with sobriety. Beth drove him home in his old Ford. The eight-lane freeway, the bridge, the four-lane suburban highway, and finally, the pot-holed narrow road. The front screen door banged home and Michael moved among his own things again. His children's naïve masterpieces hung along the hall wall. The window-frames he had sanded and painted twice greeted him with heat-cracked paint. A vase of roses on the table filled his lungs. His cat, unthought-of this last month, moved ahead of him into the kitchen. Nothing reclaimed him yet.

House looks great, Beth.

Does it? Needs a good cleaning.

She filled the kettle and poured coffee beans into the grinder. Buzzed and poured them into the cafetière. Her thick blonde hair swinging, her sturdy brown legs under her white shorts, her green eyes looking at him with direct simplicity. (Like her mother in appearance, he thought, not for the first time.) Outside, wind chimes tinkled like they always did, but this time he heard them and it added to his sense of unreality. The magic kingdom enveloped him and he yawned as if no amount of yawning could bring sufficient oxygen into his lungs.

Wake up, Dad, have something to eat before you conk out. And later tell me everything. One phone call wasn't enough. I want to know about Brendan. And this place you were staying in.

There isn't much else to tell. Like I said in the car, Brendan will come home when he feels like it, meanwhile he's more than fine. Just broke a small law about immigration, but he'll learn. Or he won't. Oh, won't have sugar in mine.

Back on a diet thing, Dad?

She poured the coffee with a flourish.

Back on something.

Much later, feeling the airlessness of his bedroom, he opened the window as wide as it would go. Stars, but not many. The price of suburban living. And dark so early, the price of living in a country closer to the equator. He unpacked some T-shirts that had dried in another century, on a clothes-line in Kate's back garden. He lifted them to his face and breathed in Atlantic air, cotton, and a slight manure undertone from the hen run near the line. Went to bed because suddenly he could not hold his head up any more, but did not sleep.

Till he slept.

PART THREE

Home is where you go when
you've nowhere to go.

Bette Davis

In the deserts of the heart
Let the healing fountain start.

W. H. Auden

Your house is your larger body.
It grows in the sun and sleeps in the stillness of night,
And it is not dreamless.

K. Gibran

Patrick Gets Love

If his mother did not love him, Patrick didn't care. He didn't know to care. He was three months old. He had no expectations, floated from one event to another, obeyed his instinct to survive, gave out signals and received responses. Was fed, held, washed, rocked, clothed. Learnt something new every second. What was love? What was a mother?

He ate and when the novelty of the world tired him, he slept. He slept a lot. Cat naps, all day and night. There were times when he was awake and not hungry or sore, and if the room was calm, he would have a little look around. Take it in, with his serious dark eyes.

The self he'd been in the womb was still there, he was the same Patrick. He wavered sometimes, neither here nor there, not as ethereal as he'd been in the early months of development, but not completely substantial yet either. He watched the people around him. He was curious and liked eyes.

The world was a strange place and he was an adventurer, wise and wary. What was the world? Anything, anything at all. He quickened to new sensations.

One day, Kate sang softly to him, and she nestled his head

in the crook of her arm. He could feel her heartbeat and the vibrations of her singing, low and melodic.

Something happened!

A warm sensation poured into his chest, his heart beat faster, his eyelids fluttered in a swoon of ... what? What was this? Overwhelming, more overwhelming than the bliss of milk filling his belly or his bowels emptying or trapped wind escaping. He smiled.

This was a new thing and it was a good thing.

Some Airmail Letters

Michael's (unsent) letter to Kate:

July 14, 99

Dear Kate:

Sorry I haven't written sooner. I can't explain how far away Gairloch seems. I took no photographs of you and I have to admit to some doubt that you actually exist. I have a photo of your house from the beach and it is possible you are in it somewhere in the shadows. Impossible to tell, but I study it sometimes.

Are you out there? As I write, are you really feeding the hens, cleaning out your fireplace, reading your book? Was Patrick really born on the landing while I slept? I never told you how I felt when I saw your record collection – the dusty Nick Drake, Pink Floyd, Jefferson Airplane, John Martyn, *High Tide Green Grass* and *Rubber Soul*. Mine are dusty too. It made me feel I knew you.

Listen. You are like a dream I want to go back into, I ache with wanting to shut my eyes and recapture you. All this California-ness just interferes. It's like bad static, I'm not receiving you at all, and this letter feels hopelessly inadequate, I don't know why I'm writing at all.

Michael's (sent) letter to Kate, on a Sierra card of a waterfall in Yosemite:

July 18th

Dear Kate –
Well, here I am, back in sunny old California. Actually, it's a little too sunny, I could do with some of your rain. Not too much, but a bit. It hasn't rained for months and everything looks dusty and dirty and the sky isn't even blue anymore, just a burnt-out white.

I wanted to thank you for your hospitality, and ask how you and your daughter (Vari? Varey? I can never spell these garlic names) are getting on with Patrick. His birth made my trip – honestly – a lifetime memory, that!

Brendan writes and phones, I feel more in contact with him than I used to when he lived across the bay. And the trip to see him made Scotland seem not so far away. Only time, also money, but still. I don't feel we have lost him anymore.

Anyway, take care of yourselves, Michael
P.S. I haven't been to Yosemite.

Kate's (unsent) letter to Michael:

July 14, 99

Dear Michael,
You've been gone more than a month now, and haven't

written or phoned, so I guess you don't even remember me. Who am I? Good question. Nobody really. Just a lady you crawled into bed with once, who later crawled into your bed. I just wanted to let you know I do not normally do things like that, that you were not one of a long series of casual lovers. You may be like that, but I am not. On the other hand, if you are not writing because you fear I may make some claim on you, that I have fallen in love with you (!) please don't flatter yourself.

I do not regret any of it. I just wanted you to know it was an aberration, but I have put it behind me. You mean as little to me as I do to you. Less, maybe.

Not-in-love-two-night-stand, Kate

Kate's (sent) postcard of Big Sands to Michael:

Aug. 1, 99

Michael,
Thanks for your letter. Glad to know all is well Stateside. Things are fine here too, if you don't count broken nights, endless laundry, a crabbit daughter. Patrick is thriving anyway, and the weather has been incredibly hot. See you, Kate
P.S. You've been to Big Sands

Michael Fetches the Beer

When Michael didn't believe Gairloch was real, his pulse fluttered, he was frightened. And daily it faded. To Beth he'd only been away a while, checking on Brendan, having a vacation. She did not expect him to change so he did not. For her, he was the same.

It was August, Marin County was deep in the pit of summer. While Kate burned scones and Mhairi turned up her CD player to drown out Patrick's cries (for, real or not to Michael, these things were happening simultaneously), Michael walked to the supermarket through waves of pungent heat. It was thick stuff, full of moisture, exhaust fumes, barbecue lighter fluid, suntan lotion, eucalyptus trees, oleander. The air was a substance and he could not get a clear breath. Telling himself not to panic, he just took slow shallow breaths and tried to concentrate on the beauty. California was a beautiful place. Marin County was a beautiful place. Lush, warm, an overabundance of Renault Espaces and Cherokee Jeeps, long-legged blonde women and tall bronzed men. Healthy helmeted children rode mountain bikes, swerving between headbanded joggers.

He was in his old neighbourhood, where he and Marcia had begun family life, where he'd pushed the strollers and driven the children to Little League and Brownies while she learnt about high finance in wealthy counties. He took the long way to the store, by the point, and stopped to admire the view of San Francisco Bay. He'd always loved this. But it didn't work. The fruit was overripe. The affluence felt immoral. The houses, ostentatious.

The bay was pretty and the city skyline pleasing, but it was all there and there was no subtlety. Nothing shadowy to lure and sustain him. He'd never known he liked shadow. Damp air and barren shores. Honed-down landscape. He shook his head and entered the store, got blasted with air-conditioning. Paid for his gallon of milk and six-pack of beer and bag of Fritos.

Went back to Marcia's house, his old house, and started the barbecue for the party while Marcia arranged flowers in vases. Just a neighbourhood thing, Beth had said on her way to college that morning, not a big deal. Something she'd arranged with her mother, who was the perfect feminist ex-common-law-wife and claimed that, though apart now, they were still best friends and even gave occasional family parties together.

But he knew a neighbourhood thing was at least forty people, in their separate family units of approximately two LL Beaned adults, two Gap-clothed kids, one golden retriever or politically correct rescued mongrel. They'd all bring nice cooled Sonoma wines and Mexican beers, potato and avocado salads, and his job was clear. Trendy scented charcoal briquettes, the lighter fluid, the meat. And meat alternatives. Also, to pretend nothing essential had changed from the old days.

Here, I'll do all that, Dad. Go get yourself a glass of vino. I'm really into barbecuing these days. Go on.

His other son, being frighteningly capable, depriving him of his illusion of purpose. Michael bowed to his superior ability and went into the kitchen, wondering what his job was now. Marcia would know, but she was nowhere in sight. The party was in full flow. No longer so many small people running about, but the same general party babble there'd always been. Raised voices, wine glasses sloshing over, smokers out on the deck, women in the kitchen, old Eric and Glen arguing about football. Stanford and Berkeley.

Michael, run and get some more lemonade and hamburger buns, will you? We're just about out. Would you mind? asked Marcia, who had suddenly appeared, flushed, in party mode.

And off he went to the store again. Relieved, really. Rarely did he feel more superfluous than at these parties everyone else seemed to enjoy so much. Surely he had enjoyed them himself, long ago. Yes, a definite recollection of pride at being able to afford this kind of relaxed decadence. But it had been a long time since he'd felt in a party mood. A this-kind-of-party mood.

He was tempted just to go home, but he was reliable and duly purchased the hamburger buns and lemonade. He lugged the paper bag back to the house and unloaded it on the kitchen counter. He indicated to Marcia with a gesture that it was there. She responded with a huge smile and thumbs up as if he'd performed the fishes and loaves trick. He blinked, couldn't bear seeing himself through her eyes. Went upstairs to what used to be the marital bedroom.

Sat on the bed, looked at the white wall, remembered the wallpaper with little purple daisies in Kate's bathroom, felt awful.

Jamie

Today the train goes clickety-clack and it is warm and the seat is soft and it empties his mind. The metal cage of the train dissolves and it is just Jamie and he glides along the rails as far as his ticket takes him. Achnasheen. He disembarks, stands still on the platform for a moment and watches the train disappear towards Kyle. Though it is still morning, it is very hot. Bees in the gorse along the tracks give the air a hum and the yellow blossoms give it a whiff of coconut. He cocks his head, listening and smelling, not trembling, more like a deer sniffing the wind, waiting for his next instinct. Then he picks up his bag and walks out, passing the stationmaster without a glance. He doesn't often have a ticket, but the strange thing is, when he does, he is rarely asked for it. Hence proving his theory of assumption. Assume the look of a ticket holder and you will be ignored by the ticket collector.

He keeps to the road west, to Gairloch and Aultbea. He has been west before, but never this road. It is a soft place and the air is different from the east. He feels new and his step has spring in it. His twenty-fifth birthday has just passed unnoticed, he is not a man for whom dates mean much and his own age is not a piece of information relevant to his survival. He is as old as he feels so he is not old today. There are a few cars and caravans passing him. He walks through a small wood by some derelict farm buildings and comes out by a loch with a rocky shore. He walks down to stand behind some pines and pee, then he walks to the shore, sits on a stone and eats a slice of *bread. He has an entire loaf in his bag, but it is already six days old, and he has decided to go ahead and eat as much as he likes. No point in saving mouldy bread. His mind is always working at problems like this. Calculating, shifting, predicting. He chews on his dry white bread, congratulates himself on his fine brain.*

Jamie, have ye got a single brain cell in that heid of yours, one of his mothers had always asked him, not in a mean way, but more a gentle chiding. The way she told her dog he was very very bad, in a sweet tone, and the dog would wag his tail and lick her face. Jamie turned towards kindness and used to follow this mother about, offering to do little chores for her, set the table, pour her a cup of tea. He drew her little pictures and always signed them with a dozen kisses. To Ellie, XXXXXXXXXXXX Jamie. He'd slop the tea over the picture, and she'd tsk and say, Jamie, have ye got a single brain cell in that heid of yours?

He dwelt on this picture of the inside of his skull and imagined his one brain cell rattling around like a dried up nut in a shell. He wasn't sure what his brain cell did. He was ten at the time, and age never did clear that one up. But he imagined it might feel lonely, all by itself. Maybe even doubt its own existence. Hadn't the mother herself asked if he even had one?

Jamie didn't know much, even before the disaster. He had what teachers called a moderate learning difficulty. But he did know what it felt like to be the only one. He was the only one not to get new reading books, the only one who had to leave the classroom with a special teacher three times a week to do maths and reading in another room. He was the last one to learn to tell the time.

Later, when he was a husky adolescent, surprising his various mothers with temporary good looks, he got a girlfriend. It was as easy as it was astonishing. Unlike most boys, he had not imagined and yearned and plotted. He was a child always, living from moment to moment, unhurried, absorbed. He was walking home from school just before his fifteenth birthday. He had a slow rolling but clumsy way of walking, like he was constantly learning how to do it, and could not get out of the way quick enough when a bike careened into him. He fell headlong, not even breaking the fall with his arms, on to the pavement, and his head made a sound like a full jar of marmalade cracking. The girl fell off her bike and scraped her knees but wasn't hurt. She saw Jamie lying there, handsome and unconscious, and cried. I've kilt him, please dinna be deid, oh, God, I've kilt him.

Tears washed from her face to his, as she hovered inches over him, willing life to return, and he woke to see this blurred vision of feminine distress. Thinking immediately that he had caused it, he sat upright, said, Ah, dinna greit, I'm sorry, please stop greitin. Then passed out again, into her arms. And she sat like that on the pavement for twenty minutes, stroking his fair hair and clammy forehead, waiting for the ambulance the paper-shop man had phoned.

Her name was Catriona and she had just left school to work in the dry cleaner's down the road from Jamie's house. She had a strict Catholic father and a boyfriend who picked her up punctually at seven every night for a walk down the river and quick grope and a conversationless walk back home by ten. Her mother was dead and her life was hemmed in by men who knew what was best for her to do.

Jamie never knew what anyone should do, much less himself. And Jamie had wonderful blue eyes and soft hesitant hands. His mouth was cherubic. Catriona moved silently and resolutely towards him.

Tak me out tae the pictures, Jamie, she said to him one day in front of the dry cleaner's.

Aye. Why not? He was enchanted. A new friend to play with.

When?

When? No one had ever asked her when before.

Now Catriona might or might not be dead and he is sleeping in the woods near a loch. He doesn't light a fire, knows all the land must belong to some estate and someone's eyes might be flickering out of a window over it from time to time. It doesn't matter, he is skilled at invisibility. The next morning, he washes in a burn, eats some more bread and walks and walks.

By afternoon, he has come to Loch Maree. He enters the village shop, thinking it is time to stock up. He has eighty-nine pounds — a fortune! — saved up from his little jobs, including the twenty pounds that he found lying on the floor in the multi-storey car park while he was checking the machines for change and hoping to find an unlocked car left overnight.

He is a frugal man and is going to spend his money wisely. He buys two packets of oatcakes, a quarter-pound of cheap Cheddar, bacon offcuts, two tins of value beans, a half-dozen eggs, a box of tea-bags, a box of matches. Almost buys some dried milk, then puts it back. Too dear.

He draws stares in the shop. One little girl keeps dragging her mother towards Jamie, and he is certainly worth the second look of a curious child. The lady serving is polite and expressionless, but does not take his money directly from his hand. Waits for him to deposit it on the counter, before she scoops it into the till.

Bye-bye for now, she says, in her Highland accent, which sounds so much softer than Aberdonian voices.

Goodbye, manages Jamie, and trips down the steps.

After another day of walking nearly all the way to the coast, he finds it. It feels like recognising someone. More, like he is being recognised. An empty cottage with two friendly windows, two chimneys, a door ajar. A door. Ajar.

First Signs

Mhairi could no longer bath him. His nakedness – skinny red limbs writhing – repulsed her to the point of nausea. When Kate noticed she didn't say anything, only took Patrick into the bath with her. Tried to compensate. Curved his little self into her upper chest, so his furry head tucked under her chin. Felt his heartbeat and softly kissed the skin below his ear. Splashed him gently, crooned.

Feeding him was a problem too.

Here, you feed him, he'll not suck properly and I'm not having it any longer, stormed her daughter, and she felt a stabbing pain imagining his soft hungry mouth opening for warm milky flesh and having a cold rubber teat shoved in instead. It broke her heart, but she went out and bought the bottles and formula.

Mhairi, you're only feeling the baby blues, you'll come out of it fine, just wait, she said, coming upon her collapsed daughter, wet-eyed again. But not quite believing it herself. She twice dialled the doctor's number, then hung up. What to say? That her daughter did not wash her face or get dressed or comb her hair any more? That she did not seem to love her baby or even be aware much of his existence? Was that a medical condition and was it curable? Kate thought, on the whole, not. She told herself it was only a phase. The credo of her motherhood, her response to all bad behaviour. It would pass, only ride it out. Don't make an issue.

Very occasionally Mhairi roused herself to take Patrick for a walk in his pram, or heat his bottles, but mostly she stayed in her dressing-gown on the sofa, watching afternoon talk shows and getting thinner and thinner. She only pecked at her food. Her mind seemed to sieve every thought away. She frequently walked into rooms, or up the stairs, only to stand there and wonder why she'd come. Mostly she felt dead and cared for nothing.

If she looked at Patrick, all the confusing thoughts came like crashing bumper cars. He had grandparents, aunts, uncles, possibly cousins out there, on Roddy's side. Should they be told? What was the etiquette? Would they want to know? What kind of trouble would Patrick's birth certificate bring her? Roddy's name, not Brendan's, a mere six months after their marriage? Would she go to jail? How would she ever be able to go back to college to get a decent job when her brain seemed to have packed in? Her old self was a very long way away indeed and seemed to taunt her with echoes of images. Herself, dancing in clubs, laughing with her friends, studying in the library. Never again. Impossible. And life was so long. A day, an hour, a single minute was so long. If she felt like this at eighteen, how would she endure the long years of her life to come?

She and Patrick would be a drain on her poor mother for ever, even if eventually she got a job as a fish-packer down at the pier, about all she'd ever be fit for. The future held nothing. And all because of Patrick. Whiny smelly scrap of crap.

He couldn't help it, she knew it wasn't really him. It was her. He deserved better, yet she could feel nothing for him but a growing alienation and, sometimes, an urgent wish to be rid of him. The thought of his absence teased her with its desirability.

Above all, he was not the baby girl she'd imagined. Nothing was as she'd imagined.

She curled away from these downward-swirling thoughts and switched on the television and two seconds later was riveted by an Aussie soap she never used to bother with. Would Kent ever realise Jean truly loved him, not Stormy? Would Avril find out her daughter took drugs and her lover was actually her long-lost brother?

Kate had loved Mhairi as a baby. And she sometimes found she loved strangers' babies who looked straight at her in supermarkets. A natural welling of emotion. But with Patrick it was all somehow more intense and more fraught. He was a morsel of achingly delicate bones and sweet-smelling flesh, and she craved him. Just looking at him put her in a trance of contentment. He was an aesthetic experience, a first love, a four-course French meal, a walk by the shore on a windy warm afternoon. He was three perfect notes on a harp. When Patrick and Kate gazed at each other, her pupils dilated and her mouth salivated. Mhairi's indifference mystified her but barely put a dent in her own satisfaction that Patrick was one fine baby.

One August afternoon, she was drawn up the stairs by his hunger call – piercing, hiccuping, air splitting. He was in his Moses basket, back arched, face red and covered with spit and snot, too young for tears. Eyes squeezed shut with the exertion.

A movement by the window caught her eye, and there was the alarming sight of her daughter. Staring out of the window, arms limp by her side. Empty-eyed.

Kate Misses Michael
and Doesn't Know It

Kate walked and walked, too much energy for once, and she felt the need to tire herself. To stop worrying about her daughter. It wasn't dark, though it was late. A full moon pierced the sky, dulled the stars, cast shadows. She could even see her own shadow on the road as she walked.

The moon was shocking white, bleached almost blue, and it was impossible to be unaware of it. Snatches of appropriate lyrics ran through her mind. The ridiculously handsome moon shone on the sea, laid a path of shimmering light on slow swells, so calm no sound could be heard. Just her own footsteps, her own breathing.

She wore an old army jumper of Jack's over one of his old shirts, and her long soft skirt flapped around her bare legs. She could feel the skin on her thighs chafe each other – warm and silky with the exercise. It was not cold, but she hugged herself. Crossed her chest tightly, yearned and yearned. Felt excited, expectant.

Walked too far, and tired before she got home. Fast steps still, but no spring, just the desire to be in bed. A sudden tearfulness, no matter how blue the moon.

Jamie

*He walks over the rough ground, the spongy heather and blaeberries, towards
the derelict cottage, not bothering about his feet, never taking his shining eyes
off the broken face of it. He slows when he reaches it, shy about entering.
His blood races and his pores open up to possibilities he's not been aware of
looking for. A home? Well, why not? Other people have homes. He sits on the
doorstep, stamping the nettles aside. An impossibly perfect peaty lochan twenty
yards in front. Then the hill he'd started climbing, trying to find a hidden spot
for a discreet shit. (No trees, very difficult.) Beyond the hill, not visible but
occasionally audible, the road he'd walked on since alighting from the train
in Achnasheen. Beyond that, Aberdeen. People, and their whorls of life.*

*Jamie believes in ghosts, of course. Before he goes into the cottage, he sits
in the sun for some time, trying to see the past inhabitants crossing the yard,
calling the cows, shooing the hens, hoeing the neeps. He closes his eyes and
listens for echoes of all these activities. The clang of a pot, a footfall, a cough.
He sends out his heart to all the sunny spaces and dark unknown crannies
inside. He feels faint with straining so hard after anything. A sigh.*

*But nothing. A soft breeze through summer grass, the buzz of bees from
the lurid yellow gorse. Too many winter winds and summer scaldings scouring
the place. Its emptiness rings out inside his head. Happy? Unhappy? He
can't guess.*

He goes inside to discover everything else. Corrugated iron roof partially gone on far gable end. Stairs fine, dead birds in the grate. Fresh sheep pellets in front room. Glass, miraculously, in all the windows. He clears one of the downstairs fireplaces, dumping mud and bird corpses outside. Pokes a stick up the chimney. Gathers dry heather, snaps off some dead rose-bush twigs and breaks up a rotten rowan branch. Gets a fire going, smokes but burns. Sets two flat-topped stones in the hearth with the fire crackling between them and settles his saucepan full of brown loch water on top of them.

After a cup of black tea, he fries two rashers of bacon and drips the grease on to some oatcakes. Then he goes out. It is ten o'clock, still light enough. He walks down to the lochan and kneels to splash water over his face and rub his hands together, feeling its velvety iciness. When he goes inside again, the smoke and bacon and warmth hit him like a wave of home. (Or mother.)

He brings his sleeping-bag, holdall and carrier-bag of food upstairs. Under the roof that is still alright, he brushes away the dust of decomposing insects and mouse droppings and unrolls his bed. He folds his jumper for a pillow and tucks himself up for the night. After a while he sleeps.

He wakes once to the dark and the noise of many intruders. Shuffling footsteps and heavy breathing. But a baa sends him back to sleep even happier. Guests in his house the first night. It is a good sign.

But later in the night the tent dream comes again. The one where his body has actually metamorphosed into an orange canvas tent. He is in the tent, the daylight glowing through the canvas. Then from upstairs the cartwheeling inferno rushing at him in his sleeping-bag. He tries to rise, to get away from it. But his muscles and bones are granite, with his blood beating futilely for escape. Then the flames engulf him and he sinks into sun, as he watches his own flesh melt into her body.

He wakes, trembling, his mouth leaking saliva. Rare to remember, once he'd woken.

Sometimes in the dream someone accuses him. A policeman, her father, his mother, all three. And he knows it must be true.

But he is safe here, hidden, invisible. They won't get him, no one knows where he is.

Everyone Knows Where He Is

At the crossroads, push-chairs and toddlers in tow: Hey, Joanna, remember the baking for the play-school sale. I nearly forgot the cake I'd promised. It's tomorrow.

Shit, and I thought I'd have time to watch *The Full Monty* again before I return it. Do you think I can just buy something? A sponge from the shop?

Don't think so. Think there's some kind of law about that. Has to be home-made or you'll have to do twenty duties.

Shit.

Hey – don't you have a video player in your kitchen?

No.

Wow, seriously underprivileged, or what? You should apply for a grant.

Oh, I'll have a Grant alright, he's not bad at all.

He's taken, you're always too late. Hey, did you notice the man up at old Dan's place?

Yeah, seen him a few times. Kind of slinks around, doesn't he?

What do you think he's up to?

No good, for sure.

Didn't you tell me once you used to play houses up there?

Aye, and it was derelict then. Imagine the state of it now. I think it's weird, I wish he'd go away.

Do you think he might be hiding out there?

Hardly, everyone knows he's there.

But he's a bit young to be a dosser, don't you think?

Not young enough to be a runaway, though. No, I doubt there's anyone out looking for him.

I bet he's on the run and he's got drugs up there. I just don't like it, not when I think of the kiddies and that. I mean, who is he?

Exactly. Gives me the creeps.

Mhairi Does a Very Bad Thing

One day, while Kate was out, Mhairi took Patrick out of his basket, wrapped him in two thin shawls, tucked a full bottle and nappy into her pocket, pulled a little bonnet over his head, and left the cottage. She walked without looking where her feet were going, as if she were sleepwalking. It was a clear warm morning and she wanted to walk and walk. She neglected to take the pram, did not seem even to think of it. On and on she walked. Her leg muscles ached and her arms were frozen into the position of carrying the baby. Patrick woke but did not cry, lulled by the rhythm of her steps and the unaccustomed closeness of her.

She left the coast road and walked through the heather. Oblivious to the bees she startled and to the beauty of the blue and orange butterflies. She was hot and headed for some boulders to sit down. Rocked Patrick. Then after a while, she got up and walked again. Further and further. Sometimes singing childish songs. This old man, he played one, he played knick-knack on my thumb. Knick-knack paddy whack, hey that's you, Mr Paddy Whack.

Miles and miles, almost eight miles of energetic bursts and sudden slumps. She was dizzy and did not recognise where she was, though it was familiar. Fatigue forced her to stop finally and she sat under a rowan. Her arms were sweaty from holding the baby so long. She made him a little bed under the tree. Pulled bracken over to make a nest. Imagined fairies were watching from the hill. Approving. Then settled him in. He stared up at her silently, then stared up through the branches of the tree. Red berries and gold leaves danced in front of the bold blue sky. He waved his fat fists slowly and murmured. She offered the bottle, but he only had a suck and stopped, pushed it away with his pink tongue. He was entranced with the view.

She leant back against the tree and closed her eyes. It was good to get away from the house. She felt she could just stay here. No need to do or think anything, just sleep. The most perfect activity. Better than television. She'd stop the television, it was too confusing. A small breeze caused some water nearby to lap, and the quiet rhythmic slap of water on earth sent her floating into sleep.

Kate came home from work and shopping to find the place tidied up and Mhairi reading a novel. The television was off.

Well, this is a nice surprise, darling. Are you feeling better?

Mhairi gave her a queer furtive look, said, I guess, and returned to her book. Kate unloaded the shopping, put some potatoes in the oven and made a cup of tea.

It's very quiet, Mhairi. Has Patrick been asleep a long time? No answer.

Mhairi, I said has Patrick been asleep long? He's normally up around now. I bought some rice cereal to try him on. He's growing that fast, I'm thinking he could use something solid.

She looked at her daughter. Mhairi's hands curled round her

book in an unnatural way and suddenly she doubted that any of the pages had been turned at all. She was simply frozen in a horrid tableau mocking normality.

Where is the baby? On my bed? In his basket?

He wasn't. Nor was he in the pram parked in the hall.

Kate went back to the living room, heart pounding. Mhairi. Look at me. Put that damned book down now and look at me. Where is the baby?

Mhairi looked blank.

What baby?

Jamie

He is writing on the wall by the window. He has found a piece of red sandstone and it writes well on the ancient plaster and lath. But what to say, what to write. Luckily no thoughts come, because he has forgotten how to write most words anyway. So he just writes his own name. In big letters. Then he writes it in little letters. Then he goes to another wall, by the fireplace, and writes his name there too. It is fun, and he smiles to himself. It does not feel like graffiti, it feels like a spot of interior decorating.

Someone flashes into his mind, a young woman, his own age, with dark hair and happy eyes, freckles across her face, but he doesn't know her. He blinks her away, writes his name again, with care, neat and straight up and down. Jimi this time, not Jamie. J I M I. On the line, keep on the line, Jimi my man, that's right. Now again. The young woman knows him, breathes close to him. She guides his hand as he writes.

His lips press each other, prior to pronouncing the letter M, but go no further. Then, finally, he says Mum out loud, like a question.

Mum?

Where Is the Baby?

What? What do you mean, *what baby?* Kate whispered.

Just what I said. I don't know what you're talking about. Then a silly guilty smile, as if she'd been caught telling a fib about taking sweeties.

Adrenaline spurted into Kate's bloodstream as if from a fire hose. Her face flamed, her hair roots stood up, she sprang to Mhairi and crouched by her daughter and in a controlled low tone repeated, Where is Patrick? Where have you left the baby? Think now. You have to tell me.

But Mhairi's smile left and she was empty, innocent and puzzled. I tell you, I don't know what you're talking about, Mum. What baby? There's no baby. And there's no bread either, did you buy some?

She rose to go into the kitchen and Kate slammed her back into the chair.

Where the hell is he? What have you done with him?

Fuck off. I haven't done anything with anybody. I don't know what you're talking about. How would I know where the bloody baby is? He's gone. Gone, alright?

Kate socked her. Not the slap in movies applied to victims of shock, but a real powerful sock to the jaw and Mhairi went sprawling on the floor. She screamed, then cried. Long, mournful sick-cow cries.

There is no baby could be heard occasionally through her sobs. *The baby is drowned.*

Jamie

The water is dark and deep. Black right from the shore. Jamie cannot swim. He does not walk very close to the edge any more, the embankment is steep and muddy. He fetches his drinking and washing water from a burn that runs behind the cottage and into the lochan. When he runs out of tea, he still boils the water and finds water can have flavour that is worth drinking just to taste. When he runs out of food it is a little more complicated. He has to tidy himself up as much as possible. Shave, rub icy water all over his torso to neutralise his odour, rub the dust off his shoes with dampened bracken. Then walk like a day-tripper would walk, purposefully but slowly, to the road into Gairloch.

The first time he gets up the courage for the trip, he gets to the shop only to find it closed. Peering through the window he sees a clock and it says seven thirty. He'd thought it was around tea time. With it being light so late, it is hard to tell. That time he'd been so hungry and disappointed he'd gone into a hotel and bought crisps and nuts and eaten them on the beach before walking home.

The second trip is more successful. He enters the first little shop and quickly shuffles around, piling things in his wire basket. Packets of soup, beans and sardines. Eggs, bread, marge, tea, matches. Stammers his thanks, avoiding eyes. But everyone is friendly and his eyes are at last drawn. The cashier is a round woman who fusses over putting his groceries in double carrier-bags, so they won't break.

Th-th-th-thank you, that's very kind, he says.

Not at all, now mind how you go, that's a steep step down.

Just as if he is a normal person, not a dirt-encrusted homeless freak.

He is set up for the day and strolls home leisurely. Tells himself, *I am strolling home*, and says it over and over. Makes it into a little hum. When he gets to the point where he leaves the road, he waits till there is no sound of traffic before he cuts across the hill. It is important his presence in the cottage is unknown.

He carries his provisions with tender care into the cottage and arranges them on the window-ledge, except for the perishables. They go on a large flat-topped stone he has brought in. He has fixed the door so the sheep no longer get in. The floors are swept with branches of broom, which lean against the wall, perhaps in the very same place the original occupants had kept their broom brushes. His spare set of clothes he keeps washed and hanging over a contraption he has made out of old planks he has found out back. Probably from a former byre. With an old slate, he's dug himself a shallow cesspit out the back. Nearby is a pile of stones to fill it with eventually.

He spends his days carefully rationing out his food, cleaning, sleeping and sometimes taking little walks. Beyond his hill, away from the road, is true wilderness. The jagged Torridon mountains, random irregular shapes he could never have imagined. Purple heather. Broom seed pods popping softly.

Must be coming on autumn, is the kind of thought he lets roll slowly round his head. He often speaks to himself. *Money almost gone, well, whit then, boy? Back tae the same old same old.*

And he would get out his money and his return rail ticket and his mind would spin back down the way he'd come. Then he'd tell the house, *You're a bonny house, a right bonny house, and I'll no be leavin ye just a wee while* yet. Dinna fret, I'm no going awa. And ye just never ken. Mebbe a wee jobbie around here for me.

He has the idea the house is as unloved as himself and is clinging to him. He has talked to no one but himself and the house for three weeks. Jamie's bubble.

Patrick Takes Note
of His Situation

When he woke he did not cry. He listened. There was the shushing noise a small breeze made in the rowan leaves; there was a bird singing, then squawking; there was the almost inaudible sound of the loch – the tiny echo or sense of space one gets from large bodies of water nearby. He looked straight up with his serious eyes and did not form any thoughts, merely took it all in. Red berries, gold feathery leaves, blue sky. Motion and sound. Flights of small birds, taking off and landing, taking off and landing. He slowly waved his dimpled hands and stretched his legs.

After twenty minutes all this stimulation tired him and used up his reserves of fuel. He began to fret for something to fill his stomach. He started by twisting and rocking, which only brought his knitted bonnet down over his eyes, further frustrating him. He whimpered, he whinged. Then took a big breath and screamed. He howled and keened till real tears came soaking his cheeks and snot ran into his mouth. Then as suddenly, he collapsed into sleep again. As limp as a rag, he lay while the breeze chilled his wet red face. Dreamt of eyes looking into his, and twitched with pleasure.

*   *   *

Woke again in the dark, shivering. Wailed thinly, but instinctively kept his energy outpour to a minimum. Heart slowed down, breathing went shallow. His dark eyes opened, peeking out from under the cap, watching shadows, wet mouth opening and closing. His spirit, which had sent him pirouetting when he was a mere three months from conception, sank back down, down, deep inside himself, and there he crouched, conserving his strength. An owl screeched nearby and a grey mouse met its end. The loch water gently lapped, lapped. Three rabbits ate steadily, tugging and tearing at grass. To Patrick who was ebbing, who was too young to be frightened and only knew there was absence of warmth and food, they were sounds with shapes and colours and he watched them. Vivid as opium dreams.

Then he dropped like a stone into coma-like sleep. His little fingers started to turn blue and his face a translucent white, his blood coursing through slowly, doubtfully.

The End of the World

You did what?

You heard me. I phoned the police.

Mother, you're crazy. What are you trying to do to me?

I told them we have lost the baby.

She spoke calmly, eyes wild, heart thudding. This was not her daughter, this was not happening. She had to plough through the minutes till it came right again. And somehow it was essential she did and said all the right things till then.

I had to tell them, Mhairi, they'll help find him.

They won't.

How?

Because I've killed the baby. I drowned him. He's dead. Mhairi, defiant, eyes flashing, then dissolving, the tears leaping out and splashing down her front.

Oh my God, no, no, you can't have. Don't say things like that.

Kate sat down, then stood up, everything crashing inside her. To hear the words was to give her fears solidity, and she could see too well the floating bloated angelic face, an inch under water. Eyes open. Ginger hair wavering.

You're not right. Something's seriously the matter with you. I'm calling the doctor.

Mum! (Blubbering on the floor like a five-year-old, out of control.) Mummy, I'm sorry. Don't be angry, Mum. I didn't mean it. Don't be angry.

I'm calling the doctor.

She found the number and, after three attempts, dialled it right. Said they had a serious problem and could a doctor come straight away. Yes, it was an emergency.

Had a moment's compassion, seeing her daughter prone weeping on the floor.

You'd better get to bed, Mhairi. You're not well at all. You're sick, darling. I just didn't realise. It's all my fault, everything. You're not well at all, get up now and go up to your bed. The doctor will be here in fifteen minutes.

Mhairi responded to her gentler tone. Did not notice, because she did not look, that Kate's eyes were cold as stone, and shuffled, sniffing and hiccuping up to her bed.

The police came, two young men. Raised the alert immediately. But it was late evening and without a clue where to look they were stuck. It seemed no neighbour had seen Mhairi go for her walk. They looked in the usual places babies get abandoned – bins, public doorsteps, public toilets. They talked to people. Kate did not tell them about the sea – that Patrick might be in it. She knew she should, but to hear the words out loud . . . bad enough to think them.

The doctor came and spoke to Kate, who found herself telling him the whole story. Mhairi's previous temperament, the circumstances of the birth, Mhairi's indifference to Patrick, her loss of appetite and its sudden return. The doctor did not seem to think any of it strange and nodded a lot. The first thing is, we see if she can remember where the baby is. Then I think a short spell in hospital where we can keep an eye on her would be a good idea, Mrs McKinnon.

You mean Craig Dunain?

Well, Raigmore, for now. Just till we see what's what. I can't make any kind of diagnosis just now. We'll have to see. Now, where is she?

He went upstairs and found Mhairi sound asleep with her clothes on, sucking her thumb. He turned on the low bedside lamp and Kate touched her shoulder, rocking her a little. Wake up, Mhairi. Here's someone to speak to you. Wake up now, just for a bit.

Who are you? Tell him to go away, Mum.

He's a doctor, Mhairi. He's here to help you.

I don't need help.

Patrick does, and you have to try and remember where you went with him. Was it . . . was it the beach?

No.

Was it the shops?

No, Mum, you went shopping, not me.

Did you go to anyone's house?

Course not.

Well, where did you go?

I don't know.

But—

Look, Mum, just accept the baby is gone. If there ever was a baby. Quit hassling, I'm getting another headache.

Mrs McKinnon, perhaps if you just leave myself and Mhairi, to talk a wee while.

Of course, Doctor. I'll be downstairs.

Walked quickly by the dark stain on the landing carpet where

Patrick had made his entrance. Downstairs to the kitchen. A cup of tea burned her tongue. Thought irrelevantly of Michael. A second's anger that he was not here. But why should he be? This was not his problem, Patrick not his grandson. My grandson, she thought, my grand wee son, and she ached with missing, wanting him. Cursed herself for leaving Mhairi alone with him, fool. Should've seen it coming.

She looked out of the window, down the slope to the sea that might contain one more body than it ever should have the right to own, a sweet morsel of boyhood, and knew, consciously told herself, that this was the worst. Worse than Jack dying. Nothing could approach the dread that drenched her.

Jamie

Jamie has gone shopping again, and is taking his time coming home. Tries a new route, sticking to the coast for longer, cutting up a different way through the hills. A village dog follows him for a while, then slinks back as Jamie walks beyond his boundaries. In his double carrier-bags this time are candles, bacon, oats, potatoes, sausages and a tin of soup. His thoughts are now given to ways of finding more money to stay on. Maybe something down at the harbour, something in the fish factory.

He stumbles into his house, sets out his things and lights a fire. It is late and chilly, a little haar begins to creep over the hills. Sheep baa in the mist. He makes a cup of tea and yacks away to himself. Wait till it cools, you'll burn your fuckin tongue, stupid bugger, Christ, it's cool the night, might sleep doon here, pull that pallet in tomorra, mak a wee bed. Dry it first, be bittie damp now.

On and on, till he eats his bacon and eggs and bread, another cup of weak tea, using the same bag. Counts his money again. Only twenty-eight pounds and thirty-two pence. Puts it back behind the loose stone. Goes upstairs and curls up to sleep.

He wakes around three with a painfully full bladder. Starting to get light outside, pink in the grey at the skyline, birds already at the berries. Air like ice water down his throat. Stumbles downstairs, out of the door and over to the tree where he pees. Steams rises. Sees the unfamiliar shape of the bottle first and reaches for it, sees Patrick. He screams, a high girlish wail.

Fuckin hell, oh my God, it's a fuckin baba. It's a baby, oh no, it's a deid baby.

He hops up and down. Tries twice to pick up Patrick before he can actually touch him. Terrified, never held a dead thing before, unless mice from traps count.

Finally, near crying, he cradles Patrick and takes him into the house. Chanting, Oh no, oh no, oh fuck, oh no . . .

Jesus Christ, ye poor wee fucker, where the hell did ye come from, ye poor wee divil? I canna fuckin believe it.

He rocks back and forth on his knees in front of the dead fire, spinning off into his world where everything that happens is his fault. The noise finally startles Patrick, snaps him back from his trance of survival. He opens his eyes and his arms jerk upwards.

Shit, says Jamie, nearly dropping him. Oh my fuck, you're nae deid. Oh fuckin Jesus, whit now? You're alive, so ye are, Jesus fuck.

He holds Patrick at a little distance to see his face properly and to give him the benefit of his teary smile, yellow stained teeth shining out. Patrick stares, opens his mouth, takes an experimentally deep breath and screams his head off.

Panic shoots through Jamie, worse than thinking he'd found a corpse. The noise is like a siren, piercing, gut-rendering, skull splitting.

Oh, shit. Oh, shit, shit, shit. Are ye hurt? Jesus.

He holds Patrick away from him, his ears ringing, his whole skeleton shaking.

Hungry. Must be hungry. It's only hunger you're feeling, is it? Wheesht while I sort somethin. Christ.

Holds up a loaf in front of Patrick. Bread? I dinna ken, but I doot you've any teeth to chaw it with.

Then he remembers the bottle. Just wait here a wee bittie, Christ, whit a noise, there's naethin much wrong with your lungs, is there? They can hear ye doon the toon.

He puts Patrick down on his jacket, on the floor by the hearth. Patrick's back arches and he is stiff and turning an alarming red, hiccuping and near choking with his distress. Jamie flies out of the door to the tree, finds the bottle and races back. He scoops up the baby and shoves the bottle in. Patrick takes one second to realise it is food. Then gets stuck in. Limp and damp. The silence roars.

Jamie shivers and reaches with his free hand for his jumper.

Bloody cold, you'll be frozen, wee mite. What the divil are ye anyway, quine or loon? I'm gonna have a wee look so I'm knowing whit to call ye.

He unwraps Patrick awkwardly like he is a china doll and peeks down his nappy.

Phew, what a pong. So it's a wee mannie ye are, hey? Listen, I'm gonna light a nice fire for us, warm ye up a bittie. That's what you'll be needing, sleeping ootside on a night like this'en. How did ye come there anyway? This is my house, did ye ken? Did the fairies drop ye off here, then, are ye a wee changelin for old Jamie tae mind? You're fairly fuckin enjoyin that drink, aren't ye?

Patrick lies in his arms, fixates on the rolling banter, the milk in his mouth and Jamie's dark eyes squinting down at him. When the bottle is finished, he keeps sucking air till Jamie pulls it out with a pop. He lays Patrick down again on his jacket and folds the sleeves over him. Then he piles some sticks into the fireplace, twists a bit of paper, pushes it under them and lights it. He doesn't always have good luck with fires. Finding dry wood is a problem and kindling or paper is not easy either. But this time his fingers move surely and do not overload the fuel, which is dead gorse branches. He waits till some of it catches and then gently lays more, talking all the while.

Patrick watches. The acrid smoke stings his eyes and irritates his throat.

But these sensations are overridden by the light and warmth and the friendly crackling. And Jamie's voice fucking this and fucking that, softly permeating the fabric of heat spreading outwards. Patrick's tiny muscles unclench, he lies mesmerised. He poos, then shudders like he always does after a bowel movement.

Are ye still cold, wee mannie? Come, I'll soon warm ye.

He builds up the fire and settles Patrick, jacket and all, facing into his chest, as easy as if he'd been a father years ago. He lies on his back by the fire. Patrick closes his eyes and snores gently, his cheeks rosy, his face relaxed, for all the world like he is home in his basket.

Jamie lies stiffly, back aching on the cold concrete floor, inhaling Patrick's poo.

Aside from that little boy in the train a couple of months ago, it has been a long time since he has touched another human being. He can't remember how long. Since Catriona, anyway. Sex in the dark. Furtive and quick. Her rushing off to the toilet after, to wash. And before that, only the mothers scrubbing his face with a cold flannel. A long time. Oh, wait now, there was old Bozo, one of the Aberdonian lot, a fatalistic alky who had occasionally used Jamie's shoulders to lean on, sometimes sleep on. No, that doesn't count. Real human contact has been rare, and holding Patrick, feeling his tiny pulse and his milky breath, is sending strange messages to an unused part of himself. And back and back comes the thought that this — a child to touch and care for — would have made the difference. Would've saved him.

If Catriona hadn't lost that baby . . .

He closes his eyes but doesn't sleep. Listens to the dawn and wonders what it all means.

Patrick wakes once more, farts, squirms, stretches, yawns and drifts back to sleep. It is morning, a faded yellow glow lights the dust motes. Jamie is frozen, his mind is frozen too, and it runs along like a broken record, replaying finding the baby again and again and leading up to the moment he is in, and he has to keep looking down at Patrick's downy ginger head and listen for his faint breathing. He has a baby and the baby is not dead.

First the cottage, now this.

But it makes his head swim. Where has the baby come from and why is he here with him? Then it comes to him with all the clarity of a childhood memory unearthed, whole and pristine. *Fuck if you're nae my own bairn then, the fuckin fairies have given me another chance. A life tae keep.*

And then, right on cue, Patrick, still in deepest slumber, almost smiles. Not quite, but his cheeks pucker as if he might.

Everyone Looks Everywhere

Morning found Kate on her doorstep waiting for the police again. They'd searched most of the night, with a helicopter sending searchlights like beacons over the hills and shores. Dozens of neighbours and thirty police had walked in spread formation along the beaches and over the back fields, using infrared heat detectors and bloodhounds. They shone torches under whins, in hollows, burrows, anywhere they could imagine a deranged mother might hide a baby. It had been the oddest sight, quite magical and lovely if the cause had been different. Like fire-flies alighting everywhere, the hills twinkling and echoing with the sounds of people talking softly.

They checked rubbish bins, doorways, both telephone booths, the public toilets, empty hotel rooms. How far could she have gone? Like most country kids, she hated walking.

Kate spent the night criss-crossing the hills, calling his name as if he could answer, just for something to say. Superstitiously believed if she kept calling his name he would stay alive. How could he not, with his own name floating in the air to him? If she stopped thinking about him for a minute, he might die. It was her job to worry about him and thereby keep him alive.

Mhairi was in a deep drugged sleep, swollen eyes and

lumbering snore. Patrick's things lay about the house as constant pain pricks, the sight of one tiny sock enough to reduce Kate to incoherence.

Duncan had been sent away finally after hours of searching, his face gaunt and morbid, not a face expecting to discover a living baby, but an all-set-for-the-funeral face that was no help at all to see.

Away you go, Duncan. I'll let you know first thing, whatever.

So she sat on the doorstep, to hurry the police up by looking for them. Her whole body poised to receive news. But a kind of helplessness possessed her too, as if she was suddenly incontinent. She felt it might be only minutes before she failed to hold herself together in one piece, literally. Her organs might depart via various orifices, or simply cease functioning. She was flying apart.

Two figures appeared on the track coming up to her house. She stood, tried to make out who they were, then hurried down to them, heart pounding. But it was only the Murdos.

For Godsake, not now, she groaned quietly. Then aloud, angry, Look, you two, now's hardly the time, unless you have some way to help, I just can't be doing ...

Ah, now, Kate, it's not like that, honestly, we're not imbeciles, we haven't come expecting you to entertain us, wheesht, woman, stop crying now, give me your arm and we'll go and make a good strong pot of tea and have another think about things. You're not to give up hope. That's not like you, Kate. But he had to give his bag of butteries to wee Murdo and crouch down on the ground because Kate had collapsed in a weeping heap. After a minute, she lifted her head with a semblance of her self and requested in a tiny voice, Murdo, my bones are like jelly, you'll have to help me up.

Course, my dear, take my hands, up we go, now just you lean on me, come along, Murdo, you take her other side, here we go.

Half-way up the path, Kate felt a little worm in her belly that escaped as a high-pitched giggle, imagining the picture they made. Big Murdo, constitutionally incapable of responding to stress, herself the opposite, a quivering wreck. Wee Murdo, ever a mystery, struggling with her weight and nervously yawning. Then she shrugged off both men, went ahead to the house. Put the kettle on and pushed the hysteria to a nearby place, where it clung on perilously, ready to dive back any second. Made the pot of tea. Grilled and buttered the butteries and watched the Murdos wolf them down. Began to eat one, found she could not swallow. Drank tea so strong her eyes fizzed.

Where's Mhairi now? asked big Murdo.

Upstairs. Asleep.

Big Murdo ate and drank and generally brought a sense of normality to the room. Wee Murdo merely looked out of the window mournfully and drooled some tea on to his jacket. A novel affection for them attached itself to her and she put her hand on big Murdo's grubby palm. Thanks, Murdo. For coming.

He choked and a rosy blush lit up his cheeks. For what? We done nothing, woman. Only keeping you company, like, for a wee while. We're on the alert, though. The whole village is out looking, you know. Were you out all night looking?

Aye.

A police car pulled up. The Murdos, who would've been

the first to phone the police, nevertheless could not control their allergy to uniformed authority, and left through the back door. We're off, Kate. Let us know if there's anything we can do at all. We'll be thinking and looking all along. We'll take a different route home, I'm thinking. You never know.

But she hardly heard him. Had flown to the front door.

Jamie

The day brings chaos. Patrick stinks and whinges. Jamie peeks down his nappy again and almost retches. Jesus Christ, man, but ye pong, I niver seen a green shite, whit are ye, a Martian?

Thinks about it a minute, while Patrick stares at him between hiccups that shake his entire body. Finally takes off his own jumper and T-shirt and vest. Puts the shirt and jumper back on. Studies the vest. Picks up Patrick and goes outside to the burn. Takes off the wee sweatsuit bottoms, untapes the nappy, flings it on the gorse.

Now this is gonna feel a wee bittie cold, man, so just hold tight and it'll be over in a minute, ken?

Patrick thinks this is funny and again tries to smile, then howls a death cry as he is lowered bottom first into the water. Jamie clumsily sloshes the green shit off then tucks the clean bum into a fold of his jumper and runs back into the house, Patrick's screams slicing through his bones.

Okay, here we are, we're bak, shutup noo you're no dying, you're only clean again, for Christ sake, I niver haird a noise like ye before. Fit a racket, wheesht now.

Ties the vest various ways around Patrick's shrunken blue willie and bright pink bottom. Has a brainstorm.

Ah-ha! The nappy solution!

He finds a carrier-bag and lays the vest on top of it, then the baby on top of the vest. He tucks the vest between the baby's legs, ties it at the waist. Pulls the carrier-bag up through the legs the same way, so it is leakproof. Then he fetches one of his shiny treasures, an old safety-pin, large and strong. He pins it all together in the middle, pulls the jogging trousers back over the wee legs and pats Patrick's bottom proudly. *Ya beauty!*

Breaks into song to drown out crying. Old song he thought he'd forgotten, so long ago, it seems to come from nowhere: *Katie Beardie had a coo, black and white about the moo, wasna that a dainty coo, dance Katie Beardie.*

Patrick, though clean and dry, does not shut up. Only goes into next mode up on the crying scale. A kind of breathless, almost silent howl.

Ah, puleeze, will ye no stop your gurnin, man, you're beginnin tae give me the willies, and whit do ye expect me tae do aboot it? I didna go out and fetch ye, it was you who landed on me and ye canna blame me if I havena a' the right things ye need. Ken?

Patrick stops crying long enough to yawn, cries another second, then closes his eyes and sinks back into his black world of water memories, worn out from wanting. The world is sorely disappointing him today. He has given out the feed-me signal and been denied. It is an overwhelming mystery he hopes will be resolved when he next awakes.

Jamie sits there with Patrick's limp little body in his arms and suddenly knows what he must do. He takes the baby upstairs and lays him down gently on his sleeping-bag, covers him up with the blanket he'd come wrapped up in. Fairy blanket. Fetches the money from under the stone and counts it again. Sighs and grimaces. Finally takes five pounds, puts it in his pocket. Takes one last long look at Patrick and his gently rising and falling chest, and leaves the cottage. Closes the door slowly and quietly. Poises on the doorstep a moment, then races pell-mell down the slope to the loch, up the hillock to the road. Stops for a breath, sweat pouring freely. Then runs on.

Cars and fish lorries pass him, gusting him with their air currents and exhaust, sometimes beeping him. He runs clumsily, with his arms swinging way up. Like a man running for his life, with no care for his appearance or speed efficiency. Hurtling his body through space, pounding the road with his old shoes. Then he slows, lopes half bent over, panting, then speeds up to a gallop again. It is almost seven miles, and it takes him just over an hour.

He gets to the village by seven forty, bright red and wheezing. He has to wait for the shop to open. He hops up and down on the doormat, peering into the shop and the owner who is putting out the loaves, the nice lady, takes pity on him and unlocks the door.

Come away in, you're looking desperate. What is it you're needing so early?

He falls into the shop, his sweat cooling rapidly, shivering. He begins to ask for milk but gets stuck on the letter M, then finally all the words behind it shoot out, like a dam bursting: M-mi-milk, I just think I'll be needing some milk, please. He has a vague idea ordinary milk is not the right thing but it will have to do. He grabs a two-litre plastic container and plonks it on the counter. Some overripe bananas waft up to him from their basket by the till, their rotting smell sweet. On impulse he asks, Whit are you wanting for the bananas?

Waves of heat and sweat roll off him, and trying not to breathe very deeply, she says, Oh, just have them. They're near black now. Gives him his change and watches him leave. He pauses before leaping into a gallop up the road.

Patrick All Alone

Patrick woke to silence and bright sunlight. Woodsmoke and old milk on his blanket. A strange sensation around his groin, his legs split wide by Jamie's soaking wadded vest. The strange crackling noise of the carrier-bag when he moved. He shuddered as if he'd just finished crying for a long time, then watched a moth at the window. Fluttering, scooting dust around and around, then settling on a stick. The gnawing in Patrick's stomach grew into a dull awareness, not worthy of a crisis scream. Again, like the night before under the tree, he withdrew into contemplative calm, conserving his energy. Fear, and all the calories it might consume, was a forbidden luxury. His eyes rolled into sleep before his lids shut and he looked dead for a minute. Then, his tiny fingers curled into fists, he dreamt of eyes again.

The Clue

When big Murdo and wee Murdo came into the shop that afternoon she mentioned to them casually, it was after all not the main news of the day – the missing baby was filling everyone's minds – but she did mention to them, You know that queer man biding up at old Dan's place? You know what one, mind you told me about him first. Well, he was here again this morning, looking like he'd just run a marathon, and all he bought was two litres of milk. Then off he went again, like a house on fire. I never saw the like. I was expecting him to ask for paracetamol or whisky. He doesn't really look the type, but you can never tell with folk.

Big Murdo leant on her counter, was sorry to see the ripe fruit gone, and said slowly, Ah, weel now, Alice, he'd probably brewed himself a nice pot of tea and forgot he had no milk. He's a strange one, alright, but harmless I'm sure.

Ach, I know well you're right, Murdo, only I can't help wondering about him. He can't always have been like that. Just barely hanging on to things, like.

She put his groceries in a bag. Wee Murdo seemed to be looking at the girlie magazines on the top shelf, then back away down to the newspapers.

He had a start somewhere same as the rest of us. Just maybe a harder time in between. Anyway, we're heading up to Kate's again, see if there's any news.

Aye, you do that, and give her my love. We've all been frantic, thinking about that poor wee bairn. Disappearing like that. I kept waking in the night trying to work out where he might be. It's too hard, all alone out there, cold and hungry. In a lower voice, quivering, she added, I have a terrible feeling, I'm so afraid all they're going to find is . . .

Now, don't be thinking things like that, Alice, that's no right at all. He's a sturdy lad and will be howling his head off when we find him. I'll be seeing you then, come along, Murdo.

Wee Murdo mumbled goodbye and followed him outside. They began to walk over the low hills, the more direct route to Kate's. Big Murdo's eyes roved the landscape, a frown between his eyes, his bushy eyebrows gathered like two arched-back caterpillars. Wee Murdo's eyes were on the ground, to see where to put his feet.

Hey, Murdo, he said.

Big Murdo came to a halt, so rare was the sound of wee Murdo's voice.

Aye?

Strange about the milk, Murdo.

What milk?

The milk Alice said about.

Oh, aye. How's that, Murdo?

Wee Murdo seemed to be excited, and big Murdo hoped this wasn't a prelude to a fit, like the one he'd had once before when they were miles from the road and he'd had to carry him.

Babababbies drink milk.

Whoa there, little man. Let's sit a second.

Jamie

He sees them coming, pure luck. The baby has gone back to sleep again, after another bottle of milk, and he's been taking a quick scout around for more firewood. Damn difficult with no trees at all, but he manages. Plenty dead whin and gorse, as well as bits of ancient pine root, soft and rotting. He drops to the ground when he hears their car stop on the road. He is just below the brow of the hill and can peer over, unseen. Oh fuck, Jesus fuck.

Four policemen getting out of a patrol car. Doors slamming, then the noise of talking. Pointing, the older one probably explaining. Uniforms striking terror even at this distance.

No fuckin way, you fuck bastards. He's mine.

And as the policemen spread out to approach the cottage from four directions, Jamie slithers noiselessly back down the hill, tears back to the cottage. Grabs the still sleeping Patrick, who wakes but only does his startle gesture, both arms flung out as if to grab a branch on the way down. Jamie puts him back down and grabs the bottle, shoves it in his jacket pocket; and the baby blanket, shoves it in the other pocket, trailing out. Then picks up the baby again and climbs out the back window.

Patrick gasps in the fresh air, opens his mouth as if to cry, but only yawns. After thirty hours, Jamie has taken Kate and Mhairi's place in the familiarity stakes. Jamie, the food-giver and bottom-washer and builder of smoky fires. Mama Jamie.

Jamie crouches behind a boulder to see what's what. So far, nothing. No movement, no noise. Has he moved that quick? Fuck he is fast. Fuckin wind. Thank fuck the bairn has him to look after himself. No way will he let these fuckers in uniforms steal his wee lad.

No. It is his house the boy has come to, and it is his job to protect him. Shit. One clean-cropped head comes bobbing up over the hill, followed by shoulders and torso.

Jamie waits for it to turn in the other direction, looking back west, then he runs bent over, baby tucked in under upper arm, up over the burn and into the scattered boulders and scrub. Hoping the distance squelches any noise. He cannot hear the policemen himself, so maybe the reverse is true. He stops again, hidden, about sixty metres from the back of the cottage.

Patrick starts to be a bit bored and emits a squeak, and Jamie rams the bottle in quick.

Husht, shut the fuck up now, if ye know what's good for you, there's my good wee mannie.

The policemen surround the cottage, walk importantly but with exaggerated nonchalance, as if stake-outs are their usual daily routine on the west, and they are not enjoying this, no, no, no, it is not a novelty. The oldest one shouts:

Hello, is anyone in there? Come out, please, we'd like a word. It's the police. Then to the others, Jimmy, you go look in the window, have a look inside. Bobby, go around the back. You, Angus, you come with me. We're going inside.

As if it's a fuckin armed robber in there, whispers Jamie.

Patrick burps.

Then the disaster. Jamie spots it before the man called Bobby does. The disposable nappy, still flung in the gorse. Lying like the great giveaway it is, bright greenish-yellow shit, a signal saying, Martian baby this way.

Oh my fuck. Okay. Alright. Oh Jesus. (Under his breath.) Then, he lays Patrick very slowly down on the ground in a little cleft between a big rock and some little ones. On his side with the bottle propped in his mouth. The blanket covers his entire body, but loosely over his face.

There, a wee tent for you, mannie, now just keep quiet, I'll be back in a tick, keep still for fuck sake.

He stands up, takes a deep breath, is conscious of doing the bravest most noble thing he's ever done, and coughs loudly till he has the policeman's attention. Makes as if to do his trousers up, then shouts, Hello, doon there! I niver haird ye, I was just havin a ... well, a ... relievin myself, ken.

He stumbles down to the cottage. Strides right through the burn, smiling broadly as his shoes tread through the gorse as if it is level ground, thrusting the nappy deep into the bush. Prays the sticky tapes are not adhered to his shoe, and says, How can I help ye? (In a voice he never heard before. No stammer, no twitching.)

The other policemen come around now, puzzled looks, though the leader tries to keep his you-are-a serious-criminal-and-we-have-caught-you-red-handed face on.

Are you staying here in this cottage?

Aye, just a wee while, but I'm nae fishin. You can check. No tackle or nothin.

Are you aware who this house belongs to? (Shaky ground, because he has just realised he doesn't know either.)

Aye. (What a daredevil genius he is, fuckin amazin, where has this person come from?)

And you have, er, permission?

Oh, aye. I always come here for a wee break in the summer. It's like campin, ken. Only I don't need a tent. Just a wee break from the city. I never leave any rubbish or anythin.

How long have you been here?

Three weeks.

Have you left this cottage since you came?

Well, I stock up in Gairloch, ken the wee shoppie there. But naewhere else.

And do you know anyone hereabouts?

Oh, no. The whole idea is tae get awa from the folk I ken.

The other three men just watch, one yawns.

Have you seen a young woman, at all? With a baby?

No, nae one has coom round here.

Not at all? Yesterday afternoon, this would have been.

No naebody.

What were you doing then? Were you here?

Oh, aye. Here.

What do you do here, if you don't fish?

I just walk, and I ... I write. (My name, over and over, he almost says, but stops. Some fuckin clever bastard is in control of his tongue.)

Do you now? A writer. (A smirk, as if that explains everything.) *Well, I guess we'll be going. We'd just like a quick look around inside the place, if you don't mind. Just routine.*

No, on you go. Door's nae locked.

If you do see anything of a baby, or anything suspicious at all, will you come into Gairloch, let us know?

Aye. Hope ye find the wee girl.

The policeman picks up the gender word, nods as if he has just done some heavy deductive work correctly after all, and dismisses this loony writer. What were they like, these artsy fartsy types? Jesus. But harmless.

After they creep through the four rooms of the cottage and marvel at the primitive standard of living they offer, they resurface into the August afternoon and make their way back to the patrol car just as Patrick's bottle pops out.

He is not ready to stop sucking. He takes a huge breath and begins to holler.

A millisecond after he begins, Jamie, who is still standing in the yard,

232

begins to sing. Loudly. *Oh, sole mio, oh, sole mio.*

The departing policemen glance back, startled, then quicken their pace. Strange one, that, they mutter. Imagine, kipping all by yourself in that creepy old place. If he wasn't loony to start with, that place would drive him to it, they all agree. And where does he write? No desk, no lights, no books even. And don't all writers need computers these days? Obviously not. He must be a poet, concludes the one called Bobby. Poets don't need much, they only scribble a few words no one ever reads.

Bit of a pity the milk clue hadn't panned out. It had been a long shot. Mind, a girl like Mhairi could never have walked carrying that bairn so far. Must be eight miles.

No, it wasn't a baby they'd find one day, but a corpse. If they did find it, poor bairn. The mother has hinted it might have been the beach Mhairi took it to, in which case there would be no chance of recovering the body. It would be long gone, fish food by now.

Mhairi Talks to Her Shrink

I know I've been bad, very very bad, and I should really just off myself, I am a bad little bitch. I've gone and killed a wee baby who never hurt a fly, he was so tiny, I am so bad, and he relied on me, his mum, and what did I do? I killed him. Didn't I? Where is he, then? Wasn't there a tree somewhere, and a wee bed I made him and he had his bottle and that. His powder-blue blanket. And water, a big bit of water, splashing noises, big splash, all gone. There was a baby, wasn't there?

Yes, Mhairi, you had a son.

I did have a big belly once, sure, and I know who made it that way, that prick Roddy who's probably off shagging some Eastern European *babushka*, but then what happened? This is terrible, I know I've done a terrible thing and my mum hates me now, for ever and ever, I wish I hadn't, only it's just so hard to remember. I'm glad he's gone. He was never supposed to be here, I was doing just fine till he came along, and he was going to fuck everything up for ever, no one really had the time for him, least of all me, he was ugly, oh, he was ugly as sin, and stunk, and the noise! But no more, and I'm not sorry. No. I am sorry. He was just a wee boy who never did any harm, and nothing was his fault it was all my fault, I am a bad bad girl, and I should just off myself.

Who would that hurt?

Myself, of course.

Who else?

She shrugged.

Have you ever tried any drugs, Mhairi?

No.

Not marijuana, or Ecstasy or acid? None of the recreational drugs?

No. Why, are you wanting some?

Why do you think this is a joke?

Why are you so serious?

Where is Patrick, Mhairi?

Nowhere.

Where did you put him?

Nowhere.

Is he perhaps near a hill, or a beach? You mentioned hearing waves.

Yes. No. No. Maybe.

Do you think Patrick is dead, Mhairi?

Yes.

Why?

Why? That's a stupid question, isn't it? He is because he is.

Jamie

Jamie curls up with Patrick in front of the fire, replaying his heroic moment over and over. Where had it come from, this courage? So few of his encounters with police have left him anything but angry and frightened. They were his number-one intimidating enemy. Worse than the headmistress who used to make him stand in front of the entire assembly to be lambasted for some accidental prank. Worse than the mum who'd been called Kathy, who used to twist his ear around half off his head, and march him up the stairs to his freezing room with the mouldy walls, where he'd be trapped for hours, or for what seemed hours. He'd complained about Kathy, and been moved on to another mother; never saw her again, but she hasn't left him yet.

One time he'd woken in a half-constructed building at the university, to be kicked in the stomach by a black leather shoe belonging to a uniformed sergeant who seemed almost albino, eerily colourless, transparent. Practically see his blood.

Tears had sprung to his eyes, and he'd struggled not to urinate, to get out of his bag, only to be kicked back down again.

Listen, scum, this is private property, hear? Understand what that means, fuckbrain? It means stay the fuck away. Another sharp jab to his groin. You have no fucking right to be here. Then he'd told his two cohorts to get him the fuck out of here, and they'd gleefully dragged him, still in his bag, and thrown him out of a glassless window on to a concrete pavement, full of students and professors. It felt like his bones had all cracked, and worse, back inside the building, where he dare not go now, was the rest of his stuff, his holdall, the clean socks, the shiny treasures.

And if I catch you here again, I'll not be so soft, ken? You'll end up in court.

Now he sits with the soft weight of Patrick, his own child, and feels as though it was that very same policeman he's fooled today. Him. Jamie. King Jamie.

The fire glows, his baby is safe and not hungry. Life is good.

Margaret Makes a Fuss

So where is she then? demanded Kate's mother, standing in the doorway.

Inverness, Mum. I told you on the phone.

Will they put her in prison?

Oh, Mum, come in. I'll put the kettle on. (Hadn't slept in two days, a husk.)

I tell you, Kate, this would never have happened, if . . .

Mother. Now listen Mum.

What is she doing in Inverness, then?

Mhairi is in the psychiatric ward of Raigmore Hospital for a few days, Mum. (In the careful explaining tone she seemed to be using a lot these sad days.) The doctor says she is suffering from a psychotic type of post-baby depression. A hormonal thing, kind of.

Hmph. And what can they do about it? That kettle's boiled, I'll do it, you sit down for a change. She bustled up again, set to with the pot and tea-bags.

I talked to the doctor yesterday and they are giving her a mild antidepressant for now, just letting her sleep.

Are you going in to see her? I tell you, if I went in, if I got my hands on her, she'd know.

Mother, I went in with her, settled her, but the doctor says it's better to leave it for a few days now.

Her mother thrust a cup of tea in front of her, sloshing it, then making a fuss of cleaning it up.

How on earth will they get it out of her then, just letting the lassie sleep? Heavens above, I don't know.

Get what out of her, Mum?

What she did with the baby, of course.

She said she killed it, Mother (whispering – her other new speech mode). Drowned it. She told the doctor she dropped it, him, in some water.

Oh. Oh! Dear God.

I don't know if it's true, Mother, she's awfully confused, but it's possible. Where is he otherwise? We just don't know.

Maybe someone stole him. Maybe she gave him away. Maybe she sold him. I read about that in the newspapers. All these rich Americans desperate for newborns. Check her bank account, see if she's deposited any money.

Mum. Calm down, you're getting hysterical.

Well, it's better than you – just look at yourself. Are you ready to give up on the poor wee lad just like that? I can't believe he's dead, Kate. He was such a bonny babie. Hair just like your grandfather's. (Tears again.)

Now, Mum, please. I am not giving up. I never stop thinking about where he might be. I walk miles looking. Oh, Mum, you're soaking your blouse.

Oh, why not cry, who wouldn't? Heaven's sake, girl, get us both a hankie. Not that one, a clean one, please. You'd better come and stay with me, Kate, can't stay here all alone.

Why not? I was alone before.

Because it's different now, everything's fallen apart, love. You shouldn't be on your own. Pack a few things. Keep me company, we'll help each other.

No, Mother. I'll come and visit you. Soon. Tomorrow, for lunch, alright? I want to stay here. Need to, if you know what I mean.

Margaret blew her nose. And what'll happen to Mhairi? Is she off her head for ever now? Will she be locked up in the loony bin?

Mother! I hope not. She's ill. Very ill. I don't understand what's the matter with her, but the doctor says it happens sometimes. Presumably, like most illnesses, she has a chance of getting better.

But what about the police?

What about the police?

Surely there's a law against losing your own baby?

I don't know. It depends.

On what?

On what they find.

Jamie

Last night had been a bad one. He's never been so tired, no idea one bairn could do this to him. Like a wee puncture in his old bike tyre letting out all the air overnight, leaving it flat and useless. It's midday, the sun is shining and there's even warmth with it. Patrick has had his bottle, his poo, his nap; this is the pattern of every morning, with Jamie sometimes using nap-time to race into the village for more milk and food. Afternoons are usually laundry times, sloshing the vest nappies in the burn, hanging them to dry. He's been lucky with the weather so far, and the routine has worked. The days fly, full to the brim.

But today he has spent nap-time gathering fuel for his fire, and Patrick has woken up girny. Jamie is girny too, his eyes feel sticky and his head aches. They girn together, irritated and restless. Patrick's wee arms and legs cycle around and work themselves up into a faster and faster spin. Jamie walks him around, tries singing, tries offering more milk, then plonks him down on the soft bed he's made him out of holdall and jumper.

Well, mannie, I give up on ye, I've nae idea whit you're wantin now, nae idea. You're a right whinge.

Patrick stops for a second, gives Jamie a wide-eyed stare of accusation, then closes his eyes and hollers. A kind of urgent panic grabs hold of Jamie.

Fuck this for a game of Jammie Dodgers. (Where has that expression come from? Being so tired seems to release phrases and words he never normally uses, and yet they sound so familiar.) Let's hit the road, naethin else for it, hey? When in doubt, move those bones.

And so he scoops up Patrick and leaves the cottage, heads towards the road, but within seconds, turns around and walks up the back way, over the low hills. No people just yet, best to lie low, wait. He walks. Just rocks and gorse, a few sheep. No trees, no lochs; the ground soft and spongy with rotted heather and the decayed trees of centuries ago. He walks slowly, craning over the baby to watch his step. Patrick is loving this. The rhythmic motion, the sun, the birdsong and air, which tastes of sea and moor and gorse blossoms. Every minuscule muscle is relaxed, and the ride is smoother for it.

Right, we'll stop here a wee bittie.

Jamie lowers himself down into a sun-trap, his eyes so heavy now he is having trouble seeing. Patrick, lulled by all the newness and sun, has dropped off. Jamie arranges himself and Patrick for a sleep. Patrick is wrapped in Jamie's jumper and lying alongside him, on his side. Jamie stretches out and has one minute of consciousness, during which he mutters to the sky and hills and entire west coast how fucking lovely they all are, he will love them all for ever and never forget them. Never.

And away he goes, into a dark therapeutic sea of sleep. His body instantly begins to recover, a warm protective seal steals over him, numbing him, repairing all damages, recharging all cells. The sun, the earth, this baby boy. He lies between them all, embraced, at peace. He sinks deeper.

Is that your baby? asks the young blonde woman.

Aye, he's mine, so he is.

What a fine big lad he is, you must be proud, she says, leaning against the bus shelter. No, the bar.

Aye, he's fair growing fast. He looks down at the baby , who turns his *head to look at him with knowing eyes. Pride swims through him, enormous intoxicating quantities of the stuff.*

Well, I envy you, she says, drinking her gin. No, lighting her cigarette. Damn, and she isn't blonde any more, just brunette.

He holds his baby closer, and feels his wee arms cling on to him. It's a train they're on, and it's snowing a blizzard outside.

I wish I had a son like yours. He's a smasher, she says, and saunters off in her swimsuit and dives into a perfectly blue loch.

Aye, he's my wee hero, so he is.

She doesn't leave any ripples.

He looks down at his son again, who is smiling. A smile to shower him with smiles.

WEST COAST CRACK

September tomorrow, already. The rowan's dripping in bright berries and the heather is a carpet of postcard purpleness. The salmon catch remains pathetic, but that was a non-starter anyway. The hens are still laying. I have a surplus and give them to my mother and anyone who will take them. Tourists still trickle into Lochinellie, but the main river has set course for home, wherever that may be. Germany mostly, if one can go by all the German cars about. Hopefully they all left a fair bit of cash behind.

This is normally my favourite time of year, but someone is missing and I can't think of anything else. If I write his name, it feels like a betrayal or an admittance. I can't.

The berries have gone unnoticed, I assume they are out there, I haven't actually looked. The purpleness of the heather was a fib too. See what writers are?

Still, trust me. Unseen and unappreciated by me, I promise all these early autumn events are happening. But the tourist exodus – I have noticed that because now when I am searching for him in the village, I can cross the road when I want. I can buy my groceries without waiting in a queue. I can drive quickly, walk unhindered, look for him over empty beaches and hills. I do not benefit from tourists and I will not miss them. I want the place to be empty, the wind to whistle through empty streets. The days are getting shorter. I have lit the Rayburn again, and this time will probably keep it lit all through winter till late spring. I want my house to shine out like a beacon, like a giant welcoming hearth, for him. Wherever he is. I can't shake this waiting feeling.

Maybe it will be permanent. And maybe some of you have the same feeling. There is someone you knew once who disappeared and you have to wake up every day and get dressed and go to work and cook and walk the dog, all as if things were as they used to be, and that person had not gone. Is it true? Write and tell me how you do it. I have watched someone die, and I can say it is far worse not knowing if someone is dead or alive.

It is the helplessness, the replaying of every lost loved thing, magnified by a million. Incredible how easily, how quickly, it happens. A child is mislaid and suddenly the world seems a crowded place, where something as small as a baby will certainly disappear without a trace. It seems remarkable it does not happen more often. Or does it? Is the world full of mislaid scraps of humanity? I keep thinking – if I look again, look everywhere . . . Meanwhile, I call him as I used to tell my daughter to call lost toys. The magic of yearning, please let it work.

The End of Duncan

How long is it now, Kate? I can't think.

Twelve days. Nearly two weeks.

Ah, Kate, there, there.

No, Duncan, that's alright (extracting herself from his embrace. His breath smelt of whisky, unusual for him). I'll just go to my bed, if you don't mind. Early start tomorrow.

You're not going out again?

Of course. This time, a circle up to the old stone bridge, then back by the bothy.

He stood by the window, looked old in the light. She noticed everything, though she felt nothing for him now, not even repulsion. The broken capillaries on his cheeks, the way his coarse grey hair receded over his shining scalp. The kindness in his grey eyes. He sighed. Whispered hoarsely: Kate, that ground's been well covered. You know fine he's gone.

No, Duncan, I do not know fine he's gone. Now, I'm going to my bed. Goodnight.

Would you like some company?

No thank you (concealing her surprise — had he just offered to come to bed with her? Duncan? It would be like sleeping with Murdo.)

Why don't I stay here? On the sofa, like. You shouldn't be alone just now. I wouldn't mind.

No, thank you, Duncan.

Well, I'll be round tomorrow tea-time, then. I'll bring some salmon from my freezer.

No, that'll be alright, Duncan.

I don't mind, Kate. I want to.

That's alright. I don't want you to.

So, I'll see you tomorrow, then.

No, Duncan.

What do you mean?

I will not see you tomorrow, Duncan. I do not want to see you any more. Not so often, anyway. (Soft measured tones.)

Sure, you're just upset, Kate.

I am upset. I have lost Patrick and tomorrow I will continue looking for him.

Kate.

No. Please. I'm sorry. But no.

He wouldn't budge, just stood there regarding her with stubbornness. She shrugged and went up the stairs, calling a goodnight over her shoulder. Lay in bed listening till she heard the door open and close. His car engine roaring his hurt down the track.

Secrets

Kate did not tell the police, they'd tried already anyway. She did not tell anyone. It was a piece of secret hope and if she told anyone it would disappear. She left the house, took the car out of the village and up on to the road east. Pulled into a lay-by and stopped. Walked, arms crossed against the cold breeze, up to the lochan. There was the cottage. Smoke curling out of the chimney. The ghost of old Dan sitting on the doorstep smoking his pipe. Herself a five-year-old, with her dad, looking for a good trout loch needing no licence. Old Dan spitting and saying they were welcome but it wasn't his and the warden did sometimes come. Smiling at her and smelling like old skin. Offering her an ancient piece of fudge.

Remembered bringing Mhairi and her friends here for summer picnics. They played house in the empty cottage, for by then Dan was dead and the place open to the weather. Three little girls – one played Mum, the other the baby, and Mhairi played Dad, smoking a twig and clicking an imaginary remote control.

Kate began to run. Up the hill. Concentrated on Patrick. But softly, softly, not wanting to scare away luck. Her footsteps like whispers on the heather. Did not knock on the door. But looked through the window. And there they were.

Patrick chortling up at Jamie's funny face, a half-full bottle of milk on the floor. Jamie leaning forward to touch his own cheek against Patrick's and kissing him with a loud smacking noise. A game of melodrama. Patrick laughing out loud.

She withdrew, and leant against the wall, thanking the universe and every atom in it. Then softly knocked on the door.

Jamie froze, Patrick stiffened. Prepared to cry.

Kate opened the door a crack. Smiled. Hello, may I come in just for a minute? as if she always called at this time of day.

Jamie just stared at her. Tightened his hold on Patrick who, on hearing Kate's voice, grew alert.

What a lovely wee baby you've got.

Jamie looked dumbly down at Patrick, then back at her.

He's beautiful. What's his name?

Jamie had no answer, had not even thought of a name.

Wondered if Kate, so light and quiet, was real. Maybe she was a fairy mother.

She sat on the floor, carefully folding her legs. You've made this old place very cosy. Where do you come from?

Jamie straightened his shoulders. I'm a travellin man.

Are you? How exciting. I love to travel too, not that I've done much. You are lucky. She gave him another smile.

Jamie smiled too, a confused smile. Nice lady, nice lady, he said to himself.

Patrick waited for one of the pairs of eyes to find his, then arched his back and squirmed. Farted and got ready to cry.

Kate reigned herself in. Merely yawned and asked off-handedly, May I hold your baby?

Part Four

Be it ever so humbug,
There's no place like home.

                              Noël Coward

I said some words to the close and holy darkness,
And then I slept.

                              Dylan Thomas

Not the kiss, but the hours, days, years after
Not the kiss

                        public toilet graffiti, Ullapool

Michael Fetches More Beer

What's the matter? asked Amber. Are you okay? Do you have a headache? I could give you a massage. I've got some new oils.

No, nothing's wrong, said Michael, reaching for his underpants and socks.

You seem so quiet. Wasn't it alright? I mean, I thought it was fabulous, you really are great, Mikey.

Oh, it was fine, Amber. Really. Nothing's wrong.

Why are you getting dressed?

I thought I'd go out for a walk.

Right now?

Just a short walk, I'll be right back. Don't get up.

I'll come with you if you want. I know just how you feel. If I don't do my aerobics every day, my muscles ache. Shall I come with you?

No, that's alright Amber. Stay here where it's warm.

Sure?

Yeah. I'll just head down to the Seven Eleven. Get some more beer. Won't be long.

More beer! Oh, that's a good idea, Mikey. You read my mind. We can sit up and watch an old movie. I'll make a dip and get the taco chips out.

Okay. He sighed.

The more clothes he put on, the better he felt, and by the time he let himself out of her apartment and padded down the wet dark street, he felt the best he'd felt all day. Alive, purposeful; the night hunter, stalking the midnight beer.

He headed towards the fluorescent convenience store, entered its vibrating premises (a seriously unpleasant sensation) and got the beer. Swung out of the door but after a few minutes halted. Realised he'd been heading happily the wrong way – back to his own place.

Kate, she wasn't.

Mhairi's Nice When She's High

Jamie went with Kate, back to her house. He held Patrick all the way, and she chatted continually, describing a lovely meal she would cook him, and how he was such an incredible amazing man, and Patrick owed him his life and she would never ever forget him.

Her house was warm and there were strange people in it. Strange smells and so many things everywhere, he felt crowded. Heaps of colourful clutter, walls painted warm colours and covered in pictures. It seemed a very loud house. He began to feel sleepy the instant he sat down. Patrick wakened in his arms, but likewise found all the stimulation too much, and quickly curled back down into sleep.

And there had been the daughter, a girl looking very much younger than himself, called Mhairi. He didn't believe Patrick was her baby, because she didn't reach out for him, she didn't look at the baby. She stared at himself. They sat in the kitchen, while two funny men, one fat and one thin, made a fuss of Patrick. Kate had been on the phone, telling police and neighbours and doctors and her mother the news: the baby was found.

She didn't say anything about himself. He heard her explain.

Said the baby just appeared, unharmed, on her doorstep. Someone had obviously taken care of the baby, kept him well and healthy, then had second thoughts and returned him. Jamie was not in trouble, but he was not the public hero either. Without being told, he understood this was to be kept quiet. He'd saved this child's life, and this was good, but it was a secret. For his own sake. No police interviews.

Mhairi stared at him and drank her tea. She wore a dressing-gown that had stains on it and her hair hung greasy over her shoulders. She shook out some pills from a bottle and swigged them down.

Is it time for those? asked the fat man.

Aye, last night's have worn off, I'm needing these, said the girl.

Where was he? she asked himself.

Under the tree. By the loch.

What did you do with him?

Nothing, he said defensively, thinking she was accusing him. I took him inside and fed him. Built a fire and kept him warm. He's alright, ken. Look at him. I didna do anythin wrong. I didna ken he was your baby.

She didn't respond, hardened the line of her mouth and looked at the wall.

How did ye forget him? he asked her.

I just did, right?

But he's only wee, ken.

Aye, well. What do you know.

Me, nae much. Nothin probably.

The fat man finished feeding Patrick, and came to the table to sit. Kate says you're called Jamie. My name's Murdo, and that's Murdo as well. He struck out his hand formally. Jamie stared at it, then shook it with his own hand, which he wished was cleaner until he saw the state of Murdo's hand.

Excellent job you did with this baby, he's in fine fettle. What are you doing out this way anyway? Where do you come from?

Jamie took a moment, people didn't normally talk to him like he was regular person. This man must be a little strange, or maybe something had happened to himself, and he was now one of them. A spell had lifted.

Frae Aberdeen.

Whereabouts?

Oh, all over. Then, sitting straighter – I'm a travellin man, actually.

Are you now? Well, that's a life I envy. If I was younger, I'd cut loose myself.

Patrick snored gently, tucked into Murdo's arms, while wee Murdo swished the dishes in the sink. Kate's voice drifted through from the hall, relaxed and happy.

What are your plans now? asked Murdo. Home for a spell, or carrying on up north? Do you have to be back for the college term next week?

Mhairi sat up straighter, tossed her hair back, sighed with impatience, as if to say – Can't you see this boy is no stylishly poor student?

Jamie instantly knew her thoughts because he had them himself, knew he hadn't changed, he was just different in this man's eyes. The girl knew who he was. She was the type who avoided eye-contact with his type, just quickened their pace when passing by. Nose up in the air. Her lot called his lot tinks.

Aye, he said to spite her. Another two days' campin, then back tae the old books.

Campin, he thought – that was a good name for it.

What are you studying, then? she challenged.

Environmental science.

Where?

The uni. Robert Gordon. He had no idea if such a course existed, but the words were popping out as if they'd been hiding in his mouth since some overheard conversation, biding their time till their use was required. Like the shiny treasures.

Then her pills kicked in. Lies were good. Tinks were adorable.

Good college, I heard.

Kate decided to swallow the student camping story, it did no harm, and he was young enough to bring out her maternal instincts. She insisted he spend the night on their sofa. It was the closest he'd come to conventional sleeping arrangements in about a year, and it was too good to waste in sleep. He made himself look at the wall, the pictures, the dying fire, the magazines, he tried viewing himself in the mirror with the room behind him, and imagined how he would look to someone else looking. Someone alone in the dark outside the window, looking in. Eventually fell asleep near dawn.

You take that poor boy this cup of tea, Mhairi, and you thank him, Kate insisted in the morning, as if Mhairi were a five-year-old who needed reminding about her manners.

Sure, Mum. Why not? she thought. Who cared? Everything was so easy now, with the wonder drug swimming in her blood. She floated through to the sitting room, oozing tenderness. She put it on the floor beside Jamie, who woke instantly. I take it you take sugar?

Oh aye, now and then, lifting the sweet strong tea to his lips.

Look, she said. Thanks. For looking after my baby.

But he wasna any bother, he's a grand wee man. Is he really yours, then?

Yes, the baby's mine. But. But. Listen, I know you aren't a student. I don't know how you live. I can't imagine. Don't you have any parents? Or friends with places to stay?

Oh, definitely. Loads of friends with big houses. And my parents, I've got at least a half-dozen of those, and they love me tae death, so they do. I just prefer livin rough, ken. It's mair fun.

Sorry. I should be back in the loony bin. That's where I've been on and off since. You know. I have to go back tomorrow, they only let me out for wee visits home.

How?

I tried to kill him. Patrick.

Fit? You never.

I did. I wanted him to die. I am a terrible person, Jamie. If Jamie is your name.

Aye. It is.

Just everything else was a lie?

He shrugged. Drank more tea.

Look, Jamie. Tell you what. I'll give you my address and phone number in Inverness. I might not be there, mind. Probably still be in the Craig, I am a fucking loony, I am, really. She giggled, ending on a high note, which brought her mother from the kitchen with a disapproving frown.

Later, Kate drove Jamie to Achnasheen to catch the train. Patrick was strapped in the back in a car seat that intrigued Jamie with its bulky frame. It appealed to him in a way — the structure moulded for comfort and protection. The immobility of just riding in it. He stroked Patrick on the cheek, envying him.

Kate let him out at the station, gave him a packet of sandwiches and crisps, but it wasn't till Garve that he reached in his pocket for a tissue and found the ten crisp twenties. Quickly he hid them in his sock, glanced around to see if they'd been spotted. Stretched, fidgeted, then went to the toilet to lock himself in and examine the money.

Counted them and congratulated himself. Wasn't he just the cleverest man alive? But back in his seat, staring out the window, he did not feel clever. His chest and throat began to ache, and his eyes felt sore. He missed his wee mannie, knew it and could think of no cure for it.

Kate and Patrick
Four Months Later

Her peace was hard won and consciously maintained. She avoided thinking about Mhairi. Buried the meeting with the children's panel; just ordinary people sitting around a table in an ordinary room, yet somehow more humiliating, more intimidating than the court room and sheriff scene she had to witness later. Hearing the word *section*, in connection with her own daughter. It felt vicious. And the visits to the psychiatric hospital, seeing Mhairi pale and vacant-eyed under the sheets. Or worse, seeing her in the day room, dressed like a middle-aged woman in a beige cardigan the old Mhairi would've scorned, doing mindless crafts like paint by number. Mhairi had sat in that room full of suspended lives and greeted her mother like a stranger.

Hello, Mother. How are you today? What is the weather like?

Not Mhairi. Where was Mhairi? But she had to respond, say the words back. It was like a game. You pretend you are someone else, and I will be someone else too.

Hello, dear. I'm fine, everything is fine. It's starting to rain now, but it was sunny when I left the house. Happy birthday, darling.

Oh, yes, so it is. Look what the nurses gave me (indicating a box of chocolates).

Oh, lovely. I brought you these. From me and your granny.

Thank you. Just put them on the table, I'll open them later, shall I? It'll give me something to do.

(The ultimate contrast and proof the old Mhairi was gone – from greedy and impatient to cool and detached. Oh, that alien maturity hurt more than anything else, worse than the paint-by-number sunsets.)

Any news, Mother?

Oh, well, let me see (gathering herself for normal speech), Patrick is doing well. Slept through the night last night, first time in——

Look at my picture, interrupted Mhairi, holding up a watercolour of another sunset on a sea. Look. The vacant expression gone, a cunning, desperately defiant look instead.

Oh, my, that is lovely, Mhairi. Will we get it framed?

Of course Patrick was still the apple of Kate's eye, but he was exhausting and she resented him sometimes as she had her own daughter – the feeling that she was sinking in a morass of unwashed Babygros, unfinished chores, unfinished thoughts. Bad enough when you were young and it was your own baby, bad enough to be forty-two even without a baby – but to be forty-two and have to mother your grandson, well. Once the bliss of recovering Patrick had worn off, she felt entitled to a few moans. The Murdos were the only ones who let her moan without trying to cheer her up.

This is totally fucked, Murdo.

That's right, Kate. There's no denying it, he hasn't stopped whingeing for an hour. Would drive me round the fucking bend.

Oh, shit, now what?

Never mind, Kate, it's only the bulb. The lamp seems to be fine. Sit down, I'll put the kettle on.

Never mind the kettle, Murdo, where's the bloody bottle?

There, on the table.

Not the milk bottle, idiot!

Unlike Margaret, who always made things worse, somehow.

Oh dear, Kate, what a noise that child's making. Are you sure you're winding him properly?

I don't know, Mum. He always just falls asleep after his bottle, how am I supposed to wind him? Wake him up?

Of course, dear, mustn't let him sleep with a bubble in his belly.

What? I can't hear you.

I said, you have to wind him anyway, shouted Margaret above Patrick's din.

Maybe he's hungry, I'll try feeding him.

What's that?

I said, maybe he's hungry! I'll get his bottle!

Try feeding him some food, Kate, he's maybe just needing some real food. Give him some of this soup.

It'll go right through him, Mum, he's too young.

Nonsense, a good bowl of pea soup is just what that child needs. Bring him over here.

What? Oh, no. Shit.

No need for language, Kate. Did all that vomit come out of him? Doesn't seem possible. My goodness, Kate, you're covered with it, go take your clothes off. Give me Patrick. There there, little tiddums, come to Nanny-noo-noo. He is a sweet little thing, Kate. Smashing. Not one thing wrong with this lad, nosiree. He's perfect, an easier baby doesn't exist, does it little Doodly Dumpkins?

Right, Mum. (Jesus, is that what I looked like to Mhairi when I held Paddy? She is *drooling* over that child. It *is* true about mothers and daughters. How depressing.)

Then, late October, Mhairi had decided enough was enough. Within a week, she resumed her old self, as if it had been hanging up on the door hook all this time, waiting for her to slip it on. She moved in her old way, graceful, unselfconscious. Her eyes shone with intelligence again, and good nature. She chose her clothes with care, looked pretty, asked for expensive shampoos and conditioners.

Daily visits with the psychiatrist trailed off to weekly, her prescription was not renewed. She was discharged from hospital and encouraged to continue her education. Kate, relieved but wary, found her a room in her old student flat. Her room mates, three other girls, were briefed.

Will I bring Paddy around next week? asked Kate, unloading some shopping in Mhairi's kitchen. Said it casually, looking in cupboards.

Maybe not yet, Mum. Oh, bring him if you want, I don't care. How is the wee man doing, anyway?

And that's how it began, Mhairi inhabiting her old life with only a vague recollection of the summer, but the stirrings of curiosity. The ebbing of fear.

Great, he's doing just great. Wait till you see his size.

I can imagine, with the way you like to feed people, he'll probably be a fatty. (But no overtones of jealousy, no wish for ownership. Curiosity only.) It's a miracle I outgrew my puppy fat. Did you bring any socks? I'm down to three pairs, Mum, I told you. (The familiar whine. Comforting.)

So for another few months, Patrick was Kate's, and readers of the *West Coaster* got to know him better than maybe they'd wished.

WEST COAST CRACK

Joe has lately become Joey and his hair is no longer red, but strawberry blond. His eyes are lighter blue, and his fat has burned away with his limbs constantly moving, muscles arching, stretching, reaching. There is a message in Joey's brain that begins the minute he wakes. It says, Go.

I barricade him in the sitting room with sofa cushions and chairs. He ricochets off forbidden surfaces, the Rayburn and radiators, and generally performs like a demented toy whose batteries are of the long-life variety.

I might make my Christmas cake this week. I usually make it in November, but I was too busy to make it then, and unlike my younger self, I do not feel tied to the proper sequence of rituals.

I let the days fall into whatever pattern they choose. I live with a baby. I do not fight gravity any more, but give in to it with great abandon. The minute I feel tired, I flop into the nearest chair and grab a book, any book. Cups of tea drunk while hot are a thing of the past and my house has reverted to a place of sticky surfaces. I remember this, and I know it passes. So it is not as bad this time around.

It is odd, mothering yet not being the mother. Is this how foster-mothers feel? It is very unlikely this child will spend all its childhood looking on me as his mother. He has a mother, my daughter Annie, and she will one day reclaim him. It is probable I will have little warning, it might be next month, it might be in four years, but I will have to gracefully relinquish him the minute his mother wants to be his mother. Nothing else will do. The transition, for his sake, must run smooth, seamless, from the love of one woman to the love of another. There will be aspects to rejoice about in this – less mess, less laundry, less expense, less noise, more sleep, more spaces of time with no interruptions. And yet, I foresee a heart-clenching hour or two, watching his face light on his mother's, not mine. Finding the odd sock under cushions, the odd toast crust under rugs. Ah, woe will be me. (And woe to you, who might have to read about it!)

We are still gripped by winter. The landscape is motionless, but I sense a trembling underneath, and a turn of the season, soon, all too soon . . .

Lambs will be on the road, oblivious to the dangers of drivers seeing through rain-lashed windows. Their mothers will seem indifferent, wander at will, expect the lambs to keep up, to remember which sodden heap of wool on legs is their unique mother. Snowdrops will push up in the garden, likewise oblivious to the future dangers of gales and frost. Either the trust of new things is poignant, or sleep deprivation has made me philosophical about inanities. I leave it to you, readers, to judge.

I am too old to be mothering again, but too young to deny it is a joy.

Jamie

He is always forgetting this. It is so important, so all-enveloping when it happens, but he never remembers. So bloody fucking irritating, this getting-sick business. As soon as he is well, he forgets there is such a thing as a sore head, a running nose, a hacking cough. He goes about in the rain getting soaked, he sleeps next to, inches from, some old geezer sputtering and sneezing right in his face, then wham, here he is again, fucked. He hits his own forehead, which is pounding, hating himself, hating his sickness, this cold which will now ruin his week, maybe month. Days and days of wanting to curl up and sleep somewhere warm and dry and leaving things behind on benches because he can't think and feels groggy.

He needs to blow his nose and has nothing to blow it on. It is filling, gravity is drawing it all out, and he wants it out, foul green stuff, but all he has are his clothes, and it's bloody raining again, so even these are soggy already. He stands up, holds still until he feels balanced, then ducks into an alley where he leans over, firmly presses one finger against one nostril and blows hard. A river of snot pours out. He clears the other nostril, but not quickly enough. A McDonald's employee, a young girl, has come round the alley to dump the rubbish and she jumps.

Shite! she shouts.

But it happens that she is not a shy one, no, she comes from large boisterous family and she is hard. Oh! You are so disgusting, do you know that? You're worse than an animal. Her lip curls and she makes as if to vomit. *Fuck off out of here, ya tink, or I'll call the polis.* Then she spits at him.

He does not need this. And he thought he'd already hit bottom. This is so fucked. Now he cannot remember what health feels like. He has always been ill, weak, despised, fit for nothing but the saliva of seventeen-year-old girls.

Kate Gets an Exciting Phone Call

Christmas was a beast storming through rigorously manned defences. Impossible for Kate to pretend the season had no emotional effect on her. Expectations rose and were dashed, despite the dashing being so predictable.

It was spent eating dinner with her mother and Mhairi at the Castle Hotel in Inverness, as Mhairi had sworn she could not come home, too many parties to go to. Patrick slept through it all, in his car seat on the floor. Mhairi glanced at him and politely admired his new clothes, did not pick him up, but gently stroked one cheek without visibly flinching. An improvement.

And then the bare minimum of ritual observed – the crackers pulled, the forgettable jokes about fish and ice lollies laughed at, the requisite amount of dry meat wasted, the presents (receipts attached) exchanged, and it was thankfully over. They all went to their own beds in their own houses, on their own coasts.

Margaret blamed it on the lack of men. Sipping her cocoa in bed in her silent house, with the wind doing its sad, haunting songs, she wondered why women bored each other to tears on occasions of social importance. The presence of men would have forced them to make more of an effort. To pretend it was not the worst Christmas Day ever. For even one man, they might've sparkled.

Was it not time one of them got a man?

Kate was in the kitchen finally icing the Christmas cake, and wondering if she could get away with calling it a millennium cake should anyone call around, heaven forbid. The phone rang. She checked on Patrick in the sitting room first, then answered it. Mhairi.

How's your classes going? Don't worry, you can always resit them in the spring. That's right. Oh, he's fine, just bouncing around the sitting room. Did you get to your last appointment? That's good. Yes, he phoned me when you didn't turn up last time. Yes, I know, I told him you'd probably just forgotten. Yes, well, you can ask for another one if you want, dear. Maybe you're right, maybe a woman therapist would be better. I don't know, Mhairi. You'll have to ask. Yes, I know. How much? What happened to the cheque I sent last week? On what?

And so on. As usual, she did not ask when her daughter was coming home to visit. She hung up the phone, dusted some flour off her long grey checked skirt. Picked up her wooden spoon. Patrick was head-butting a Paisley cushion and when it eventually tumbled on top of him, he hollered. Kate smiled, knowing exactly what had happened by the sound of his muffled cry. She went in the sitting room and scooped him up, kissed the top of his head. When he stopped whimpering, she tipped him backwards and kissed the spot under his chin. Nibbled him till he laughed.

The phone rang again, and this time she kept Patrick with

her, gave him her key-ring while she cradled the receiver under her chin.

Kate, it's me, Michael. He huddled in an open phone box, the freezing wind at his back.

Michael! Where are you?

Patrick stopped drooling at the sharp sound of her voice, then resumed gnawing on the door keys. Metal on gums, teeth millimetres beneath the skin aching to get a grip.

I'm here. In Inverness.

You're never.

Well, I am, actually. How are you? How are Mhairi and Patrick?

Oh, well, they're just, well, fine. Listen, are you coming out to see us?

I could come tomorrow evening. Do you want me to?

Nah, I was just being polite.

Thought so.

Patrick dropped the keys, she let him down to get them. Hung up the phone then stood there staring at it till she heard the splash that meant Patrick had found the dog's water bowl.

Jamie

He sits on the milk crate and leans against the corrugated iron of the shed.
A navy knitted cap that he'd found nesting in a cardboard box is pulled
over his head, which is bowed on to his hands. He has a temperature, his
head feels too heavy for his neck. Traffic sounds are muffled and his throat
sends a continual message of pain to a brain that has turned off its receptors.
His eyes are shut. No one is home. Home is shivering.

At the end of the close is a busy road and purposeful footfalls of vertical
beings pound by, occasionally preceded by a pram or trailing a shopping trolley.
Earlier he'd watched them, mesmerised. He is invisible and feels alright about
staring. It is as good as telly. Old ladies, fat track-suited men, squealing
babies with rubber dummies just out of reach. A baby kicked off his bootee,
powder-blue corduroy, and the mother did not notice, just strode on, smoking
furiously. Jamie had paused, then detached himself from the crate, lost his
balance, regained it, and fetched the bootee, instinctively bringing it to his face.
It smelt of fabric conditioner, but Jamie just thought it smelt clean, that this
was what normality and care smelt like. Comfort Spring Fresh Conditioner.
He trotted dizzily after the mother, and made noises.

Your bababababababy's lost his shoe, wait!

The fever made the world a different place — his vision narrowed and
wavered, so that wherever he looked, for instance at the retreating back of the
mother, he perceived a new cocoon of surreal space. The pavement undulated

under his feet, and his own voice came back to him from a distance, with a slight echo.

She glanced over her shoulder at him and just pushed the pram faster.

Now the bootee rests in his coat pocket and he has switched off and is not at home. He is deep inside, upstairs in the tent, where it is always dim, and sometimes dreams come, but mostly emptiness and absence of pain. (Meanwhile, viral cells have their hey-day — this boy has zero resistance, let's go to town, they yip.)

Despite appearances, he is not asleep. If he was, he'd fall over sideways like he does sometimes when genuine sleep overtakes him.

Later, the air changes and he stirs. Sniffs and stretches, obeying his limbs and organs, which do not wish to freeze to death before pneumonia gets a real chance. The air is warmer, and this has the ironic result of snowflakes appearing. Soft, fluffy, lacy, light, and for a minute he smiles, as charmed by them as he'd been as a child. Magic of snow, transforming everything. Dirty to clean, from cluttered and chaotic to smooth and white. One flake attaches itself to his lashes and he blinks it away, then coughs. Fuck this, he says. Snow means slush and sickness, feet and fingers like ice cubes. Frostbit nose.

Jamie organises himself. Very slowly, teetering this way and that. Sneezes, shivers, sweats. Finds his bag under the crate, straightens his cap, ties a shoelace. He stands up and begins to move off towards the town centre, drives his body to a kinder environment. The train station. Now that's a place. He'll know what to do when he gets there.

Patrick Is Sad

Patrick was having a bad day.

He sat in his push-chair facing the sea, Kate behind him somewhere, a hovering shadow, absorbed with the imminence of Michael. They could go no further, and the lack of motion was setting up a series of increasingly loud messages inside his mind.

Cry, cry, get ready to cry. Cry until motion resumed.

He stretched his neck, his arms and legs, inhaled deeply, braced himself, and began the faint wailing. Kate responded by rocking the push-chair back and forth on the rough track.

Not good enough. Real motion, changing scenery and physical vibrations required.

The faint wailing rose to a crescendo of screams.

Kate's rocking of the push-chair became almost violent, but still the view remained the same.

Right, no other option. The full whammy, then. His body went stiff as a board. He held his breath and turned bright red, all a prelude to the dreaded siren scream, the granddaddy of all screams. Nothing would do but movement. His stomach was full, his nappy was dry, he was warm, not alone, but none of these did the trick on days like this. He wanted out of his skin, he was in agony with the pain and unfairness of it. He was claustrophobic. Go go go go. Just go, move this thing, go now.

He was trapped in his body, and no matter how many times a day Kate cuddled him, rocked him, fed him, he couldn't get out. She couldn't help him.

Why? Why? His brain was so full of blood pounding, his ears so full of his own noise, he lost sight of what he was aching for; the concept itself of freedom and lost abilities swirled and drowned in all his aching sorrow.

He forgot what he was missing. Only knew he was miserable and exhausted.

Kate yanked the push-chair back up the track yet again, exasperated. Told herself he'd be back to his normal easy self soon, this would pass. He'd sleep well tonight. Maybe he'd have the same pattern tomorrow. Restless day, solid night's sleep. Giving her some time with Michael. Michael! Unless he fell asleep in the car when she went to fetch Michael off the bus, then woke thinking it was morning. The thought depressed her. Patrick's cries eased up a little as they jolted along, and soon he was hiccuping and trembling all over after each hiccup. Dog slunk behind, ignored and bored.

Jamie

He's watching the trains, stamping the snow off his shoes, up and down to keep the circulation going. It hurts to breathe and he doesn't know what day of the week it is. He vaguely wonders what his two pounds ten pence can get him in the way of fuel for his body and possible shelter, and if he can combine the two, as he did last summer on his holidays out west. But, of course, he'd had more money then. He can't recall exactly why he had more money then, but he gets a rosy glow recalling the actual trip.

Proud. He'd felt proud of being able to take care of himself, enter the unknown world of Wester Ross, find shelter, feed himself. Make a home of an old ruin. Taste the feel of four walls and roof that belonged, at least temporarily, to him alone. His castle. The relief. Then the baby, almost the receptacle of a night-time pee, thank God he'd needed to go. What if he'd had a stronger bladder? Poor baby would've been blue by morning. No, that was one fortunate bairn, and one day he'd walk up to him, tap him on the shoulder, and introduce himself. Hello, I am your saviour. Without me and my wanderings and midnight bladder emptyings, you would've stopped long ago. A few months of life, and that would've been you, mate. Kaput. Shake his hand, and not ask for anything in return, refuse all offers of reward, just wander off. The noble loner. The sunset.

Odd, how the fever brings these lucid visions, and memories too. He is not very tied to his body, and there she is …

✳   ✳   ✳

That strange lovely grey-haired lady. On top of every recollection of Patrick came the face and especially the eyes of the
lady. Skelly-eyed. One eye off to get the messages, the other
looking for the money, someone used to say. (A mother? His
own mother? But, then, who had she been talking about?)

The nice lady who took his baby. Thin, sharp-boned, but
soft somehow. Dark eyes, terrible grey marks under them, like
she slept rough too. She hadn't grabbed. Just talked, then asked
if she could hold his baby: Can I hold your baby please?

Very respectful of her to admit it was his baby. And then
she'd held the baby across her chest and rocked back and forth
and begun crying. Not with any noise, just the tears washing
over the baby's head. Patrick, she'd called the baby, and he'd
known. Of course.

How is his name Patrick?

She'd smiled through her tears, looked like she was going to
hug himself as well. Oh, he is a Patrick, do you not think so?
Look at him, does he not look like a Patrick to you?

She held the baby around so he could see his face and, sure
enough, the lady had cast a spell, and the baby was very obviously
a Patrick, could be no other.

How did ye do that? How did ye ken?

Oh, I guess . . . (She still smiled.) Aren't names funny? I didn't
know until he was Patrick, and then I immediately thought he'd
always been Patrick, right from the very beginning, it was like
meeting someone I'd already met a while ago. And who else
would he look like anyway? Names are strange, as soon as someone gets a name, that's who they are, don't you think? I mean,
can you imagine having any other name? What is your name?

Jamie.

Well, Jamie, I don't know any other Jamies, so now every time I hear that name, I'll think of you, the name will mean you and feel like you in this cottage with this baby. Jamie. I like it, it's a nice name. And you've taken such good care of this baby. I am so grateful to you. Amazed, really. After all, not many men could do it.

Whit's your name?

Kate.

Kate. Kate. (Too short, in his opinion, he wanted to call her Katie.)

My name's quite common. Now, Jamie, can I tell you a story? It's a secret story. Can I tell you? I have a daughter and she did a dreadful thing. She is not herself, she is not well, and she did a really terrible thing, so you're not to tell anyone. Have you ever done a terrible thing, something you didn't mean to do, but did anyway? We all have, really.

How did she know about the fire?

That was months ago, September. Commuters stream around his frozen body. As an object, he is only slightly inconvenient, like a postbox or bin. He is in a cloud of sickness, while watching the trains and wondering how to become one of those people who have destinations.

The Inverness train comes in. The piece of paper with the Inverness address, in his pocket, soft and worn.

He watches a young woman struggle with her pram. Puts his bag down, and encouraged by her distracted air of gratitude, helps her lift the pram up the steps into the carriage. It is crowded, and he finds himself shuffling along into the aisle. Inverness has such good associations, he doesn't mind, wants to be among Inverness-bound people for a few seconds. They might even assume he is one of them. He sways, feverish and dizzy, then before he can negotiate his way back off the train, the doors slide to and close.

The train begins its pre-departure vibration, its hum, and a fact tries to storm through Jamie's muffled brain, succeeds when his eyes alight on his safety-pinned holdall sitting on the wet platform. His holdall, holding all his clothes, food, shiny treasures, his world. For a confused second, he has a vision of Kate's car, with Patrick's head just visible, driving away from Achnasheen, himself standing alone and bereft. Paddy's eyes and forehead and hair sliding away, away, just a speck, then gone.

And underneath, always running like a determined current, ignored but always there, is the echo of all the doors closing to him, and locking. Thud, click.

I'm sorry. Sweat now pouring off him, he shoves his way to the door. I have tae get off, have tae get off quick, excuse me. Tries to open the doors, no luck. They are electric, no handles. The train begins to move out of the station and he panics, pounds on the door and shouts to a man who is standing on the platform, waving to a woman in the train.

Tell the driver tae stop!

The man just shrugs and mimes his frustration.

Jamie, wondering if this is a nightmare and he is still on the crate in the alley, shouts hoarsely, For Christ's sake, tell the fuckin driver tae stop the train, will ye? I need tae get off!

The man slides out of view, and Jamie hears his own loud voice in the quiet compartment. He looks at the sea of stiff, affronted faces. Heart pounding, he turns to the passenger nearest him, a bearded spectacled man, and says, I'm sorry I shouted in your ear, ken, it's just . . .

I'm sorry you took the name of the Lord in vain.

Whit?

Jamie is in danger of fainting. The worst thing imaginable has just happened. He is lopsided, deformed, grotesquely unbalanced. He backs into the carriage and sits down. The bearded man follows him, a maniacal gleam in his eyes. Jamie looks out of the window at Aberdeen rushing past, hoping he'll wake up soon, with his bag in his hand.

The Lord is your shepherd, you must be careful how you speak of him.

Jamie turns his sore and heavy head. The bearded man is sitting right next to him. The words enter, revolve slowly, make sense. Then something occurs to him and he finds, to his amazement, words coming out of his own mouth: I didna tak the name of the Lord in vain. I said fuckin.

Ah, but you said Christ's sake first.

No I didna.

Did, I'm afraid. The bearded man smiles gently.

Did I? Suppose I did, I canna mind. Is that a swear?

My son, it was so automatic, you did not hear it but the Lord heard it. The Lord hears everything. Every cry, every prayer.

No way.

Yes way. The Lord loves you. Did you know that?

Jamie, with great effort, turns his head away and looks out of the window again. Houses rush past, streets shrink and disappear.

Oh, yes, son, you belong to the Lord whether you know it or not. Lost sheep are his speciality.

Something happens to Jamie's eyes, and he has to shut them for a while, they are burning. The bearded man's sermon turns into a lullaby.

When the ticket collector comes for tickets and Jamie is jostled awake, the bearded man reaches into his pocket and takes out a wallet. Miracle! He offers him a ticket to Inverness and — double miracle — a place to stay there.

When Jamie blurts out his tragedy, bearded man tells the conductor, who radios back to Aberdeen. The bag is retrieved, not having ever been in real danger of theft. Who would've wanted to touch such an unsavoury-looking item? It would've sat in the lost luggage unclaimed for six weeks and ended up in St Bart's charity shop, where some wifey, lip curling, would have *thrown the lot — shiny treasures and all — into a big black bin.*

Jamie wonders if he will end up in the bearded man's church, on his knees. What is the man's name? Of course, and this is the funny thing, it is the same name as his own, only he calls himself James, which has a totally different feel to it, just as that lady, the bairn's granny said. Names are strange things indeed. Now he could never be a James, not in a million years. But James is a good person to know, if he doesn't expect much in return.

He lives alone in a bare council house; boxes of Tesco value corn flakes on the mantle, toothbrush in a mug over the kitchen sink, no woman's touch. He gives Jamie an old Scouts sleeping-bag for the lumpy sofa. In the morning, Jamie has a bath with all the works, including a shave and haircut and a liberal splash of Lynx. James fries a good breakfast. Then gives Jamie a five-pound note and directions into town, to have a look-see, the idea being he might spend a little time here.

God works in mysterious ways, he tells Jamie, gripping his hand tight. Don't worry about your bag, I've got all you need here, come back when you want.

Jamie gets lost several times, but eventually finds the roads winding down to the pedestrian precinct. Finds a concrete bench to sit on.

Church with James might be nice. Coloured light filtering through, a choir singing 'Amazing Grace', the notes lifting high into the air, floating up to the dome where white doves might sail slowly around and around.

He gives himself a little shake, the doves turn into snowflakes. Stands up, but quickly sits down again. Dizzy. And he begins to cough a cough that rips membranes and strains muscles and makes his eyes water.

He yearns for his bag, his piece of property, his treasures. Its absence is like a limb torn out.

Michael and Kate Act Like Idiots

Sex, or love, or whatever is a combination of these and eludes vocabulary, might make eyes shine and skin glow and hearts beat, but its overwhelming feature is its ability to bring on stupidity. This was Kate's first thought when she saw Michael on the eight o'clock bus; she could feel her brain shrink, could hear it fade away. See you later, it called from a distance.

He hadn't seen her yet, so she got a good look. And it did her no good. Her body remembered too well the last time, so annoying when she'd done her best just to forget it. A little episode that was such a minor blip compared to the dramas Patrick's life had unleashed. Chemical changes took place in her body, even before he got off the bus. Her blood pressure rose, her facial muscles tensed, pupils dilated. Her posture straightened and she breathed rapid shallow breaths. Years fell off and a stupid grin emerged, even as she despised it. High as a kite, she would only get by through mimicking sobriety, now. Not give him the satisfaction of thinking his presence had wrought the change. Not that he could see much anyway, it was pitch dark but for the headlights. Hey, Kate, you look great. He threw one burly arm around her, the other holding a bag.

And more blushing, more eye sparkling, despite the fresh

awareness of the flat tones of his accent. This would never do.

Michael seemed the same, but because she'd known him for only a week, six months ago, it was hard to tell. He smelt the same, clean and cottony.

Michael, who thought she looked older, repeated, Honestly you do, you look great.

Well, that's a change, then. Get your bag, I've left Paddy asleep in the car.

Who? This is my bag.

You travel light. Paddy. You know. Mhairi's son.

Ah, Patrick.

They got into the car and quietly drove to the cottage. Michael did not recognise Paddy. Patrick the fairy infant had departed completely, leaving a robust round-cheeked thug in his place. He snored softly.

Kate told Michael to leave his bag in the sitting room, thought that was a good neutral place for the bag of a man when you were not sure where he was going to sleep. It gave nothing away, anyway.

Are you just going to leave Paddy in the car?

Ach, he'll be alright a wee while, till I put the kettle on anyway. He'll waken when I bring him in, and we won't get much peace then I can tell you.

But it's freezing. He'll be blue.

Not likely. He's tons of layers on, plus his own layer of fat. She took off her jacket and switched the kettle on. Go sit by the fire, Michael, in fact, throw some coal at it.

He sat, then stood. I'll get him, you sit.

Kate opened her mouth to protest, then closed it and sank into an armchair, punctured, undone.

An American is here, she wrote her column in her head, and I am adding to my knowledge of their race. They are bossy. They always do what they want, often impulsively. When they think they are right, they don't listen to anyone. They do it with a smile and with good manners, but with total resolve and righteousness. That's why they are always having little wars, and sometimes big ones. That's why a guest in my house sets me right about my own grandson.

After he'd settled a wakened Patrick on Kate's lap, he watched her feed him a bottle. Thought: She barely remembers who I am. No good memories, anyway. I just imagined the whole thing. We are strangers. Coming was a mistake.

Since she was baby-bound, he switched on some lamps, checked the fire, made cups of tea. Whistling all the while, as if he was at ease.

You're happy, she said, but as if that was bad thing to be.

Ah, well, why not? I'm glad to be here.

How long are you staying, if I can ask?

Not long, I'll head back tomorrow. There's a bus taking shoppers to some Dingwall supermarket, about noon. Apparently I can sneak on.

Oh. When is your flight? You came here for two days?

No, I'm here for a week. Just to sort out Isabel's things. She's coming back with me.

Isabel? (Not me, not me. Fool!)

Brendan's girlfriend in Inverness.

I remember her. Why does she need help?

Brendan can't help her, and I guess I'm a soft dad.

Why can't Brendan?

You didn't hear? How could you not know? He got deported. Mhairi blew the whole deal, told her shrink, told the immigration, everyone. Brendan's back in California and I'm helping Isabel join him. She's given up her flat.

Patrick pulled away from his bottle with his usual loud pop. He looked over at Michael, his blue eyes wide and curious. His full stomach signalled sleep again, but with his last seconds of alertness, he concentrated on this newcomer with a deep voice. Michael stared back, did not make a silly face or baby voice. Gave him a man-to-man look, then smiled. Nightie-night, fella, he said softly.

Patrick's eyelids dropped as if Michael had hypnotised him. His cheeks fat and rosy from sucking and his limbs flopped out, Kate's own face changed watching him. This was her true love, love with no ambiguity, no grey areas or caution. She curled him into her chest and leant back and sighed. I didn't know any of this, Michael. Mhairi, well ...

I know about it, Kate. Brendan told me. I know about her getting the post-partum blues, or whatever. It happens. But what a nightmare for you, and so lucky this little guy was found and returned. I can't imagine. I kept wanting to phone you, see if he'd been found.

Why didn't you?

I don't know. Brendan was phoning almost daily by that point, so I knew I'd hear the news from him anyway. But I thought about you continually.

Did you?

I even dialled the number a few times, but no one answered and I kind of gave up.

You wrote once.

And you wrote back once.

That was something.

I wish I'd phoned again, till I got you. (Looking around at the unchanged room, smelling the coal fire and dog hair.) I've missed this, Kate.

She smiled, despite herself. Is it being here that made you say that? You sound surprised, as if you didn't know you had till this second.

Maybe.

And now you have to go back tomorrow?

That's right. (She looks relieved, I'm sure she looks relieved.) Things to do. Escorting my future daughter-in-law.

And why does she need you again? She always struck me as an independent young woman.

Ah, well, you think you know someone. Look at Mhairi, what a shock she must've given you. How is she now, anyway?

The funny thing is, she's very well indeed. I can't believe it, but she's doing fine, phones every week, not that she tells me much. She gets good grades, she's seeing a boy called Gerald now, he's on the electrician's course near her.

Good, that's good. Brendan didn't say much, of course, he doesn't know much, not being here any more.

How is he? Does he miss Scotland?

Talks of nothing else, but I expect he'll get over it. He was starting to mention Canada a few weeks ago. Though if he marries Isabel, he won't be able to marry a Canadian girl for citizenship. He'll be bit more limited. I should've answered your postcard, Kate. I should've written you a proper letter.

Well, never mind.

And suddenly she was tired and empty. There was no infatuation to hide. Were her feelings really so fickle that they could come and go without a trace? Was middle age just another phase of adolescence? It was somehow humiliating to have the mood swings without the consolation of an unlined face and firm flesh.

I'm taking this wee man off to bed, Michael. While his sleep is deep. She levered herself slowly out of the chair, keeping Patrick steady.

What are the nights like?

She looked up sharply, then realised his meaning. All right some nights, horrendous others. He was up three times last night. Hellish. I just took him in with me.

Best way. Marcia should've done that with our lot. She used to let them scream, till the whole house would wake up, then she'd walk the floors.

Ah, well, maybe grannies are lazier.

I'd hardly call you lazy, Kate.

Why not?

And I wish you'd stop calling yourself granny.

But I am.

You're hardly the typical gran, Kate. You could easily be taken for Paddy's mother.

Well, that's sweet to say, but nonsense.

It isn't nonsense. Any word from the dad, what was his name – Roddy?

Nothing. I doubt we'll hear from him now. It doesn't matter, it's his loss, not ours. Paddy belongs to us.

Does Mhairi show any interest in him yet?

A little. But I'm sure she'll come round. He's such a gorgeous boy, she's bound to fall in love with him eventually. Maybe she was like those cats who give birth at six months, and just drop their kittens anywhere, totally uninterested. Just kittens themselves still, not ready yet. Absentmindedly she kissed the top of Patrick's furry head.

Michael didn't reply, just tilted his head and frowned to see her lips nuzzling.

I'll be right back, Michael. There's some soup on the Rayburn if you want to help yourself.

She climbed the stairs slowly, lowered Patrick an inch a minute into his cot, held her breath, willed him to carry on dreaming. Backed softly out of the bedroom, breath still held. Tripped over Dog, who had followed her up, fell against the door. Patrick, with a one-second preamble while he took in enough breath, launched into his air-raid-siren scream.

Oh, fuck.

Everything alright up there?

Fine, Michael. But I'll need to settle him now.

Picked him up, lay on her bed with him, curled her body around his, covered them both with the feather quilt. Hoped the heat would send him off again. He stopped wailing, snuggled in. When his breathing seemed the slow sleeping kind, she inched away from him, slowly, slowly, but his desertion radar was alerted and he went into instant panic again. Kate considered bringing him downstairs. Considered and considered how she would entertain his tired demanding little brain and at the same time have a conversation with a stranger she'd once been intimate with. He was so big, she'd forgotten that bit, he was so tall and broad, she wondered if there was enough soup and bread and then and then and then.

She fell asleep.

Patrick lay somewhere on the border of sleep and wakefulness. His little being, tired of beating against the restraints of his body, tried weakly to settle. To adjust to who he had become. To surrender.

Luckily the distractions of life around and in him – the breathing of Kate, the wind against the window; the sensation of his milk being digested, the feel of the quilt and the warmth of Kate's body – all these combined to soothe him. He lowered his guard, forgot what he'd been, trusted. His fist slowly uncurled as he sank into real sleep.

Night in Kate's cottage. Mice gnawing through ancient beams, a rose-bush scratching the kitchen window, the sea a rhythmic roar, but only when listened for. Otherwise a hush. A quiet and a darkness outside that was almost absolute. The fire lit a space, and Michael got down on the floor and stretched near it, then curled up against a bean-bag like an enormous cat. Except he was not content, he was agitated. His stomach hurt just under his rib-cage, a tight little knot gnawed his membranes, just like the mice at the old wood.

What was he doing here again? There was no place he'd wanted to come more.

It was very quiet up there. Was his heart stone still lying in the drawer of the little table in the box room? Who had he been when he put it there, and why?

He went into the kitchen, ladled his soup, buttered his bread, came back to the sitting room. Slurped the soup, chewed the bread, poured himself a glass of wine from the bottle he'd brought and forgotten to give.

He'd leave the next day, he'd go back and make his house into a home again. Let Beth go off and make her own life, try to make something of this last third of his life. He felt old and deliciously melancholy at this thought, and that almost, but not quite, calmed him.

He couldn't quite recall what he'd hoped for with this return visit (a scene with some swoon in it?) but he was sure it hadn't happened. He had certainly thought about their lovemaking, especially the second and last time, but that first kiss, on the track when they'd leant into each other, that kiss had haunted him. The seconds before that kiss haunted him. The falling sensation, the headiness, the promise. It was still happening. But he could not connect this memory with the woman up the stairs. Maybe it had just been a forgettable episode for her, and he was only wanting it be mutually dramatic. So hard to tell wishful thinking from truth.

She must have gone to sleep herself.

Yes, I can hear two sets of snores. No, three. Dog must be up there too. Don't think she remembered me at all. Not really.

He took off his shoes and jeans, lay on the sofa in front of the fire and pulled an old quilt around himself. Noticed a framed photo on the mantelpiece he didn't recall from last time. He leant closer to see. A smiling man with red cheeks and one hand on Dog. Jack? He blinked, turned away, as if to look had been an intrusion. There had never been a place for him here. After a short time of feeling lousy and sorry for himself, he slept.

✳   ✳   ✳

Kate was up twice with Patrick. He had long since stopped waiting for the smell of his mother – breastmilk and cheap perfume. He was past expecting Jamie, with his cold-milk bottles. Hunger now signalled a need for the smell and touch of Kate, a deeply familiar being, one he had known since five months before birth. The first time he woke from the cold, having kicked off the quilt. She tucked him in again and he fell quickly back to sleep.

She got up, got undressed, pulled on her nightgown and groggily gave Michael a thought. Not a long thought, just a two-second dreamy query, and crawled back into bed.

The second time Patrick woke he was hungry and the minute after he worked up steam for a cry, she popped the rubber teat into his open mouth. He sucked noisily till he pulled air, then belched and fell back asleep. She rolled him on to his side, put a pillow between him and the edge of the bed, then curled up for a last hour of sleep before morning. But sleep did not come this time. Her eyes were wide open in the dark.

She wanted to rush out of her bedroom and find where Michael lay sleeping. She hadn't even made up the bed in Mhairi's room for him – why? Would that have seemed too decisive? Too direct a message saying stay out of my bed? She wanted to hold him. Kiss the space between each eye and hairline, that little indent on the side of his head. And the spot below his earlobe. They'd have to be lying down for her to do this. She wanted to slide her hands under whatever he was wearing, to believe he was real and not just her wish fulfilment come to taunt her.

But when an hour had passed and she kept almost (but not) doing these things, she was afraid. Who was he? A man she had known briefly, months ago. A stranger in every sense. Today he would leave, and Paddy would give her all the cuddles she needed for a good while yet. Better not to risk either rejection or – worse – acceptance. Hold tight, hold tight.

Morning. Dark still, and wind blasting the windows, but seven o'clock, and Kate stood in the doorway of the sitting room, watching Michael. Stared at him sleeping. His mouth was slightly open and one hand had fallen off the side of the sofa, giving him something of the defenceless look of Patrick. Again, she ached to touch him. Her throat closed up against a swell. But she kept drawing away, back to other rooms, tending the domestic round, the washing, the feeding, the hanging up of wet clothes. Coming back to stare and sigh and going away. Inside a trumpet heralded, urging her to fling herself on this man, yet hundreds of invisible anchors fixed her to the ground. Hold tight. Steady.

Once he stirred and coughed, and she fled, lest he catch her looking at him.

Once he woke to see the back of her skirt, swinging out of the room. He stared at the empty space, the air she left in her wake.

A Grand Start to the Day

Coming out of the Sea View Hotel in the wee hours, the two Ians paused in the car park, debated which of them was the safest bet to drive.

But you know what? said one, swaying towards his friend with a leer.

What?

Something's up at Kate's house the night.

No. What?

Ah, now, that's the question.

What're you on about, man? Gie us a cigarette.

I'm on about true love, man, a subject you know fuck all about.

What a load of old bollocks you talk.

Ah, you do know about true love, I see. A load of old bollocks indeed. Apologies my friend.

Fuck off.

Will I drive then?

Aye, why not?

They rolled down their windows, laughed and sang, set all the farm dogs to barking.

Jamie

Jamie sits on the concrete bench outside Marks again, after another night at James's house. It is early afternoon, but the Christmas lights are on. (Though Christmas was ten days ago. Where had he spent Christmas Day? In a fever dream of sugar-plum houses, coated with icing snow.) His skin under his clothes feels great, scrubbed again in James's bath. Light-headed still and dizzy, but he decides this might be a good day after all. A day to make decisions, to do things. Thinks of checking out some second-hand shops to find some old clothes that aren't quite so old, to match his newish skin. Could use a new pair of trainers, but hard to get those second-hand. His current pair is down to a fluke, found them like manna, lying on the ground in the park. Usually shoes had to be the charity-shop stiff leather ones, dead men's shoes.

He has a notion to look that girl up, the skelly-eyed Kate's daughter. Well, if she isn't in that crazies' place. He still has her address and phone number, scrawled on an envelope. College Road. On a lucid day, action must be taken, because who knows when the next lucid day will come? Sludge awaits, he well knows, so he doesn't waste any more time.

(Meanwhile, not far away, it is seconds from snowing and Mhairi is hanging up clothes. Winter is often full of these deceptive days. Glimpses of blue sky, but a trick. She knows she'll end up bringing them back in later, just as damp, probably damper. But the impulse to hang them up, to see them hanging up as if it is not winter, is too strong, and she carries on pegging.)

Jamie likes Inverness. It is smaller and cleaner than Aberdeen, and the accent is so clear and soft. It is a friendly place. Not much further north, but something about the light and air makes it seem like a much more northern place. He feels so good he almost buys a Big Issue from a smiling old man in front of Clarke's, but then reins in his impulse. A pound is a pound, after all. Merely smiles at the vendor, gives him what he hopes is a conspiring wink, and has a coughing fit.

The buildings and pavement all rock as he coughs, as if it is the world that is walking around the streets with pneumonia, not him. He leans against the wall till it passes, till the pavement calms itself, and weakly moves on.

Morning Is a Time for Mourning

How long did I sleep?

I don't know. Fourteen hours, I think.

He squinted against the bright light, and she stood with Patrick on her hip, a cup of tea in her hand.

Here. I couldn't remember if you took milk or not. So I chanced it. But no sugar, right? (Still the light bantering tone she couldn't to seem to lose.)

Right. Milk is fine. Thanks.

Look, I'm sorry I fell asleep last night, putting Paddy back to sleep. I meant to make up a bed for you. Were you warm enough?

Oh, I was fine. I built up the fire, I was roasting.

He felt drunk with over-sleep, as if he'd travelled too far in forgotten dreams to come back to the surface with ease. He wished she wouldn't look at him right now, looking as he must. He sat up quickly, bent over his tea to hide himself.

Jet travel is a bitch, he said.

Is it? (Poor you, rich American, having to travel by jet.)

People who don't fly never believe it. (And always feel superior in your deprivation.) But it is true. You'll see.

Will I? Maybe.

Anyway. This tastes great. He yawned and stretched. Not a great start to the day.

Have a bath if you want. The water's hot. I thought we might go for a little walk, but the weather.

He looked out of the window and saw that what he had first taken to be bright sun was actually blinding snow flurries. Sun somewhere reflecting on it, but soft dry snow sticking to the glass.

Jesus, it's snowing. And felt stupid for stating the obvious.

Aye. Been snowing on and off since just before Christmas, but it doesn't stay. Too close to the sea here. Then she turned and left, Patrick's drool spinning out behind her.

He got up, had a bath, felt a little restored, but the feeling that it was all wrong, that there was not a place for him here, was stronger. He felt like he had died. The man he had been with her was dead and he was now just a ghost, hovering around the edges, looking for a way in and finding none. His absence had left not the smallest gap. It was an illusion. Nothing existed like he imagined it did, but he kept making the mistake of forgetting this. He looked in the mirror and felt panicky to be elsewhere soon. To be in mind-numbing motion.

Listen, Kate, what time is it? I don't want to miss that shopper's bus. The next Westerbus isn't till tomorrow morning.

Of course he would go, and he would never be seen or heard of again, and she would spend her days looking after Patrick and listening to the sea and her own sad stories. Oh, God, she would probably even let Duncan come back.

Short visit.

Well, I just wanted to come and see you again, Kate. See how you were getting on.

Thanks for coming (revert to manners, always handy when in doubt). It was nice of you. Come again any time you're in the country.

Thanks. Might do that. One day.

Good, you do that.

He straightened up from zipping his bag and they beamed their mouths at each other. Ratatatatat. Her eyes met his at last, and they were not smiling.

You too. You could come and visit me. (A small whine entering his voice.)

His heart was pounding. He had to get away, be away right now, who was he? He was beginning to disintegrate right in front of this puzzled woman. Wrong, all wrong.

How it Ends

He looks in the shop windows, at Waterstone's and Menzie's, at Burton's and Millet's. At all the shiny products he has been taunted with for years, but today they are not irritants, they are proof that the world is thriving and wholesome, a place that awaits his participation. He too will one day walk through these doors and pick up shiny products, these crisp odourless clothes and stiff books and clean shoes, and no shop detective will approach him, no assistant will regard him with veiled suspicion. He has rarely felt so close to admittance to the human race. Is that the power of a bath and a night spent indoors? Or is it the fever? Is he delirious?

He even feels the stirring of sexuality, blood coursing through his groin, and greets it like a long-lost friend. Must be a sign, a mate was waiting for him somewhere. The long-haired girl hitcher? Hennaed hair Patrick's-mum-Mhairi? He has done it all before, after all. Didn't Catriona think he was the thing, once?

Unfortunately, this euphoria has the effect of making him look stoned, and pedestrians give him a wide berth. His arms and legs are swinging wildly. His right arm, which still misses the weight of the holdall, swings especially wildly.

He heads down Academy Street, mistakenly assuming it will lead to a road with the word College in it. Asking for directions is still beyond him.

*   *   *

The shopper's bus is swinging down the glen, towards the village, and Kate's car is winding its way around the hairpin corners towards the village from the other side. Patrick concentrates on his bowels, Michael mentally checks to make sure he hasn't left anything in Kate's bathroom. He has bad luck with toothbrushes.

Near the train station is one of those pubs that open early and close late and a man stumbles out into the watery wintry sunshine, walks over to the station car park, where he has parked illegally, and gets into his Ford Escort van. He is not late for work, he had a job yesterday but today he does not, and he is careless about things. He pulls up to Academy Street, looks down it to check traffic, sees none and pulls too quickly on to the road, too quickly to stop before he hits and runs over a young man who is trying to cross.

Less than a mile from Jamie, Mhairi is making a cup of coffee before she goes out to her maths class. She lives across the road from the college, and is able to leave these things till the last minute. She looks slender and pale, but attractively so. Her eyes are a little vague, she is preoccupied with laundry and college and what to buy at the shops. Nowhere about her is the look of a mother of an eight-month-old. And yet, she is not quite as she was. Hard to say where the imprint is. She has not aged visibly anywhere, but there is a difference. Maybe in her movements, which are a trifle weary, as if in readiness for the moment she will no longer be able to put off.

Kate's car turns the last corner. There it is, she says to Michael, in a high pre-tears voice. She gives him an apple, her hand touching his briefly, and he tucks it into his pocket. A glossy Granny

Smith. Tell Brendan I'm sorry it didn't work out for him here. Good luck to him and Isabel.

And good luck to your Mhairi – it sounds like she'll be fine. She'll get her degree, get a job, meet Mr Right.

Patrick, still strapped into his car seat, begins to howl.

Well, she might, you never know.

Oh, aye, she'll get on fine probably, she says.

Michael swings his bag over his shoulder and climbs on to the bus. He's lost fifteen pounds since the spring, and now, finally, she notices this. He moves differently. His muscles are closer to the surface, changing the shape of his legs and arms. Lost chances taunt her.

He sits in a window-seat and arranges himself. No thoughts but to act casual till out of sight of Kate. This woman who has yet to fit the shape he'd given her in his imagination. The Kate-and-Michael reunion scenes he'd imagined mock him. Her looking up into his eyes and literally swooning, him gathering her up, their kiss, the low-coombed bedroom, curtains blowing in the sea breeze, wildly waving and welcoming him back home where he belonged.

And that was it. In California he'd longed for Gairloch. California had never really fitted him. Changeling in a family of millions. Like son, like father.

But that apparently is an illusion too, for here he is, running away as fast as he can from the shock of reality colliding with dreams. The truth is he belongs nowhere, and if he never arrives in Inverness, it will be some time before anyone misses him. Beth is grown, he is essential to no one's life. He could be dead and it would make no difference. His skin wavers into transparency, unreal, unsubstantial. A thoroughly dispensable man.

The bus starts up. He coughs to summon the facial muscles needed for the farewell smile and nonchalant wave.

But Kate has her back turned, she is tending Patrick, wiping his face. She gets into her car and drives off. He turns back to contemplate the back of the seat in front of him. Brown velour, with vomity-coloured specks, no doubt designed to camouflage vomit. His stomach lurches, anticipating the bus winding around the coast and up the glen to Loch Maree.

Oh, fuck, fuck, fuck, chants Kate. All the way back to the cottage, where she stops and puts her face in her hands and visualises turning the car round and heading back down the road at high speed. Paddy would protest with a scream. Not just hunger, but a sore bum and gut-ache from all the tension. No sense of humour, that kid.

She would catch up with the bus just past Kinlochewe, where the road curves by the unlikely wooden tourist shop that was always closed. Now she was behind it she didn't know what to do. What did they do in films? Force the bus off the road? Honk and make wild gestures? In the end, all she would have to do was catch the eye of big Murdo and wee Murdo, who would be sitting on the back seat of the bus, having decided to see what was on offer at the supermarket, maybe special offers on whisky. They would ask in shrugs and pointing fingers if they were to come with her instead, and she would indicate YES with a big smile and nod. They would tell the driver and the bus would stop in the lay-by as the road inclined.

What to do now, what would she do now? She had no idea. She would put one foot in front of the other and sit back to watch herself perform. Patrick would have conveniently cried himself to sleep.

Michael would notice the two Murdos get up and then he would see Kate. Her face would be agitated, two spots of pink on her cheeks, dark eyes darting. She would let the Murdos off the bus but not answer any of their questions, and they would stand puzzled on the slushy verge, watching while she continued through the bus till she came to Michael, who would suddenly blush thinking he must've forgotten his passport or something and put her to great inconvenience. He would have a look of apology. Kate, what is it? he would ask in a whisper. All eighteen people on the bus would stare and wait.

Michael, I need to tell you, look. She would crouch on the aisle floor and lower her voice, making as private a space between them as possible. The silence would roar. Even the driver would turn off his Strawbs tape to listen.

What is it, Kate, did I leave something?

No. Listen, she would say. Why don't you stay a little longer?

You want me to?

Yes. Please.

She would smile. He would say something but just then jets would come out of nowhere and fill the sky with noise. What? she would shout, and all eighteen heads would bend closer.

Yes. I will! I'd love to! Michael would shout into the quiet wake of the jet noise.

The bus would erupt into cheers and Kate would have to turn and shout at them, It wasn't a marriage proposal, you gits, Jesus, what a sad bunch you are. But she would blush and they would ignore her, and throw things at them as they left the bus. Bits of torn tissue paper, pennies, an empty lager tin. Michael would wonder out loud if this was another strange Highland custom.

Outside, she would shove the two Murdos back on to the bus. No, she would slip them each a fiver for their outing in Inverness, then shove them back on to the bus. The sun would burst out, a rainbow would arch across the glen, all her wrinkles would be gone, she would have a heaving young bosom, and from nowhere, a track from an old Beatles album would start up. Here comes the sun. No, no. The Ritchie Havens version.

Of course, she would be too ecstatic to enjoy the exquisiteness of the moment, but would look forward to looking back and enjoying it later.

Kate lifts her head from her hands, removes her arms from the steering-wheel, considers her house now coated in white like a lacy shawl.

They would return here, settle into a routine, have some fairly good sex, which would soon settle into mediocre routine sex, some misunderstandings, they would squabble, she would resent him rearranging anything in her house, he would resent having to feel a guest in his new home, and after a decade or so, they would learn to ignore each other, especially when engaged in activities that made them physically disgusting to each other, like washing hair, picking noses. They would not be happy but would be too old by then, and set in their ways, to hope for anything else, and they would rub along, like she and Jack had. Probably he would grow fat and she would get even thinner, and they would stop embracing as their figures became less conducive to any kind of joining.

Because although Michael made her feel alive right now, it was only the prospect of Michael, the imagined life with Michael that made her heart beat fast, and in the end, it would only be the same hours, days, years filled with the minutiae of living, and her heart would beat normally, not race.

The house stares back at her, as it disappears under its white shroud, softly rounded as there is no wind yet, and the snow clings to itself around edges. Like the icing on a gingerbread house. The windows are black and look reproachfully at her. There should be a yellow glow shining from them, grey smoke should be drifting from the chimney, the kettle should be singing. The snow will melt soon, it never stays, though she wishes and wishes it would.

The phone rings.

What? asks Mhairi. Yes, that's my name, but I don't know what you're talking about. A man has been hit by a car and he had my phone number in his pocket? What's his name? No idea at all? No, no, it's just I don't remember giving my number to anyone. In fact, I make a point of not giving my number out, especially to men. One blue baby bootee? And a train ticket from Aberdeen? Look, I don't know anyone from Aberdeen, and I certainly don't know anyone who has a baby. What does he look like? Uh-huh. I think you've made a mistake. That's alright, no, really, I'm sure. No, I'm not coming to hospital. I don't know him. Goodbye.

Genuinely puzzled, and more — *irritated*: how dare a stranger go and get himself hurt and implicate herself? But a niggling afterwards. A dangerous unpleasantness is stirring up, which soon topples into languor, her old response to anxiety. She decides to have a nap. Her maths class had been exhausting, after all. Sits on her bed and looks at nothing. Then she yawns, and her eyes catch a framed photo of Patrick and herself. Where had that come from? Kate. At first she just notices her hair, which was a lot longer then, and wonders if she should grow it out again. Was she prettier then? Then it is the baby she sees, his rounded smallness, the way he was curled up into her jumper. If she didn't know better, if she didn't know who these people were, she would think the snuggling baby and young mother loved each other. They looked the part perfectly.

She takes a breath, smells his first sweet smell again and closes her eyes while it pours back into her. Extraordinary how it is exactly like being filled, she thinks, and lets it keep coming till it is no longer Patrick's infant smell, but everything, and none of it hurts this time. Lies back on her pillows and lets her thoughts run where they will. First they head towards Jack, and she notes with a dreamy detachment that she feels only tenderness. No anger. She says the things she has been waiting to say to him, but finds they are only trivial chatty things. As if she had seen him yesterday. Her new boyfriend's pierced nose, the fact she is putting on weight, the cost of a good cup of coffee.

Roddy dips into her stream of thoughts, but only for a second, and his face is blurred. Nothing, only his aftermath. A rock-hard stomach, the dark landing carpet, a howling. Hers and Patrick's. A series of Patricks, all crying. At night, during the day, in bed, in his pram, in the bath, in the shops, while she was trying to watch television.

But he wasna any bother, he's a grand wee man. Is he really yours, then?

Someone said that.

Jamie is away. He keeps coming back, but mostly he is away, in a place of no dreams, no memories, no desires. It's the morphine, but he has no thoughts to think that. He only knows he doesn't hurt. Monitors register his continuing presence with little bleeps and lights, but do not penetrate his mind.

Then a minute chemical change occurs, and he does hurt, and he does know he is in a hospital bed, though in which city and under what circumstances, he has no idea. He knows that his body is damaged and does not obey him.

He hums a lullaby to himself, eyes closed, does not see the nurses who stand alert over him, doing things with tubes and switches. He hums and imagines he is rocking. He is upstairs in his orange tent. Then, as the painkillers increase their hold, he is in his own little house, his cottage by the loch. He belongs here. This is his place, and he is not alone. There is a fire in the grate, and for a second it swells into an inferno, his heart panics (the machines record this) but then it is alright again, a small blaze. In his arms, pinning them down so they are numb and he cannot feel them any more, is a small boy body, wrapped in an old cotton shirt.

Her whitewashed house sits in the slope of the hill, going down to the sea, coated with unlikely snow. Its gable end points seaward, braces itself with stone and beam against the weather, while the vulnerable front, with its windows, door, porch, faces gentler south. The wind-warped plum and rowan are dark on one side, white on the other. Stone walls, likewise half white, do not pen in sheep – they scatter everywhere – but divide up the surrounding landscape like parentheses.

Kate is sitting in her car still, and riding into the future. She sees that she is still living here. Despite a touch of arthritis, she rides her bike to the shops some days, but mostly she is either in her house looking out of the windows, or she is outside working in the garden, glancing at her house from time to time. It is an ordinary stone house, thousands like it, and it clothes her. Safe and snug. There she is at the window now, the kitchen window. Is she alone? But the door is shut, and curtains are being drawn.

Wait, what if there are two heads silhouetted? Whose would they be? Perhaps it is Michael after all. Perhaps she decided that she could not cancel out the future just because she could not imagine a sufficiently good one. Or that the prospect of sharing her life, no matter how inevitable the fading of romance, was preferable to living alone. To merge spheres, to create and live in that imperfect place where two lives meet. It is possible she took her chances with the unknown and summoned him back. And he came.

Or it might be Patrick, grown-up, a good grandson who hoes the veg plot and occasionally has dinner with her.

Maybe it is Jamie, mysteriously reappeared on her doorstep, to talk about things. He seemed to enjoy talking with her.

Or maybe is it just Kate and her shadow, taking down mirrors, choosing not to watch herself grow old.

Patrick is quiet but not asleep. His dark eyes scour the inside of the car, and he is wandering, his eyes roll in their sockets and the lids finally lower. Images float and merge, dissolve and re-form, till a young man in a damp cottage comes up. Patrick's inner focus firms up. He is being swaddled in a T-shirt, and sung to and he is breathing the rancid sharp air of an unwashed young man who is afraid and ecstatic at the same time. Woodsmoke permeates, stings his eyes, but he feels good and his face shows happiness. He is safe. Saved.

He dies, he has always been dying. He dies again and again. He is on the street, he is looking for some walls, a roof, a hearth, he shivers naked, dies again, and like the foetal Patrick not understanding his own physical limitations, he swoops over the surface of the earth and surveys all the roofs, all the smoking chimneys, looking, looking for one that beckons. Two friendly windows, a door, two steps leading up to it. A door that does not lock, but opens. He looks and he looks. Old houses shudder in his wake, their beams creak and their windows rattle.

Then the machine begins to bleep again, and he is back in his skin and hurting. White-dressed women he will never know send up a little cheer, as if his continuing life is a winning lottery ticket.

Kate watches white stuff stick to her house till she can bear the sight of her own reproachful dark windows no longer. She removes her sleeping grandson from his car seat, opens the door to her house (it is never locked), goes inside and up the stairs. Lays the baby on her bed and silently removes his snowsuit. Covers him with a blanket and tiptoes downstairs to Dog's tail wagging welcome. Switches on lights, lights the sitting-room fire, checks the Rayburn, puts on the kettle. The house begins to lose its chill loneliness, feels occupied, its air is moving around busily, and yet Kate finds it hard to settle. It is only three o'clock, but the day is drawing in, and she decides to cook a complex and tasty meal to eat by candlelight. Maybe open that bottle of good wine still left over from Jack's funeral.

She begins slicing onions, when a knock on the door brings Michael (who had got off the bus and walked back to her house through snow flurries, who did not really know why he was doing it but was too miserable to care), and Kate and Michael say nothing, confronted with each other's presence after an hour apart. Merely fling their bodies against each other, her sharp bones impacting on his soft solidity against their will, as if they have no choice. He is standing one step down from the door, so while they embrace, her feet leave the ground and she is suspended, bound tightly to nothing and nobody but him.

Mhairi gets up from bed. Shakes herself, rubs her forehead, then runs her hands through her hair. Reaches for her coat and boots. It is a long walk and the wind stings her face and especially her ears. By the time she arrives, she is tingling and numb. Opens the door to the intensive-care ward and walks into a welcoming blast of hot air. A hospital sirocco.

Is this your friend? asks the nurse.

No. No, not a friend. He's ... he's Jamie.

He doesn't hear her voice. And yet his name (indifferent, a separate entity) enters his ears and comes home to roost upstairs in the tent. Becomes a heartbeat.

Patrick sleeps. He has kicked off his blanket but is not cold. The room wraps round him, the sea wind tries but cannot penetrate.

He sleeps and dreams unimaginable dreams.

Now you can buy any of these other
Review titles from your bookshop or
direct from the publisher.

FREE P&P AND UK DELIVERY
(Overseas and Ireland £3.50 per book)

Hens Dancing	Raffaella Barker	£6.99
The Catastrophist	Ronan Bennett	£6.99
Horseman, Pass By	David Crackanthorpe	£6.99
Two Kinds of Wonderful	Isla Dewar	£6.99
Earth and Heaven	Sue Gee	£6.99
Sitting Among the Eskimos	Maggie Graham	£6.99
Tales of Passion, Tales of Woe	Sandra Gulland	£6.99
The Dancers Dancing	Éilís Ní Dhuibhne	£6.99
After You'd Gone	Maggie O'Farrell	£6.99
The Silver River	Ben Richards	£6.99
A History of Insects	Yvonne Roberts	£6.99
Girl in Hyacinth Blue	Susan Vreeland	£6.99
The Long Afternoon	Giles Waterfield	£6.99

TO ORDER SIMPLY CALL THIS NUMBER

01235 400 414

or e-mail orders@bookpoint.co.uk

Prices and availability subject to change without notice.